LONGMAN LITERATURE

The Mac Laverty Collection

Bernard Mac Laverty

Editor: Hamish Robertson

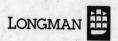

Longman Literature
Series editor: Roy Blatchford

Novels

Jane Austen   *Pride and Prejudice*   0 582 07720 6
Charlotte Brontë   *Jane Eyre*   0 582 07719 2
Emily Brontë   *Wuthering Heights*   0 582 07782 6
Charles Dickens   *Great Expectations*   0 582 07783 4
F Scott Fitzgerald   *The Great Gatsby*   0 582 06023 0
Nadine Gordimer   *July's People*   0 582 06011 7
Graham Greene   *The Captain and the Enemy*   0 582 06024 0
Thomas Hardy   *Far from the Madding Crowd*   0 582 07788 5
Aldous Huxley   *Brave New World*   0 582 06016 8
Robin Jenkins   *The Cone-Gatherers*   0 582 06017 6
Doris Lessing   *The Fifth Child*   0 582 06021 4
Joan Lindsay   *Picnic at Hanging Rock*   0 582 08174 2
Bernard Mac Laverty   *Lamb*   0 582 06557 7
Brian Moore   *Lies of Silence*   0 582 08170 X
George Orwell   *Animal Farm*   0 582 06010 9
            Nineteen Eighty-Four   0 582 06018 4
Alan Paton   *Cry, The Beloved Country*   0 582 07787 7
Paul Scott   *Staying On*   0 582 07718 4

Plays

Alan Ayckbourn   *Absurd Person Singular*   0 582 06020 6
J B Priestley   *An Inspector Calls*   0 582 06019 2
Terence Rattigan   *The Winslow Boy*   0 582 06019 2
Willy Russell   *Educating Rita*   0 582 06013 3
            Shirley Valentine   0 582 08173 4
Peter Shaffer   *The Royal Hunt of the Sun*   0 582 06014 1
Bernard Shaw   *Arms and the Man*   0 582 07785 0
            Pygmalion   0 582 06015 X
            Saint Joan   0 582 07786 9
Oscar Wilde   *The Importance of Being Earnest*   0 582 07784 2

Short stories

Jeffrey Archer   *A Twist in the Tale*   0 582 06022 2
Bernard Mac Laverty   *The Mac Laverty Collection*   0 582 08172 6

Contents

Longman Group UK Limited,
Longman House, Burnt Mill, Harlow,
Essex CM20 2JE, England
and Associated Companies throughout the world.

This educational edition first published 1991
Second impression 1992

Editorial Material set in 10/12 pt Helvetica Light Condensed
Produced by Longman Singapore Publishers (Pte) Ltd
Printed in Singapore

ISBN 0 582 08172 6

Consultant: Geoff Barton

The writer on writing

A critic once declared that a work of art should not 'mean' but 'be'. Bernard Mac Laverty, in common with some other writers, steadfastly and rightly refuses to interpret what his work might mean. Readers must bring their own thoughts and responses to his stories and novels which have a life of their own, a 'unity of being'.

D H Lawrence also echoed this: 'Never trust the teller, trust the tale.' It was his way of warning that any work of art is 'open': that it can never totally be 'explained' by reference to its sources, or to the life of the writer.

Nevertheless, readers are always interested in what lies behind the composition of any work of art, and provided that 'the background' is never seen as wholly important, our enjoyment, as readers, will always be deepened by an appreciation of the artistic shaping of the background.

Bernard Mac Laverty was born in Belfast in 1942. He spent his formative years there and was a pupil at St Malachy's grammar school. He worked for some years as a medical technician, and later studied English at Queen's University. Then followed a move to Scotland, to Edinburgh, which provides the setting for his story **A Time to Dance**. A later move to the island of Islay off the west coast of Scotland no doubt provided the setting and perhaps inspired the images found in **Remote**. He now lives and works as a full-time writer in Glasgow, with his wife and family.

He has written two powerful and highly praised novels, *Cal* and *Lamb*. Both of these have been made into successful films for which he also wrote the screenplays. Three collections of his short stories, *Secrets*, *A Time to Dance*, and *The Great Profundo*, have been published, the last two being the sources of the stories in this volume.

These stories have taken root, consciously or subconsciously, in one mind – a product of experiences, impressions, memories of one, or more than one, distinct culture.

v

Capturing the child's eye view

Mac Laverty is now in his late forties, a warm personality with a robust sense of humour, confirmed by audiences who have heard him speak in schools and at many literary festivals. Yet he also still remains uncannily in touch with his own childhood. He captures the child's eye view of the world as few other writers have done, as is evident in stories such as My Dear Palestrina, The Beginnings of a Sin, A Time to Dance and More than just the Disease.

A Radio Four interview by Frank Delaney revealed just how immediate and intimate his own memories of childhood are: the hot summer days in Atlantic Avenue, Belfast; the large Victorian house shared with his grandparents, great aunt, his father, mother and younger brother Peter; its interior decorated with items from the cinema gleaned by his father who worked there, doing posters. There were familiar smells – the smells of old people – and the predominant colour of brown. There was the security of voices, many voices, heard as, during the illness occasioned by rheumatic fever, he drifted off to sleep. There was also the pervasive sense of religion, or religious observance, which brought ghostly presences and fear.

And there was Sectarianism. This Catholic boy was aware of religious–tribal loyalties and often tells the story of when he and his friends met a group of Protestant boys in a wood on Cave Hill, a mountain in Belfast. To negotiate a safe passage out would be difficult, and the question 'Are youse Catholics?' would normally have been a prelude to more violent behaviour; but the tension was quickly relieved by a child philosopher who declared 'We all believe in the same God, don't we?' and a very small child who soon became the focus of attention because he was 'able to boak (vomit) whenever he wanted'. The mixture of God, philosophy, Fair-Isle pullovers and bizarre humour somehow seems to not only occupy this writer's memories, but also to inspire some of his stories.

In another recent interview with George Watson, Bernard Mac Laverty also revealed that he had read that definitive study of an Irish Catholic upbringing, James Joyce's *Portrait of the Artist as a Young Man*. Although impressed by it, he didn't need it as a model for his own portraits of Catholic youth. He had merely to switch on his own 'retrieval system from the past', out of which came authenticity and accuracy, even down to minute detail – all Catholic schools were 'painted throughout a pale hospital green above shoulder level, and below, a dark hospital green'.

We only have to read **The Beginnings of a Sin** to be aware of the accuracy of the writer's memory and the power of religious mystery:

After tea they always said the Family Rosary. Colum would half kneel, half crouch at the armchair with his face almost touching the seat. The cushion smelt of cloth and human. He tried to say the Rosary as best he could, thinking of the Sacred Mysteries while his mouth said the words...

pages 26–7

Although it was a modern house, it was full of old things. A picture of the Assumption of Our Lady in a frame of gold leaves hung by the front door. The furniture in Father Lynch's room was black and heavy. The dining room chairs had twisted legs like barley sugar sticks.

page 30

The 'Troubles'

Another potent source behind some of Mac Laverty's work is the desperate and ongoing tragedy of Northern Ireland. In the interview with George Watson, Mac Laverty showed that he, like other Northern Irish writers, was fully aware of the possible artistic dangers in writing directly about the 'Troubles'. Would he be accused of simply exploiting a situation which is sufficiently tragic in itself? Or would it be seen as glamourising violence, however unintentionally, or possibly oversimplifying the complexity of things?

Instead, Mac Laverty has preferred to approach the whole issue obliquely (with the one notable exception of his novel *Cal*). In his first novel, *Lamb*, the inexorable fate of the two main characters and the tragedy of Ulster seem linked in the possibility that 'each man kills' – or is capable of killing – 'the thing he loves'. George Watson observes that this famous phrase of Oscar Wilde's 'may apply as much to certain Irish nationalists in their attitude to Ireland, as to Michael's love for Owen.' Indeed one only has to read the description of the nationalist town of Strabane to realise this:

> *Tall terraces of shops with charred rafters for roofs, crumbling gables, slogans sprayed*
> *everywhere, men with nothing to do sheltering from the rain in doorways …*
> *A town bent on self-destruction. Cutting off its nose to spite the British Government's*
> *face. The air was full of a savage and bewildered gloom.*
>
> Bernard Mac Laverty, *Lamb*

In this collection, the human consequences of bigotry and violence are highlighted in **Some Surrender** and in that uncompromising, chilling tale, **Father and Son**:

> *I take my son's limp head in my hands and see a hole in his nose that should not*
> *be there. At the base of his nostril. My son, let me put my arms around you.*
>
> page 7

Yet, however dark and horrifying such incidents may be, it is also true that the hallmarks of Bernard Mac Laverty's writing are understatement, clarity and above all, compassion. He has said, significantly, 'you've got to think through your own humanity accurately'. George Watson found this:

> *a most powerful statement of the function of the literary artist. He wishes us to think*
> *ourselves into the position of others quite unlike ourselves at first appearance, and*
> *then to realise what elements of common humanity we share with them.*

Readers of Mr Mac Laverty's published work to date will not, surely, dispute this assertion. After all, the child in the wood did say:

> *We all believe in the same God, don't we?*

Introduction

The short story

It is often assumed that the short story is a dying literary genre with a decreasing readership. Apparently more preferred are novels of literary acclaim which win awards on television, or full length – even overgrown – blockbusters which are equally subject to marketing hype and are then filmed as serials or soaps. Short stories can survive only as short filmed units; slot-fillers in a busy, nightly television schedule of 'essential' news, feature films and other 'entertainments' for mass audiences.

But current broadcasting, and Bernard Mac Laverty's work to date, deny this assumption. Not only have his two full-length novels been filmed effectively and successfully, but so also have two of the stories in this collection, **My Dear Palestrina** and **More than just the Disease**. Also, his other stories are works of consummate craftsmanship which can compete with the best fiction written during this century. Can anyone walk into an art gallery and ignore the individual pictures in favour of the 'total effect'?

Characters

Bernard Mac Laverty's stories are rich portraits of people who demand our attention and sympathy: a murdered victim, a truanting schoolboy who is blind to reality, a peculiar sword swallower immortalised by Matisse, a parish priest with an unforgivable secret ... the catalogue seems endless.

Children are often portrayed, too, as centre-focus characters whose innocence and naivety reflect ironically on the lives of their elders and 'betters', but who never serve to fully condemn them. Think especially of Colum in **The Beginnings of a Sin**.

Compassion, pity for the old, the forgotten and the lonely are also evident, particularly in **Remote, Eels, Words the Happy Say** and **Across the Street**. In each of these stories the main character is alone, adrift in a sea of circumstances which serve only to exaggerate this condition, and only the reader is left to fully recognise his or her plight. Yet these stories are never sentimental; the style is spare, economical, and the tone is always of understatement rather than emotional excess. We are never told what to think or feel, we are simply invited to see the action, listen to the dialogue and draw our own conclusions.

Themes

These are the key issues which a writer, or artist, wishes to illuminate for his/her audience. In Bernard Mac Laverty's work the issue which most immediately springs to mind is that of bigotry and sectarianism in Ulster, Northern Ireland. Only in *Cal*, however, does Mac Laverty directly engage, as a writer, with the Irish 'Troubles': a sadly inaccurate euphemism for the endless reality of divided loyalties and terrorist violence. In *Lamb* this reality is also present, but is more deeply embedded within the plot.

Father and Son and **Some Surrender** in this collection do seem, like *Cal*, to confront the subject, but at a deeper level these stories show much more: the shifting, often unstable relationships between parents and their children; relationships often disrupted by circumstances beyond the control of either. This concern is not only found in Ulster, it is universal.

It should also be stressed that Mac Laverty's stories do not often deliver a clear message. What we find instead are ideas: revealed areas of the human condition, curious paradoxes and even unanswered debates which tick like time-bombs within the layers of narrative. These can vary from the direct but subtle portrayal of isolation in **Remote** to the complexity of ideas found in **My Dear Palestrina**: isolation, innocence, prejudice, social class barriers, potential revolution, the problem of identity and the essential growth towards understanding by children, and indeed, by all readers.

The writer's craft

George Watson, whilst commenting on *Lamb*, defined the virtues of a good short story writer:

> ...*tight narrative construction, clean and clear visualisation, the ability to suggest much through the telling use of tiny detail, the laconic ease of dialogue.*

These are indeed the hallmarks of Mac Laverty's work, but he is also prepared to be unconventional, to experiment. Look at the narrative techniques in **Father and Son, Some Surrender** and **The Great Profundo**, and the manipulation of tone and genre in **Profundo** and **End of Season** respectively. Think also of the totally unforced use of descriptive detail in the tightly-narrated story **Remote** which concentrates on a single incident: a lonely old woman arranges a lift to a local village where she can post a letter to herself.

> *The road spun past, humping and squirming over peat bogs, the single track bulging at passing places – points which were marked by tall black and white posts to make them stand out against the landscape.*

page 39

The single-track road is her single-track life, after the death of her husband. The passing places where human contact is subsequently made are important, but few and far between. An apparently inconsequential description of a remote landscape expands to include the remote figure who sees it, and we, the readers who see her – watching.

Thinking about our own humanity

Kafka said that stories come from 'the depths of blood and fear'. Tennessee Williams said, 'I give you truth in the pleasant disguise of illusions'. Both statements are probably true of Bernard Mac Laverty's work, although it could be argued that there is more truth than illusion and that **The Great Profundo** debates precisely that point.

What is true is that his stories entertain us, tantalise us, and above all make us, in Mac Laverty's own words, 'think through our own humanity accurately'.

■ Reading log

One of the easiest ways of keeping track of your reading is to keep a log book. This can be any exercise book or folder that you have to hand, but make sure you reserve it exclusively for reflecting on your reading, both at home and in school.

As you read the short stories, stop from time to time and think back over what you have read.

- Is there anything that puzzles you? Note down some questions that you might want to research, discuss with your friends or ask a teacher. Also note any quotations which strike you as important or memorable.

- Does your reading remind you of anything else you have read, heard or seen on TV or the cinema? Jot down what it is and where the similarities lie.

- Have you had any experiences similar to those narrated in the story? Do you find yourself identifying closely with one or more of the characters? Record this as accurately as you can.

- Do you find yourself really liking, or really loathing, any of the characters? What is it about them that makes you feel so strongly? Make notes that you can add to.

- Can you picture the locations and settings? Draw maps, plans, diagrams, drawings, in fact any doodle that helps you make sense of these things.

- Now and again try to predict what will happen next in the story. Use what you already know of the author, the genre (type of story) and the characters to help you do this. Later record how close you were and whether you were surprised at the outcome.

- Write down any feelings that you have about the book. Your reading log should help you to make sense of your own ideas alongside those of the author.

The Mac Laverty Collection

Father and Son

BECAUSE I DO not sleep well I hear my father rising to go to work. I know that in a few minutes he will come in to look at me sleeping. He will want to check that I came home last night. He will stand in his bare feet, his shoes and socks in his hand, looking at me. I will sleep for him. Downstairs I hear the snap of the switch on the kettle. I hear him not eating anything, going about the kitchen with a stomach full of wind. He will come again to look at me before he goes out to his work. He will want a conversation. He climbs the stairs and stands breathing through his nose with an empty lunch box in the crook of his arm, looking at me.

This is my son who let me down. I love him so much it hurts but he won't talk to me. He tells me nothing. I hear him groan and see his eyes flicker open. When he sees me he turns away, a heave of bedclothes in his wake.

'Wake up, son. I'm away to my work. Where are you going today?'
　'What's it to you?'
　'If I know what you're doing I don't worry as much.'
　'Shit.'

I do not sleep. My father does not sleep. The sound of ambulances criss-crosses the dark. I sleep with daylight. It is safe. At night I hear his bare feet click as he lifts them, walking the lino. The front door shudders as he leaves.

My son is breaking my heart. It is already broken. Is it my fault there is no woman in the house? Is it my fault a good woman should die? His face was never softer than when after I had shaved. A baby pressed to my shaved cheek. Now his chin is sandpaper. He is a man. When he was a boy I took him fishing.

2

I taught him how to tie a blood-knot, how to cast a fly, how to strike so the fish would not escape. How to play a fish. The green bus to quiet days in Toome. Him pestering me with questions. If I leave him alone he will break my heart anyway. I must speak to him. Tonight at tea. If he is in.

'You should be in your bed. A man of your age. It's past one.'
    'Let me make you some tea.'
    The boy shrugs and sits down. He takes up the paper between him and his father.
    'What do you be doing out to this time?'
    'Not again.'
    'Answer me.'
    'Talking.'
    'Who with?'
    'Friends. Just go to bed, Da, will you?'
    'What do you talk about?'
    'Nothing much.'
    'Talk to me, son.'
    'What about?'

My son, he looks confused. I want you to talk to me the way I hear you talk to people at the door. I want to hear you laugh with me like you used to. I want to know what you think. I want to know why you do not eat more. No more than pickings for four weeks. Your face is thin. Your fingers, orange with nicotine. I pulled you away from death once and now you will not talk to me. I want to know if you are in danger again.

'About . . .'
    'You haven't shaved yet.'
    'I'm just going to. The water in the kettle is hot.'
    'Why do you shave at night?'
    'Because in the morning my hand shakes.'

Your hand shakes in the morning, Da, because you're a coward.

3

You think the world is waiting round the corner to blow your head off. A breakfast of two Valium and the rest of them rattling in your pocket, walking down the street to your work. Won't answer the door without looking out the bedroom window first. He's scared of his own shadow.

Son, you are living on borrowed time. Your hand shook when you got home. I have given you the life you now have. I fed you soup from a spoon when your own hand would have spilled it. Let me put my arm around your shoulders and let me listen to what is making you thin. At the weekend I will talk to him.

It is hard to tell if his bed has been slept in. It is always rumpled. I have not seen my son for two days. Then, on the radio, I hear he is dead. They give out his description. I drink milk. I cry.

But he comes in for his tea.

'Why don't you tell me where you are?'
'Because I never know where I am.

My mother is dead but I have another one in her place. He is an old woman. He has been crying. I know he prays for me all the time. He used to dig the garden, grow vegetables and flowers for half the street. He used to fish. To take me fishing. Now he just waits. He sits and waits for me and the weeds have taken over. I would like to slap his face and make a man out of him.

'I let you go once – and look what happened.'
'Not this again.'
The boy curls his lip as if snagged on a fish-hook.

For two years I never heard a scrape from you. I read of London in the papers. Watched scenes from London on the news, looking over the reporter's shoulder at people walking in the street.

I know you, son, you are easily led. Then a doctor phoned for me at work. The poshest man I ever spoke to.

'I had to go and collect you. Like a dog.'

The boy had taken up a paper. He turns the pages noisily, crackling like fire.

'A new rig-out from Littlewoods.'

Socks, drawers, shirt, the lot. In a carrier bag. The doctor said he had to burn what was on you. I made you have your girl's hair cut. It was Belfast before we spoke. You had the taint of England in your voice.

'Today I thought you were dead.'

Every day you think I am dead. You live in fear. Of your own death. Peeping behind curtains, the radio always loud enough to drown any noise that might frighten you, double locking doors. When you think I am not looking you hold your stomach. You undress in the dark for fear of your shadow falling on the window-blind. At night you lie with the pillow over your head. By your bed a hatchet which you pretend to have forgotten to tidy away. Mice have more courage.

'Well I'm not dead.'

'Why don't you tell me where you go?'

'Look, Da, I have not touched the stuff since I came back. Right?'

'Why don't you have a girl like everybody else?'

'Oh fuck.'

He bundles the paper and hurls it in the corner and stamps up the stairs to his room. The old man shouts at the closed door.

'Go and wash your mouth out.'

He cries again, staring at the ceiling so that the tears run down to his ears.

My son, he is full of hatred. For me, for everything. He spits when he speaks. When he shouts his voice breaks high and he is like a woman. He grinds his teeth and his skin goes white about his mouth. His hands shake. All because I ask him where he goes. Perhaps I need to show him more love. Care for him more than I do.

I mount the stairs quietly to apologise. My son, I am sorry. I do it because I love you. Let me put my arm around you and talk like we used to on the bus from Toome. Why do you fight away from me?

The door swings open and he pushes a hand-gun beneath the pillow. Seen long enough, black and squat, dull like a garden slug. He sits, my son, his hands idling empty, staring hatred.

'Why do you always spy on me, you nosey old bastard?' His voice breaks, his eyes bulge.

'What's that? Under your pillow?'

'It's none of your fucking business.'

He kicks the door closed in my face with his bare foot.

I am in the dark of the landing. I must pray for him. On my bended knees I will pray for him to be safe. Perhaps I did not see what I saw. Maybe I am mistaken. My son rides pillion on a motor-bike. Tonight I will not sleep. I do not think I will sleep again.

It is ten o'clock. The news begins. Like a woman I stand drying a plate, watching the headlines. There is a ring at the door. The boy answers it, his shirt-tail out. Voices in the hallway.

My son with friends. Talking. What he does not do with me.

There is a bang. A dish-cloth drops from my hand and I run to the kitchen door. Not believing, I look into the hallway. There is a strange smell. My son is lying on the floor, his head on the bottom stair, his feet on the threshold. The news has come to my door. The house is open to the night. There is no one else. I go to him with damp hands.

'Are you hurt?'

Blood is spilling from his nose.

They have punched you and you are not badly hurt. Your nose is bleeding. Something cold at the back of your neck.

I take my son's limp head in my hands and see a hole in his nose that should not be there. At the base of his nostril.

My son, let me put my arms around you.

A Time to Dance

NELSON, WITH A patch over one eye, stood looking idly into Mothercare's window. The sun was bright behind him and made a mirror out of the glass. He looked at his patch with distaste and felt it with his finger. The Elastoplast was rough and dry and he disliked the feel of it. Bracing himself for the pain, he ripped it off and let a yell out of him. A woman looked down at him curiously to see why he had made the noise, but by that time he had the patch in his pocket. He knew without looking that some of his eyebrow would be on it.

He had spent most of the morning in the Gardens avoiding distant uniforms, but now that it was coming up to lunch-time he braved it on to the street. He had kept his patch on longer than usual because his mother had told him the night before that if he didn't wear it he would go 'stark, staring blind'.

Nelson was worried because he knew what it was like to be blind. The doctor at the eye clinic had given him a box of patches that would last for most of his lifetime. Opticludes. One day Nelson had worn two and tried to get to the end of the street and back. It was a terrible feeling. He had to hold his head back in case it bumped into anything and keep waving his hands in front of him backwards and forwards like windscreen wipers. He kept tramping on tin cans and heard them trundle emptily away. Broken glass crackled under his feet and he could not figure out how close to the wall he was. Several times he heard footsteps approaching, slowing down as if they were going to attack him in his helplessness, then walking away. One of the footsteps even laughed. Then he heard a voice he knew only too well.

'Jesus, Nelson, what are you up to this time?' It was his mother. She led him back to the house with her voice blaring in his ear.

She was always shouting. Last night, for instance, she had

started into him for watching T.V. from the side. She had dragged him round to the chair in front of it.

'That's the way the manufacturers make the sets. They put the picture on the front. But oh no, that's not good enough for our Nelson. He has to watch it from the side. Squint, my arse, you'll just go blind – stark, staring blind.'

Nelson had then turned his head and watched it from the front. She had never mentioned the blindness before. Up until now all she had said was, 'If you don't wear them patches that eye of yours will turn in till it's looking at your brains. God knows, not that it'll have much to look at.'

His mother was Irish. That was why she had a name like Skelly. That was why she talked funny. But she was proud of the way she talked and nothing angered her more than to hear Nelson saying 'Ah ken' and 'What like is it?' She kept telling him that someday they were going back, when she had enough ha'pence scraped together. 'Until then I'll not let them make a Scotchman out of you.' But Nelson talked the way he talked.

His mother had called him Nelson because she said she thought that his father had been a seafaring man. The day the boy was born she had read an article in the *Reader's Digest* about Nelson Rockefeller, one of the richest men in the world. It seemed only right to give the boy a good start. She thought it also had the advantage that it couldn't be shortened, but she was wrong. Most of the boys in the scheme called him Nelly Skelly.

He wondered if he should sneak back to school for dinner then skive off again in the afternoon. They had good dinners at school – like a hotel, with choices. Chips and magic things like rhubarb crumble. There was one big dinner-woman who gave him extra every time she saw him. She told him he needed fattening. The only drawback to the whole system was that he was on free dinners. Other people in his class were given their dinner money and it was up to them whether they went without a dinner and bought Coke and sweets and stuff with the money. It was a choice Nelson didn't have, so he had to invent other things to get the money out of his mother. In Lent there were the Black Babies; library fines were worth the odd 10p, although, as yet, he had not taken a book from the school library – and anyway they didn't have to pay fines, even if they were late; the Home Economics Department asked them to bring in money to buy their ingredients and Nelson would always add 20p to it.

'What the hell are they teaching you to cook – sides of beef?' his mother would yell. Outdoor pursuits required extra money. But even though they had ended after the second term, Nelson went on asking for the 50p on a Friday – 'to go horse riding'. His mother would never part with money without a speech of some sort.

'Horse riding? Horse riding! Jesus, I don't know what sort of a school I've sent you to. Is Princess Anne in your class or something? Holy God, horse riding.'

Outdoor pursuits was mostly walking round museums on wet days and, when it was dry, the occasional trip to Portobello beach to write on a flapping piece of foolscap the signs of pollution you could see. Nelson felt that the best outdoor pursuit of the lot was what he was doing now. Skiving. At least that way you could do what you liked.

He groped in his pocket for the change out of his 50p and went into a shop. He bought a giant thing of bubble-gum and crammed it into his mouth. It was hard and dry at first and he couldn't answer the woman when she spoke to him.

'Whaaungh?'

'Pick the paper off the floor, son! Use the basket.'

He picked the paper up and screwed it into a ball. He aimed to miss the basket, just to spite her, but it went in. By the time he reached the bottom of the street the gum was chewy. He thrust his tongue into the middle of it and blew. A small disappointing bubble burst with a plip. It was not until the far end of Princes Street that he managed to blow big ones, pink and wobbling, that he could see at the end of his nose, which burst well and had to be gathered in shreds from his chin.

Then suddenly the crowds of shoppers parted and he saw his

mother. In the same instant she saw him. She was on him before he could even think of running. She grabbed him by the fur of his parka and began screaming into his face.

'In the name of God, Nelson, what are you doing here? Why aren't you at school?' She began shaking him. 'Do you realise what this means? They'll put me in bloody jail. It'll be bloody Saughton for me, and no mistake.' She had her teeth gritted together and her mouth was slanting in her face. Then Nelson started to shout.

'Help! Help!' he yelled.

A woman with an enormous chest like a pigeon stopped. 'What's happening?' she said.

Nelson's mother turned on her. 'It's none of your bloody business.'

'I'm being kidnapped,' yelled Nelson.

'Young woman. Young woman . . . ' said the lady with the large chest, trying to tap Nelson's mother on the shoulder with her umbrella, but Mrs Skelly turned with such a snarl that the woman edged away hesitatingly and looked over her shoulder and tut-tutted just loudly enough for the passing crowd to hear her.

'Help! I'm being kidnapped,' screamed Nelson, but everybody walked past looking the other way. His mother squatted down in front of him, still holding on to his jacket. She lowered her voice and tried to make it sound reasonable.

'Look Nelson, love. Listen. If you're skiving school, do you realise what'll happen to me? In Primary the Children's Panel threatened to send me to court. You're only at that Secondary and already that Sub-Attendance Committee thing wanted to fine me. Jesus, if you're caught again . . .'

Nelson stopped struggling. The change in her tone had quietened him down. She straightened up and looked wildly about her, wondering what to do.

'You've got to go straight back to school, do you hear me?'
'Yes.'

'Promise me you'll go.' The boy looked down at the ground.

13

'Promise?' The boy made no answer.

'I'll kill you if you don't go back. I'd take you myself only I've my work to go to. I'm late as it is.'

Again she looked around as if she would see someone who would suddenly help her. Still she held on to his jacket. She was biting her lip.

'Oh God, Nelson.'

The boy blew a flesh-pink bubble and snapped it between his teeth. She shook him.

'That bloody bubble-gum.'

There was a loud explosion as the one o'clock gun went off. They both leapt.

'Oh Jesus, that gun puts the heart sideways in me every time it goes off. Come on, son, you'll have to come with me. I'm late. I don't know what they'll say when they see you but I'm bloody taking you to school by the ear. You hear me?'

She began rushing along the street, Nelson's sleeve in one hand, her carrier bag in the other. The boy had to run to keep from being dragged.

'Don't you dare try a trick like that again. Kidnapped, my arse. Nelson, if I knew somebody who would kidnap you – I'd pay *him* the money. Embarrassing me on the street like that.'

They turned off the main road and went into a hallway and up carpeted stairs which had full-length mirrors along one side. Nelson stopped to make faces at himself but his mother chugged at his arm. At the head of the stairs stood a fat man in his shirtsleeves.

'What the hell is this?' he said. 'You're late, and what the hell is that?' He looked down from over his stomach at Nelson.

'I'll explain later,' she said. 'I'll make sure he stays in the room.'

'You should be on *now*,' said the fat man and turned and walked away through the swing doors. They followed him and Nelson saw, before his mother pushed him into the room, that it was a bar, plush and carpeted with crowds of men standing drinking.

14

'You sit here, Nelson, until I'm finished and then I'm taking you back to that school. You'll get nowhere if you don't do your lessons. I have to get changed now.'

She set her carrier bag on the floor and kicked off her shoes. Nelson sat down, watching her. She stopped and looked over her shoulder at him, biting her lip.

'Where's that bloody eyepatch you should be wearing?' Nelson indicated his pocket.

'Well, wear it then.' Nelson took the crumpled patch from his pocket, tugging bits of it unstuck to get it flat before he stuck it over his bad eye. His mother took out her handbag and began rooting about at the bottom of it. Nelson heard the rattle of her bottles of scent and tubes of lipstick.

'Ah,' she said and produced another eyepatch, flicking it clean. 'Put another one on till I get changed. I don't want you noseying at me.' She came to him, pulling away the white backing to the patch, and stuck it over his remaining eye. He imagined her concentrating, the tip of her tongue stuck out. She pressed his eyebrows with her thumbs, making sure that the patches were stuck.

'Now don't move, or you'll bump into something.'

Nelson heard the slither of her clothes and her small grunts as she hurriedly got changed. Then he heard her rustle in her bag, the soft pop and rattle as she opened her capsules. Her 'tantalisers' she called them, small black and red torpedoes. Then he heard her voice.

'Just you stay like that till I come back. That way you'll come to no harm. You hear me, Nelson? If I come back in here and you have those things off, I'll *kill* you. I'll not be long.'

Nelson nodded from his darkness.

'The door will be locked, so there's no running away.'

'Ah ken.'

Suddenly his darkness exploded with lights as he felt her bony hand strike his ear.

'You don't ken things, Nelson. You *know* them.'

He heard her go out and the key turn in the lock. His ear

15

sang and he felt it was hot. He turned his face up to the ceiling. She had left the light on because he could see pinkish through the patches. He smelt the beer and stale smoke. Outside the room pop music had started up, very loudly. He heard the deep notes pound through to where he sat. He felt his ear with his hand and it *was* hot.

Making small *aww* sounds of excruciating pain, he slowly detached both eyepatches from the bridge of the nose outwards. In case his mother should come back he did not take them off completely, but left them hinged to the sides of his eyes. When he turned to look around him they flapped like blinkers.

It wasn't really a room, more a broom cupboard. Crates were stacked against one wall; brushes and mops and buckets stood near a very low sink; on a row of coat-hooks hung some limp raincoats and stained white jackets; his mother's stuff hung on the last hook. The floor was covered with tramped-flat cork tips. Nelson got up to look at what he was sitting on. It was a crate of empties. He went to the keyhole and looked out, but all he could see was a patch of wallpaper opposite. Above the door was a narrow window. He looked up at it, his eyepatches falling back to touch his ears. He went over to the sink and had a drink of water from the low tap, sucking noisily at the column of water as it splashed into the sink. He stopped and wiped his mouth. The water felt cold after the mint of the bubble-gum. He looked up at his mother's things, hanging on the hook; her tights and drawers were as she wore them, but inside out and hanging knock-kneed on top of everything. In her bag he found her blonde wig and tried it on, smelling the perfume of it as he did so. At home he liked noseying in his mother's room; smelling all her bottles of make-up; seeing her spangled things. He had to stand on the crate to see himself but the mirror was all brown measles under its surface and the eyepatches ruined the effect. He sat down again and began pulling at the bubble-gum, seeing how long he could make it stretch before it broke. Still the music pounded outside. It was so loud the vibrations tickled his feet. He sighed and looked up at the window again.

16

If his mother took him back to school, he could see problems. For starting St John the Baptist's she had bought him a brand new Adidas bag for his books. Over five pounds it had cost her, she said. On his first real skive he had dumped the bag in the bin at the bottom of his stair, every morning for a week, and travelled light into town. On the Friday he came home just in time to see the bin lorry driving away in a cloud of bluish smoke. He had told his mother that the bag had been stolen from the playground during break. She had threatened to phone the school about it but Nelson had hastily assured her that the whole matter was being investigated by none other than the Headmaster himself. This threat put the notion out of his head of asking her for the money to replace the books. At that point he had not decided on a figure. He could maybe try it again some time when all the fuss had died down. But now it was all going to be stirred if his mother took him to school.

He pulled two crates to the door and climbed up but they were not high enough. He put a third one on top, climbed on again, and gingerly straightened, balancing on its rim. On tip-toe he could see out. He couldn't see his mother anywhere. He saw a crowd of men standing in a semicircle. Behind them were some very bright lights, red, yellow and blue. They all had pints in their hands which they didn't seem to be drinking. They were all watching something which Nelson couldn't see. Suddenly the music stopped and the men all began drinking and talking. Standing on tip-toe for so long, Nelson's legs began to shake and he heard the bottles in the crate rattle. He rested for a moment. Then the music started again. He looked to see. The men now just stood looking. It was as if they were seeing a ghost. Then they all cheered louder than the music.

Nelson climbed down and put the crates away from the door so that his mother could get in. He closed his eyepatches over for a while, but still she didn't come. He listened to another record, this time a slow one. He decided to travel blind to get another drink of water. As he did so the music changed to fast. He heard the men cheering again, then the rattle of the key in

17

the lock. Nelson, his arms rotating in front of him, tried to make his way back to the crate. His mother's voice said,

'Don't you dare take those eyepatches off.' Her voice was panting. Then his hand hit up against her. It was her bare stomach, hot and damp with sweat. She guided him to sit down, breathing heavily through her nose.

'I'll just get changed and then you're for school right away, boy.' Nelson nodded. He heard her light a cigarette as she dressed. When she had finished she ripped off his right eyepatch.

'There now, we're ready to go,' she said, ignoring Nelson's anguished yells.

'That's the wrong eye,' he said.

'Oh shit,' said his mother and ripped off the other one, turned it upside down and stuck it over his right eye. The smoke from the cigarette in her mouth trickled up into her eye and she held it half shut. Nelson could see the bright points of sweat shining through her make-up. She still hadn't got her breath back fully yet. She smelt of drink.

On the way out, the fat man with the rolled-up sleeves held out two fivers and Nelson's mother put them into her purse.

'The boy – never again,' he said, looking down at Nelson.

They took the Number Twelve to St John the Baptist's. It was the worst possible time because, just as they were going in, the bell rang for the end of a period and suddenly the quad was full of pupils, all looking at Nelson and his mother. Some sixth-year boys wolf-whistled after her and others stopped to stare. Nelson felt a flush of pride that she was causing a stir. She was dressed in black satiny jeans, very tight, and her pink blouse was knotted, leaving her tanned midriff bare. They went into the office and a secretary came to the window.

'Yes?' she said, looking Mrs Skelly up and down.

'I'd like to see the Head,' she said.

'I'm afraid he's at a meeting. What is it about?'

'About him.' She waved her thumb over her shoulder at Nelson.

'What year is he?'

'What year are you, son?' His mother turned to him.

'First.'

'First Year. Oh, then you'd best see Mr MacDermot, the First Year Housemaster.' The secretary directed them to Mr MacDermot's office. It was at the other side of the school and they had to walk what seemed miles of corridors before they found it. Mrs Skelly's stiletto heels clicked along the tiles.

'It's a wonder you don't get lost in here, son,' she said as she knocked on the Housemaster's door. Mr MacDermot opened it and invited them in. Nelson could see that he too was looking at her, his eyes wide and his face smiley.

'What can I do for you?' he said when they were seated.

'It's him,' said Mrs Skelly. 'He's been skiving again. I caught him this morning.'

'I see,' said Mr MacDermot. He was very young to be a Housemaster. He had a black moustache which he began to stroke with the back of his hand. He paused for a long time. Then he said,

'Remind me of your name, son.'

' – Oh, I'm sorry,' said Mrs Skelly. 'My name is Skelly and this is my boy Nelson.'

'Ah, yes, Skelly.' The Housemaster got up and produced a yellow file from the filing cabinet. 'You must forgive me, but we haven't seen a great deal of Nelson lately.'

'Do you mind if I smoke?' asked Mrs Skelly.

'Not at all,' said the Housemaster, getting up to open the window.

'The trouble is, that the last time we were at that Sub-Attendance Committee thing they said they would take court action if it happened again. And it has.'

'Well, it may not come to that with the Attendance Sub-Committee. If we nip it in the bud. If Nelson makes an effort, isn't that right, Nelson?' Nelson sat silent.

'Speak when the master's speaking to you,' yelled Mrs Skelly.

'Yes,' said Nelson, making it barely audible.

19

'You're Irish too,' said Mrs Skelly to the Housemaster, smiling.

'That's right,' said Mr MacDermot. 'I thought your accent was familiar. Where do you come from?'

'My family come from just outside Derry. And you?'

'Oh, that's funny. I'm just across the border from you. Donegal.' As they talked, Nelson stared out the window. He had never heard his mother so polite. He could just see a corner of the playing fields and a class coming out with the Gym teacher. Nelson hated Gym more than anything. It was crap. He loathed the changing rooms, the getting stripped in front of others, the stupidity he felt when he missed the ball. The smoke from his mother's cigarette went in an arc towards the open window. Distantly he could hear the class shouting as they started a game of football.

'Nelson! Isn't that right?' said Mr MacDermot loudly.

'What?'

'That even when you are here you don't work hard enough.'

'Hmmm,' said Nelson.

'You don't have to tell me,' said his mother. 'It's not just his eye that's lazy. If you ask me the whole bloody lot of him is. I've never seen him washing a dish in his life and he leaves everything at his backside.'

'Yes,' said the Housemaster. Again he stroked his moustache. 'What is required from Nelson is a change of attitude. Attitude, Nelson. You understand a word like attitude?'

'Yes.'

'He's just not interested in school, Mrs Skelly.'

'I've no room to talk, of course. I had to leave at fifteen,' she said, rolling her eyes in Nelson's direction. 'You know what I mean? Otherwise I might have stayed on and got my exams.'

'I see,' said Mr MacDermot. 'Can we look forward to a change in attitude, Nelson?'

'Hm-hm.'

'Have you no friends in school?' asked the Housemaster.

'Naw.'

'And no interest. You see, you can't be interested in any subject unless you do some work at it. Work pays dividends with interest . . .' he paused and looked at Mrs Skelly. She was inhaling her cigarette. He went on, 'Have you considered the possibility that Nelson may be suffering from school phobia?'

Mrs Skelly looked at him. 'Phobia, my arse,' she said. 'He just doesn't like school.'

'I see. Does he do any work at home then?'

'Not since he had his bag with all his books in it stolen.'

'Stolen?'

Nelson leaned forward in his chair and said loudly and clearly, 'I'm going to try to be better from now on. I am. I am going to try, sir.'

'That's more like it,' said the Housemaster, also edging forward.

'I am not going to skive. I am going to try. Sir, I'm going to do my best.'

'Good boy. I think, Mrs Skelly, if I have a word with the right people and convey to them what we have spoken about, I think there will be no court action. Leave it with me, will you? And I'll see what I can do. Of course it all depends on Nelson. If he is as good as his word. One more truancy and I'll be forced to report it. And he must realise that he has three full years of school to do before he leaves us. You must be aware of my position in this matter. You understand what I'm saying, Nelson?'

'Ah ken,' he said. 'I know.'

'You go off to your class now. I have some more things to say to your mother.'

Nelson rose to his feet and shuffled towards the door. He stopped.

'Where do I go, sir?'

'Have you not got your timetable?'

'No sir. Lost it.'

The Housemaster, tut-tutting, dipped into another file, read a card and told him that he should be at R.K. in Room 72. As he left, Nelson noticed that his mother had put her knee up against the Housemaster's desk and was swaying back in her chair, as she took out another cigarette.

"Bye, love,' she said.

When he went into Room 72 there was a noise of oos and ahhs from the others in the class. He said to the teacher that he had been seeing Mr MacDermot. She gave him a Bible and told him to sit down. He didn't know her name. He had her for English as well as R.K. She was always rabbiting on about poetry.

'You, boy, that just came in. For your benefit, we are talking and reading about organisation. Page 667. About how we should divide our lives up with work and prayer. How we should put each part of the day to use, and each part of the year. This is one of the most beautiful passages in the whole of the Bible. Listen to its rhythms as I read.' She lightly drummed her closed fist on the desk in front of her.

'"There is an appointed time for everything, and a time for every affair under the heavens. A time to be born and a time to die; a time to plant and a time to uproot . . ."'

'What page did you say, Miss?' asked Nelson.

'Six-six-seven,' she snapped and read on, her voice trembling, '"A time to kill and a time to heal; a time to wear down and a time to build. A time to weep and a time to laugh; a time to mourn and a time to dance . . ."'

Nelson looked out of the window, at the tiny white H of the goal posts in the distance. He took his bubble-gum out and stuck it under the desk. The muscles of his jaw ached from chewing the now flavourless mass. He looked down at page 667 with its microscopic print, then put his face close to it. He tore off his eyepatch, thinking that if he was going to become blind then the sooner it happened the better.

The Beginnings of a Sin

I BELIEVE HE'S LATE again thought Colum. He took a clean white surplice from his bag and slipped it over his head, steadying his glasses as he did so. It was five to eight. He sat on the bench and changed his shoes for a black pair of gutties. Father Lynch said that all his altar-boys must move as quietly as shadows. When he was late he was usually in his worst mood. Sometimes he did not turn up at all and Miss Grant, the housekeeper, would come over and announce from the back of the church that Father Lynch was ill and that there would be no Mass that day.

At two minutes to eight Colum heard his footstep at the vestry door. Father Lynch came in and nodded to the boy. Colum had never seen anyone with such a sleep-crumpled face in the mornings. It reminded him of a bloodhound, there was such a floppiness about his deeply wrinkled skin. His whole face sagged and sloped into lines of sadness. His black hair was parted low to the side and combed flat with Brylcreem. Colum thought his neat hair looked out of place on top of the disorder of his features.

'Is everything ready?' Father Lynch asked him.

'Yes, Father.'

Colum watched him as he prepared to say Mass. He began by putting on the amice, like a handkerchief with strings, at the back of his neck. Next a white alb like a shroud, reaching to the floor. The polished toe-caps of his everyday shoes peeped out from underneath. He put the cincture about his waist and knotted it quickly. He kissed the embroidered cross on his emerald stole and hung it round his neck. Lastly he put on the chasuble, very carefully inserting his head through the neck-hole. Colum couldn't make up his mind whether he did not want to stain the vestments with hair-oil or wreck his hair. The chasuble was emerald green with yellow lines. Colum liked the feasts of the martyrs best, with their bright blood colour. Father

Lynch turned to him.

'What are you staring at?'

'Nothing, Father.'

'You look like a wee owl.'

'Sorry.'

'Let's get this show on the road,' Father Lynch said, his face still like a sad bloodhound. 'We're late already.'

None of the other altar-boys liked Father Lynch. When they did something wrong, he never scolded them with words but instead would nip them on the upper arm. They said he was too quiet and you could never trust anybody like that. Colum found that he was not so quiet if you asked him questions. He seemed to like Colum better than the others, at least Colum thought so. One day he had asked him why a priest wore so much to say Mass and Father Lynch had spoken to him for about ten minutes, keeping him late for school.

'Normally when people wear beautiful things it is to make their personality stand out. With a priest it is the opposite. He wears so much to hide himself And the higher up the Church you go, the more you have to wear. Think of the poor Pope with all that trumphery on him.'

After Mass Father Lynch asked him how the ballot tickets were going.

'Great. I've sold – '

'Don't tell me. Keep it as a surprise.'

In the darkness Colum stood at the door waiting. He had rolled up a white ballot ticket and was smoking it, watching his breath cloud the icy air. He pulled his socks up as high as he could to try and keep his legs warm. There was a funny smell from the house, like sour food. The woman came back out with her purse. She was still chewing something.

'What's it in aid of?'

'St Kieran's Church Building Fund.'

'How much are they?'

'Threepence each.'

25

The woman hesitated, poking about in her purse with her index finger. He told her that the big prize was a Christmas hamper. There was a second prize of whiskey and sherry. She took four tickets, finishing his last book.

'Father Lynch'll not be wanting to win it outright, then.'

He was writing her name on the stubs with his fountain pen.

'Pardon?'

'You're a neat wee writer,' she said. He tore the tickets down the perforations and gave them to her. She handed him a shilling, which he dropped into his jacket pocket. It was swinging heavy with coins.

'There's the snow coming on now,' said the woman, waiting to close the front door. He ran the whole way home holding on to the outside of his pocket. In the house he dried his hair and wiped the speckles of melted snow from his glasses. Two of his older brothers, Rory and Dermot, were sitting on the sofa doing homework balanced on their knees and when he told them it was snowing they ran out to see if it was lying.

He took down his tin and spilled it and the money from his pocket on to the table. He added it all together and counted the number of books of stubs. For each book sold the seller was allowed to keep sixpence for himself. Over the past weeks Colum had sold forty-two books around the doors. He took a pound note and a shilling and slipped them into his pocket. He had never had so much money in his life and there was still a full week to sell tickets before the ballot was drawn.

His mother stood at the range making soda farls on a griddle. When they were cooked they filled the house with their smell and made a dry scuffling noise as she handled them. He heard the front door close and Michael shout 'Hello'. At eighteen he was the eldest and the only wage earner in the house.

'Come on, Colum,' said his mother. 'Clear that table. The hungry working man is in.'

After tea they always said the Family Rosary. Colum would half kneel, half crouch at the armchair with his face almost touching the seat. The cushion smelt of cloth and human. He tried to say the Rosary as best he could, thinking of the Sacred Mysteries while his mouth said the words. He was disturbed one night to see Michael kneeling at the sofa saying the prayers with the Sunday paper between his elbows. Colum counted off the Hail Marys, feeding his shiny lilac rosary beads between his finger and thumb. They were really more suitable for a woman but they had come all the way from Lourdes. Where the loop of the beads joined was a little silver heart with a bubble of Lourdes water in it – like the spirit level in his brother's tool kit.

When it came to his turn to give out the prayer Colum always waited until the response was finished – not like his brothers who charged on, overlapping the prayer and the response, slurring their words to get it finished as quickly as possible. They became annoyed with him and afterwards, in whispers, accused him of being 'a creeping Jesus'.

At the end of each Rosary their mother said a special prayer 'for the Happy Repose of the Soul of Daddy'. Although he had been dead two years, it still brought a lump to Colum's throat. It wouldn't have been so bad if she had said father or something but the word Daddy made him want to cry. Sometimes he had to go on kneeling when the others had risen to their feet in case they should see his eyes.

It was Colum's turn to do the dishes. They had their turns written up on a piece of paper so that there would be no argument. He poured some hot water into the basin from the kettle on the range. It had gone slightly brown from heating. He didn't like the look of it as much as the cold water from the pump. In the white enamel bucket under the scullery bench it looked pure and cool and still. Where the enamel had chipped off, the bucket was blue-black. If you put your hand in the water the fingers seemed to go flat.

He dipped a cup into the basin, rinsed it out and set it on the table. Father Lynch had funny fingers. He had tiny tufts of black hair on the back of each of them. They made Colum feel strange as he poured water from a cruet on to them. The priest would join his trembling index fingers and thumbs and hold them over the glass bowl, then he would take the linen cloth ironed into its folds and wipe them dry. He would put it back in its creases and lay it on Colum's arm. He had some whispered prayers to say when he was doing that. Colum always wondered why Father Lynch was so nervous saying his morning Mass. He had served for others and they didn't tremble like that. Perhaps it was because he was holier than them, that they weren't as much in awe of the Blessed Sacrament as he was. What a frightening thing it must be, to hold Christ's actual flesh – to have the responsibility to change the bread and wine into the body and blood of Jesus.

He dried the dishes and set them in neat piles before putting them back on the shelf. Above the bench Michael had fixed a small mirror for shaving. Colum had to stand on tip-toe to see himself. He was the only one of the family who had to wear glasses. He took after his father. For a long time he had to wear National Health round ones with the springy legs that hooked behind his ears, but after months of pleading and crying his mother had given in and bought him a good pair with real frames.

He went to the back door and threw out a basinful of water with a slap on to the icy ground. It steamed in the light from the scullery window. It was a still night and he could hear the children's voices yelling from the next street.

The kitchen was warm when he came back in again. Radio Luxembourg was on the wireless. Colum took all his money in his pocket and put the stubs in a brown paper bag.

'I'm away, Mammy,' he said.

She was having a cigarette, sitting with her feet up on a stool.

'Don't be late,' was all she said.

He walked a lamp post, ran a lamp post through the town until he reached the hill which led to the Parochial House. It was a large building made of the same red brick as the church. He could see lights on in the house so he climbed the hill. It was still bitterly cold and he was aware of his jaw shivering. He kept both hands in his pockets, holding the brown bag in the crook of his arm. He knocked at the door of the house. It was the priest's housekeeper who opened it a fraction. When she saw Colum she opened it wide.

'Hello, Miss Grant. Is Father Lynch in?'

'He is busy, Colum. What was it you wanted?'

'Ballot tickets, Miss. And to give in money.'

She looked over her shoulder down the hallway, then turned and put out her hand for the money.

'It's all loose, Miss,' said Colum, digging into his pocket to let her hear it.

'Oh, you'd best come in then − for a moment.'

Miss Grant brought him down the carpeted hallway to her quarters − she had a flat of her own at the back of the house. She closed the door and smiled a jumpy kind of smile − a smile that stopped in the middle. Colum emptied the bag of stubs on the table.

'There's forty-two books . . .' he said.

'Goodness, someone has been busy.'

'. . . and here is five pounds, five shillings.' He set two pound notes and a ten shilling note on the table and hand-fulled the rest of the coins out of his pocket. They rang and clattered on the whitewood surface. She began to check it, scraping the coins towards her quickly and building them into piles.

'All present and correct,' she said.

Colum looked at the sideboard. There was a bottle of orange juice and a big box of biscuits which he knew was for the ticket sellers. She saw him looking.

'All right, all right,' she said.

She poured a glass of juice and allowed him to choose two biscuits. His fingers hovered over the selection.

'Oh come on, Colum, don't take all night.'

He took a chocolate one and a wafer and sat down. He had never seen Miss Grant so snappy before. Usually she was easygoing. She was very fat, with a chest like stuffed pillows under her apron. He had heard the grown-ups in the town say that if anybody had earned heaven it was her. They spoke of her goodness and kindness. 'There's one saint in that Parochial House,' they would say. For a long time Colum thought they were talking about Father Lynch.

In the silence he heard his teeth crunching the biscuit. Miss Grant did not sit down but stood by the table waiting for him to finish. He swallowed and said,

'Could I have ten more books, please?'

'Yes, dear.' She put her hands in her apron pocket and looked all around her, then left the room.

Colum had never been in this part of the house before. He had always gone into Father Lynch's room or waited in the hallway. Although it was a modern house, it was full of old things. A picture of the Assumption of Our Lady in a frame of gold leaves hung by the front door. The furniture in Father Lynch's room was black and heavy. The dining room chairs had twisted legs like barley sugar sticks. Everything had a rich feel to it, especially the thick patterned carpet. Miss Grant's quarters were not carpeted but had some rugs laid on the red tiled floor. It was the kind of floor they had at home, except that the corners of their tiles were chipped off and they had become uneven enough to trip people.

'Vera!' he heard a voice shout. It was Father Lynch.

Vera's voice answered from somewhere. Colum looked up and Father Lynch was standing in the doorway with his arm propped against the jamb.

'Hello, Father.'

'Well, if it isn't the owl,' said Father Lynch.

He wasn't dressed like a priest but was wearing an ordinary man's collarless shirt, open at the neck.

'What brings you up here, Colum?'

He moved from the door and reached out to put his hand on a chair back. Two strands of his oiled hair had come loose and fallen over his forehead. He sat down very slowly on the chair.

'Ballot tickets, Father. I've sold all you gave me.'

30

Father Lynch gave a loud whoop and slapped the table loudly with the flat of his hand. His eyes looked very heavy and he was blinking a lot.

'That's the way to do it. Lord, how the money rolls in.'

He was slurring his words as if he was saying the Rosary. Miss Grant came into the room holding a wad of white ballot tickets.

'Here you are now, Colum. You'd best be off.'

Colum finished his juice and stood up.

'Is that the strongest you can find for the boy to drink, Vera?' He laughed loudly. Colum had never heard him laugh before. He slapped the table again.

'Father – if you'll excuse us, I'll just show Colum out now.'

'No. No. He came to see me – didn't you?'

Colum nodded.

'He's the only one that would. Let him stay for a bit.'

'His mother will worry about him.'

'No she won't,' said Colum.

'Of course she won't,' said Father Lynch. He ignored Miss Grant. 'How many books did you sell?'

'Forty-two, Father.'

The priest raised his eyes to heaven and blew out his cheeks. Colum smelt a smell like altar wine.

'Holy Saint Christopher. Forty-two?'

'Yes.'

Miss Grant moved behind Colum and began to guide him with pressure away from the table.

'That calls for a celebration.' Father Lynch stood up unsteadily. 'Forty-two!'

He reached out to give Colum a friendly cuff on the back of the head but he missed and instead his hand struck the side of the boy's face scattering his glasses on the tiled floor.

'Aw Jesus,' said the priest. 'I'm sorry.' Father Lynch hunkered down to pick them up but lurched forward on to his knees. One lens was starred with white and the arc of the frame was broken. He hoisted himself to his feet and held the glasses close to his sagging face, looking at them.

'Jesus, I'm so sorry,' he said again. He bent down, looking for the missing piece of frame, and the weight of his head seemed to topple him. He cracked his skull with a sickening thump off the sharp edge of a radiator. One of his legs was still up in the air trying to right his balance. He put his hand to the top of his head and Colum saw that the hand was slippery with blood. Red blood was smeared from his Brylcreemed hair on to the radiator panel as the priest slid lower. His eyes were open but not seeing.

'Are you all right, Father?' Miss Grant's voice was shaking. She produced a white handkerchief from her apron pocket. The priest shouted, his voice suppressed and hissing and angry. He cursed his housekeeper and the polish on her floor. Then he raised his eyes to her without moving his head and said in an ordinary voice,

'What a mess for the boy.'

Miss Grant took the glasses which he was still clutching and put them in Colum's hand. Father Lynch began to cry with his mouth half open. Miss Grant turned the boy away and pushed him towards the door. Both she and Colum had to step over the priest to get out. She led him by the elbow down the hallway.

'That's the boy. Here's your ballot tickets.'

She opened the front door.

'Say a wee prayer for him, Colum. He's in bad need of it.'

'All right, but – '

'I'd better go back to him now.'

The door closed with a slam. Colum put his glasses on but could only see through his left eye. His knees were like water and his stomach was full of wind. He tried to get some of it up but he couldn't. He started to run. He ran all the way home. He sat panting on the cold doorstep and only went in when he got his breath back. His mother was alone.

'What happened to you? You're as white as a sheet,' she said, looking up at him. She was knitting a grey sock on three needles shaped into a triangle. Colum produced his glasses from his pocket. Within the safety of the house he began to cry.

'I bust them.'

'How, might I ask?' His mother's voice was angry.

'I was running and they just fell off. I slipped on the ice.'

'Good God, Colum, do you know how much those things cost? You'll have to get a new pair for school. Where do you think the money is going to come from? Who do you think I am, Carnegie? Eh?'

Her knitting needles were flashing and clacking. Colum continued to cry, tears rather than noise.

'Sheer carelessness. I've a good mind to give you a thumping.'

Colum, keeping out of range of her hand, sat at the table and put the glasses on. He could only half see. He put his hand in his pocket and took out his pound note.

'Here,' he said offering it to his mother. She took it and put it beneath the jug on the shelf.

'That'll not be enough,' she said, then after a while, 'Will you stop that sobbing? It's not the end of the world.'

The next morning Colum was surprised to see Father Lynch in the vestry before him. He was robed and reading his breviary, pacing the strip of carpet in the centre of the room. They said nothing to each other.

At the Consecration Colum looked up and saw the black congealed wound on the thinning crown of Father Lynch's head, as he lifted the tail of the chasuble. He saw him elevate the white disc of the host and heard him mutter the words,

'Hoc est enim corpus meum.'

Colum jangled the cluster of bells with angry twists of his wrist. A moment later when the priest raised the chalice full of wine he rang the bell again, louder if possible.

In the vestry afterwards he changed as quickly as he could and was about to dash out when Father Lynch called him. He had taken off his chasuble and was folding it away.

'Colum.'

'What?'

'Sit down a moment.'

He removed the cincture and put it like a coiled snake in the drawer. The boy remained standing. The priest sat down in his alb and beckoned him over.

'I'm sorry about your glasses.'

Colum stayed at the door and Father Lynch went over to him. Colum thought his face no longer sad, simply ugly.

'Your lace is loosed.' He was about to genuflect to tie it for him but Colum crouched and tied it himself. Their heads almost collided.

'It's hard for me to explain,' said Father Lynch, 'but . . . to a boy of your age sin is a very simple thing. It's not.'

Colum smelt the priest's breath sour and sick.

'Yes, Father.'

'That's because you have never committed a sin. You don't know about it.'

He removed his alb and hung it in the wardrobe.

'Trying to find the beginnings of a sin is like . . .' He looked at the boy's face and stopped. 'Sin is a deliberate turning away from God. That is an extremely difficult thing to do. To close Him out from your love . . .'

'I'll be late for school, Father.'

'I suppose you need new glasses?'

'Yes.'

Father Lynch put his hand in his pocket and gave him some folded pound notes.

'Did you mention it to your mother?'

'What?'

'How they were broken?'

'No.'

'Are you sure? To anyone?'

Colum nodded that he hadn't. He was turning to get out the door. The priest raised his voice, trying to keep him there.

'I knew your father well, Colum,' he shouted. 'You remind me of him a lot.'

34

The altar-boy ran, slamming the door after him. He heard an empty wooden coat-hanger rattle on the hardboard panel of the door and it rattled in his mind until he reached the bottom of the hill. There he stopped running. He unfolded the wad of pound notes still in his hand and counted one – two – three – four of them with growing disbelief.

Remote

Around about the end of each month she would write a letter, but because it was December she used an old Christmas card, which she found at the bottom of the biscuit tin among her pension books. She stood dressed in her outdoor clothes on tiptoe at the bedroom window waiting for the bird-watcher's Land Rover to come over the top of the hill two miles away. When she saw it she dashed, slamming the door after her and running in her stiff-legged fashion down the lane on to the road. Her aim was to be walking, breathing normally, when the Land Rover would indicate and stop in the middle of the one-track road.

'Can I give you a lift?'

'Aye.'

She walked round the front of the shuddering engine and climbed up to sit on the split seat. Mushroom-coloured foam bulged from its crack. More often than not she had to kick things aside to make room for her feet. It was not the lift she would have chosen but it was all there was. He shoved the wobbling stick through the gears and she had to shout – each month the same thing.

'Where are you for?'

'The far side.'

'I'm always lucky just to catch you.'

He was dressed like one of those hitch-hikers, green khaki jacket, cord trousers and laced-up mountain boots. His hair was long and unwashed and his beard divided into points like the teats of a goat.

'Are you going as far as the town this time?'

'Yes.'

'Will you drop me off.'

'Sure. Christmas shopping?'

'Aye, that'll be right.'

The road spun past, humping and squirming over peat bogs, the single track bulging at passing places – points which were marked by tall black and white posts to make them stand out against the landscape. Occasionally in the bog there were incisions, a black-brown colour, herring-boned with scars where peat had been cut.

'How's the birds doing?' she shouted.

'Fine. I've never had so many as this year.'

His accent was English and it surprised her that he had blackheads dotting his cheekbones and dirty hands.

'Twenty-two nesting pairs – so far.'

'That's nice.'

'Compared with sixteen last year.'

'What are they?'

He said what they were but she couldn't hear him properly. They joined the main road and were silent for a while. Then rounding a corner the bird-man suddenly applied the brakes. Two cars, facing in opposite directions, sat in the middle of the road, their drivers having a conversation. The bird-man muttered and steered round them, the Land Rover tilting as it mounted the verge.

'I'd like to see them try that in Birmingham.'

'Is that where you're from?'

He nodded.

'Why did you come to the island?'

'The birds.'

'Aye, I suppose there's not too many down there.'

He smiled and pointed to an open packet of Polo mints on the dashboard. She lifted them and saw that the top sweet was soiled, the relief letters almost black. She prised it out and gave it to him. The white one beneath she put in her mouth.

'Thanks,' she said.

'You born on the island?'

'City born and bred.' She snorted. 'I was lured here by a man forty-two years ago.'

39

'I never see him around.'

'I'm not surprised. He's dead this long time.' She cracked the ring of the mint between her teeth.

'I'm sorry.'

She chased the two crescents of mint around with her tongue.

'What did he do?'

'He drowned himself. In the loch.'

'I'm sorry, I didn't mean that.'

'On Christmas Day. He was mad in the skull – away with the fairies.'

There was a long pause in which he said again that he was sorry. Then he said, 'What I meant was – what did he do for a living?'

'What does it matter now?'

The bird-man shook his head and concentrated on the road ahead.

'He was a shepherd,' she said. Then a little later, 'He was the driver. There should always be one in the house who can drive.'

He let her off at the centre of the village and she had to walk the steep hill to the Post Office. She breathed through her mouth and took a rest halfway up, holding on to a small railing. Distances grew with age.

Inside she passed over her pension book, got her money and bought a first-class stamp. She waited until she was outside before she took the letter from her bag. She licked the stamp, stuck it on the envelope and dropped it in the letter box. Walking down the hill was easier.

She went to the Co-op to buy sugar and tea and porridge. The shop was strung with skimpy tinselled decorations and the music they were playing was Christmas hits – 'Rudolf' and 'I saw Mammy Kissing Santa Claus'. She only had a brief word with Elizabeth at the check-out because of the queue behind her. In the butcher's she bought herself a pork chop and some bacon. His bacon lasted longer than the packet stuff.

When she had her shopping finished she wondered what to do to pass the time. She could visit young Mary but if she did that she would have to talk. Not having enough things to say she felt awkward listening to the tick of the clock and the distant cries of sea birds. Chat was a thing you got out of the habit of when you were on your own all the time and, besides, Mary was shy. Instead she decided to buy a cup of tea in the café. And treat herself to an almond bun. She sat near the window where she could look out for the post van.

The café was warm and it, too, was decorated. Each time the door opened the hanging fronds of tinsel fluttered. On a tape somewhere carols were playing. Two children, sitting with their mother, were playing with a new toy car on the table-top. The cellophane wrapping had been discarded on the floor. They both imitated engine noises although only one of them was pushing it round the plates. The other sat waiting impatiently for his turn.

She looked away from them and stared into her tea. When they dredged him up on Boxing Day he had two car batteries tied to his wrists. He was nothing if not thorough. One of them had been taken from his own van parked by the loch shore and the thing had to be towed to the garage. If he had been a drinking man he could have been out getting drunk or fallen into bad company. But there was only the black depression. All that day the radio had been on to get rid of the dread.

When 'Silent Night' came on the tape and the children started to squabble over whose turn it was she did not wait to finish her tea but walked slowly to the edge of the village with her bag of shopping, now and again pausing to look over her shoulder. The scarlet of the post van caught her eye and she stood on the verge with her arm out. When she saw it was Stuart driving she smiled. He stopped the van and she ducked down to look in the window.

'Anything for me today?'

He leaned across to the basket of mail which occupied the

passenger seat position and began to rummage through the bundles of letters and cards held together with elastic bands.

'This job would be all right if it wasn't for bloody Christmas.' He paused at her single letter. 'Aye, there's just one.'

'Oh good. You might as well run me up, seeing as you're going that way.'

He sighed and looked over his shoulder at a row of houses.

'Wait for me round the corner.'

She nodded and walked on ahead while he made some deliveries. The lay-by was out of sight of the houses and she set her bag down to wait. Stuart seemed to take a long time. She looked down at the loch in the growing dark. The geese were returning for the night, filling the air with their squawking. They sounded like a dance-hall full of people laughing and enjoying themselves, heard from a distance on the night wind.

My Dear Palestrina

'COME ON, LOVE, it's for your own good,' she said. Rooks from the trees above set up a slow, raucous cawing. Cinders had spilled on the footpath and they cracked and spat beneath their shoes, echoing in the arch of the trees overhead, as they walked the mile from the town to Miss Schwartz's place. The boy stayed one pace behind and slightly to the left of his mother. To show her determination, she had begun by taking his hand but it seemed foolish to be seen dragging a boy of his age. Although now they were separate they were so far gone along the road that she knew she had won. The boy stopped at the old forge and stared at the door into the dark, listening to the high pinging of the blacksmith's hammer.

'Don't have me to go back, Danny, or I'll make an example of you.' She waited, looking over her shoulder at him. His eyes were still red from crying.

Miss Schwartz had a beautifully polished brass knocker on her black front door. It resounded deep within the house. It seemed a long time before she answered. When she did, it was with politeness.

'Yes, can I help you?'

The boy's mother smiled back and nodded down the path to where the boy was standing.

'I want him to have piana lessons,' she said.

Mrs McErlane, panting after the walk, fell into an arm-chair, propped her bag on her knee and listened as Miss Schwartz struck single notes for her Danny to sing. His voice was clear but not rich and still had reverberations of the long afternoon's crying in it. Her long pale finger poked about the piano and no matter where it went Danny's voice followed it. Then she played clusters of notes and Danny repeated them. She asked the boy to turn away and struck a note.

'Can you find that note?' and Danny played it. She did this again and again and each time the boy found it. At the doorstep

44

on the way out Miss Schwartz said that the pleasure in teaching would be hers. *Auf wiedersehen.*

'Did you hear that?' said Mrs McErlane on the way home. 'Anyway it will be good for you. It's a lovely thing to have. The others is too old to learn now.'

Danny said nothing but hunched his shoulders against the darkness and the cold of the night that was coming on.

'I hated to think of that piana going to waste,' she said.

Because the McErlanes had a boy young enough to learn, it was they who got the piano when Uncle George died. They also got a lawn mower and a vacuum cleaner, even though they had no carpet in the house.

The piano came in the night when Danny was in bed. When he had visited Uncle George, Danny would slip into the front room on his own and climb up on the piano stool and single-finger notes. He liked to play the white ones because afterwards, when he struck a black note it was so sad that it gave him a funny feeling in his tummy. The piano stool had a padded seat which opened. Inside were wads of old sheet music with film stars' pictures on the front.

Bing Crosby, Johnny Ray, Rosemary Clooney. He had heard her singing on the radio.

> A cannon-ball don't pay no mind
> Whether you're gentle or you're kind.

It was about a civil war. He liked the way she twirled her voice. When he tried to sing that song he always put on an American accent.

> Two brothers on their way
> One wore blue and one wore grey.

After school he walked to his first lesson on a road that fumed with dry snow and wind. The door of the forge was closed and the place silent. On the way out a car passed him, returning to town. A white face pressed itself up against the back window. White hair, blue glasses and a red tongue sticking out at him. Mingo. Danny hated Mingo, with his strange eyes and white fleshy skin. Some of the boys in school had told him that Mingo was from Albania and they were all like that there.

Miss Schwartz had a warm fire blazing in her front room.

'You must be cold,' she said. 'Come, warm your hands.'

Danny held out his chapped hands and felt the heat on them. He rubbed the warmed palms on his bare knees, trying to thaw them out. Miss Schwartz smiled.

'You are such a good-looking boy,' she said. Danny stood embarrassed, his brown eyes averted, looking down at the fire. His blond hair had been cuffed and ruffled by the wind and gave him a wild look.

'You look like the Angel Gabriel,' she said and pulled her mouth into a wide smile. 'Sit down – near the fire – and let me tell you about music.' She spoke with a strange accent, as if some of her words were squeezed into the wrong shape. Her mouth was elastic. Danny knew every word she said but it was not the way he had heard anybody talk before.

'What kind of music do you like?'

'I dunno,' said Danny after a moment's thought.

'Do you have a favourite singer?'

'I like Elvis.'

'Rubbish,' she said, still smiling. 'What I am going to tell you now you will not believe. You will not understand it, but I have to tell you all the same. I will teach you about things. I hope I will nurture in you a love you will never forget.' The smile had disappeared from her face and her eyes widened and drilled into Danny's. 'Music is the most beautiful thing in the world. Today beautiful is a word that has been dirtied, but I mean it truly. Beautiful.' She let the word hang in the air between them.

'Music is why I do not die. Other people – they have blood put in their arms,' she stabbed a fingernail at the inside of her elbow, 'I am kept alive by music. It is the food of love, as you

46

say. I stress that you will not believe me, but what you *must* do is *trust* me. I will show it to you if you will let me. Rilke says that music begins where speech ends – and he should know.'

Danny looked at her and the two pin-head reflections of the fire in her eyes. She was good-looking, with a long thin face and a broad mouth which she was constantly contorting as she wrestled to make the strange words clear. She did not wear lipstick like his mother. Her jet black hair was pulled back into a knot at the back of her neck and her parting was straight, as if ruled. Danny had seen her from the back when she played the organ in church and occasionally when she had come into the town shops, a dark figure hardly worth notice, her basket on her stiff forearm, her wrist to the sky. But here she seemed to fill the room with her talk and her flashing hands. All the time she sat on the edge of her chair, leaning towards him, talking into him. He swayed back as far as his stool would let him.

'Wait,' she said. She got up and went over to a bureau and took out a sheet of paper from a typewriter. She held it up.

'Look. Look hard at this.'

Danny looked but could see nothing, only the slight curl at the bottom of the page where it had lain in the machine.

'I give you a white sheet of paper. It is nothing. But the black marks . . . The black marks, Danny. That is what makes it important. The music, the words. They are the black marks,' she said, and her whole face blazed with passion. 'I am going to teach you those marks. Then I am going to teach you to make the most wonderful music from them. Come, let us begin.' As she sat down at the piano she snorted, 'Elvis Presley!'

When the lesson was over Miss Schwartz got up and went out, saying that they both deserved a cup of tea. Danny sat on the piano stool and looked at the room. It was a strange place, covered in pictures. Behind the pictures the wallpaper was dark brown, or else so old that it looked dark brown. There were plants in pots standing in saucers all over the place. Large dark green spikes with leathery leaves, small hanging plants, one with a pale flower on it. The wind pressured round the house and buffeted in the chimney. He could hear the ticking of fresh snow on the windows and the drone of a lorry taking the hill.

'I hope it lies,' he said to himself. The fire hissed and blew out a small feather of flame.

Miss Schwartz, carrying a tray, closed the door with her toe, which peeped out from her dressing-gown. It was of black silk, long to the floor and hanging loosely about her body. On the back it had a strange Chinese pattern in scarlet and green and silver threads. It reminded Danny of the one the magician wore in the Rupert Bear strip in the *Daily Express*.

'Now, while we drink our tea I will have to play you some music,' she said. She lifted the lid of one of the pieces of furniture and put on a record. She turned it up so loud that the music bulged in the room. Danny had never heard anything like it and he hated it. It had no tune and he kept waiting for somebody to sing but nobody did. He ate two biscuits and drank his tea as quickly as he could. Then she let him go.

On his way home the January wind cut his face and riffled the practice music he carried clenched under his arm. In the telephone wires above he heard the sounds of a peeled privet switch being whipped through the air again and again and again. At the forge he crossed the road to have a closer look. It was more of a shack than a building, with walls made of corrugated iron and hardboard of different faded and peeling colours. Someone had cleaned a paintbrush by the door or had tried out various colours on the wall. The place was surrounded by bits of broken and rusting machinery from farms. From the dark came the rhythmic sound of hammering. Danny edged into the open doorway and it stopped. A man's voice came out of the blackness.

'What do you want, lad?'

Danny jumped.

'C'mere,' said the voice. Danny moved to the threshold, trying to see into the gloom. 'What can I do for you?'

'Just looking.'

'Well, you'll never see from out there. Come in.'

The place smelt of metal and coke fumes and oil. Danny could make out a man in a leather apron. He looked too young to be a blacksmith, with his tight black curly hair.

'What's your name?' he asked. When Danny told him he thought for a moment. 'Your Da's a bus driver? Am I right or am I wrong?'

The man talked as he worked, heating a strip of metal in the coke of his fire and hammering it while it was red. Each hammer blow pulsed through Danny's head like the record at Miss Schwartz's.

'And what has you up this end of town?' Danny told him he was going to music.

'To Miss Warts and all?' he shouted. 'I wonder would she like this song?' He began to sing loudly, and bang his hammer to the rhythm, 'If I was a blackbird'. When he came to the line 'And I'd bury my head on her lily white breast', he winked at Danny. He had a good voice and could get twirls into it – like Rosemary Clooney. When he had finished the song, he asked Danny about school. He didn't seem to think much of it because he said it was the worst place to learn anything. He talked a lot and Danny helped him to work the bellows for his fire. When he took the red hot metal out of the fire, it had tiny lights that flashed and disappeared. The man said that that was the dust touching it and burning up. As the smith worked, Danny looked at his arms, not muscled, but tight with sinews and strings, pounding at the metal. He shouted to make himself heard over his work.

'The schools make the people they want. They get rid of their cutting edge. That's how they keep us quiet.' He nodded that he wanted Danny to pump harder. 'It'll not always be like that. Our time will come, boy, and it'll not be horseshoes we'll be beating out. No, sir.'

Danny was breathless with the pumping. The blacksmith looked at him, raising one eyebrow.

'Are you the lad that was very ill not so long ago?'

Danny breathed and nodded.

'Then maybe you better quit and be off home.'

Danny picked up his music from the cluttered bench and blew the brown rust from it. As he left the man shouted after him,

'Just give us a call any time you're passing, son.'

Danny tried to walk the road in step to the fading ring of his hammer.

When he came through the back door his mother yelled at him, 'Where's the good cap I knitted for you?'

'Oh, sorry, I left it behind.'

She began to help him unbutton his coat, scolding with concern.

'You are not strong yet, you know. I don't know what that woman was thinking of, letting you out without it. Are your ears not freezing?'

'I'm O.K.'

'You are not indeed. I never met your equal for catching things. There's not much the doctors don't know about that you haven't had. Twice over maybe. You must look after yourself, Danny.'

The boy went up to his room and lay on the bed. His mother was right. He seemed to be constantly ill. The last time had been the worst. The one nice thing he could remember about it was having the bed made while he was in it. He would lie there while his mother pulled all the bed-clothes off, then she would straighten the sheet beneath him, tugging it with exaggerated grunts. 'The weight of you!' she would say. He would run his fingers fan-like across the smoothness under him. His mother, separating out the clothes and standing at the end of the bed, would flap the upper sheet to make it fall soothingly on top of him. It came slow and cool and milky down over him with a breath of cotton-smelling air. It was almost transparent and he could look down at his feet and see himself in a white world – his tent, his isolation. The light came through, but he was cut off. He made no attempt to take the sheet down from his face. He heard her voice, then felt the heavier blankets fall across his

50

body, the light disappearing. Only then would he turn back the sheet and look at her. He had wanted to remain suspended in the moment of the sheet, in its relaxation and whiteness, but it always came to an end. He knew that he made peaks at his head and at his toes. He had seen furniture covered this way, and his grandfather in the hospital morgue.

'Now sit up for your medicine.' It had been white too. Cloying sweetness trying to disguise a revolting base flavour. His father gave him sixpence if he could keep it down. After a week he had a shilling on his bedside table. His mother opened *her* mouth when she gave him the stuff. She set the spoon down and lifted the bowl in readiness. His tongue furred with the mixture. Little squirts of warm saliva came into his mouth and he gagged but it stayed down. 'Good boy. Another sixpence. Sure, you'll be rich by the end of the bottle.'

Now he rolled off the bed and decided to go downstairs and let his mother hear what he had learned that day.

'First, empty that,' she said. Danny went to the compost heap at the bottom of the garden with the scraps. On the way back he swung the empty colander and listened to the quiet hoot and whine of the wind through its holes. He liked listening to things. In the room with the two clocks he liked to hear how the ticks would catch up with one another, have the same double tick for a moment and then whisper off into two separate ticks again. The hiss of Miss Schwartz's dressing-gown as she moved. The thin squeak of his compass as he opened its legs. The pop his father's lips made when he was lighting his pipe. He left the empty colander on the draining board.

'Are you ready?' he asked her. His mother listened to his scales, her head cocked to one side, drying her hands on her apron. He played them haltingly.

'There's not much of a tune to that,' she said. 'How much do you have to practise?'

'Until I get it right, she says.'

'Who's "she", something the cat brought in?'

'Miss Schwartz.'

'Have a bit of respect, Danny.'

Danny seemed to get it right with little effort, but what little he did he had to be goaded into by his mother. There was nothing Miss Schwartz taught him that he couldn't do after several attempts. So, in the first months, Miss Schwartz increased the level of difficulty and the duration of his practice pieces. And he was always able for them.

Along the sides of the lane that led to her house Danny saw the yellow celandine and the white ones with the strange smell. Wild garlic, she had called them. He met Mingo coming down the lane to where his father had parked the car. Mingo made a vulgar noise with his mouth as they passed but Danny ignored him. Miss Schwartz held the door open and he gave her the envelope with the clinking money in it.

Seated at the piano, he asked,

'Is Mingo any good?'

'Mingo?'

'The boy with the white hair that's just left.'

'Is that what you call him? That boy . . .' she paused, 'is average.'

'Is he as good as me?'

'Do not worry about other people. You will go forward as fast as you are able.' She smiled at him the way he looked at her, then added, 'You knew more on your first day than Mingo, as you call him, will in all his life. Now let me hear you play.'

Danny played his piece and when he had finished she shrugged and smiled.

'It is perfect,' she said, 'but still it is mechanical. Danny, you are a little machine. A pianola. Listen.' She sat on the stool and began to play. Danny listened, watching her closed eyes, the almost imperceptible sway of her body as she stroked music from the notes. 'At this point it must sing. *Cantabile*.' She talked over her playing, pointing out to him where he had gone wrong. 'Now try it again.'

Danny played the piece again and when it was over Miss Schwartz's eyes sparkled.

'That was much better,' she said. 'Beautiful. You learn so quickly.'

'I can't play like that at home,' he said, 'but here it's different.'

'I think,' said Miss Schwartz, 'it is time for an examination. It will please your mother. And I think it will please you because we will get a trip to the city. And . . .' she added after more thought, 'it will please me. I will write a note to your mother. Although I will not say this in the letter, if you have any difficulties with the bus fare I will pay it myself. Do not say it, of course, if there are no difficulties.'

They began to work on a new piece by her darling Schubert and when she felt they had accomplished enough she got up and made tea.

Alone in the room, Danny stared at the picture. Silhouettes, she called them. Jet black outlines of composers she had named. Beethoven, Mahler on the tips of his toes, Schubert. He liked Beethoven the best, the way his hair sprouted in all directions.

As they drank their tea she played again the record that she had played at their first lesson. Now Danny knew it and could hum the melody as it played.

Some weeks ago, when she had come back in with the tea, she had found Danny in the corner, crouched looking at her records. She kept them in a huge set of books, each page with a circular hole in it so that you could see the label of the record. Danny turned the stiff pages of the records, carefully looking at the labels, scarlet ones with a dog barking into a horn, green ones with the title in tilted writing. He took out a record and looked closely at its surface, angling it to the light. Intense black with light shining in the grooves. She handled them like eggs. When she came in all she said was, 'Be careful, Danny.' She poured the tea and then continued her sentence, 'or they will

53

end up like this.' She leaned over and lifted a record which had a large bite out of its side.

'Some boys who come here are not as careful as you. Goodbye, Dinu Lipatti. I think I will have to make a flowerpot out of you. You see?' She pointed to one of her plants. A record had been folded up in some way to make a container. 'You heat it and you mould it until it is the shape you want. I hate to waste anything. That's what comes of the war.' She bit into her gingersnap and said through her chewing,

'I would like to stand on his glasses.'

Danny liked to dip his into his tea and bite the warm, mushy sweetness.

When he handed Miss Schwartz's note to his mother, she ruffled his hair with her hand.

'You're losing your blondness,' she said, 'but the sun in the summer should bring it back again.' When she had finished the letter, the boy looked at her for a decision.

'Yes, you can go,' she said. 'But you'll have to stay the night. I'll not have you travelling that much in one day. Maybe your Aunt Letty would keep you.'

In the city they went to the Assembly Rooms and Danny passed his examination with the highest commendation. On the way down the steps, Miss Schwartz took his hand and although he made a slight attempt to take it away, she held tightly on to it. Then without looking at him, staring straight ahead into the rush hour traffic, she said,

'It's *not* too late. You can be great. If you try you can be really great.' She squeezed his hand so hard it hurt. Then she let it go.

'Did you say that to me?' asked Danny.

'Yes, Danny. To you.'

Afterwards they met a friend of Miss Schwartz's and went for tea in The Cottar's Kitchen. Danny had never seen her in such a joyful mood. She laughed and talked and praised him so much that he became embarrassed. She called him *'mein Lieber'* and introduced him to her friend as her star pupil, her *Wunderkind*.

'. . . and this is Mr Wyroslaski. He plays the cello in a symphony orchestra.'

He was a tall man with a very thin face. He had dark brown eyes, deep eyes, not unlike Miss Schwartz's own. His hair was very long, almost like a woman's.

'Why do all music people have funny names?' Danny asked.

'Like what?' asked Miss Schwartz.

'Like Schwartz and Wyro . . . Wyro – your name,' he said, nodding at her friend, 'and all those composers.'

'Names do not matter; you, *mein Lieber*, will be a great musician one day.'

'My name is Dandy McErlane,' and the way he said it made them all laugh. Miss Schwartz leaned across the table and smacked a kiss off Danny's forehead. He blushed and looked down at his plate.

'Besides,' said Mr Wyroslaski, 'there is John Field. He is an Irish composer. Names do not matter. What matters is the heart, the mind. Did you ever hear of a composer called Joe Green?'

Danny nodded that he hadn't.

'That is English for Giuseppe Verdi.'

'Who's he?' asked Danny. He joined uncertainly in the laughter his question had started. Mr Wyroslaski looked at him and produced a large handkerchief from his pocket. He slowly folded it into a pad which he licked and leaned over to Danny.

'Marysia, you leave your mark on everyone.' He rubbed Danny's forehead hard. It surprised Danny that Miss Schwartz had a first name. He sounded it over in his mind, Maur-ish-a, Maur-ish-a. He never imagined himself calling her anything but Miss Schwartz.

Today she looked different. When she had come out of the Ladies' Room her black hair was down, falling over her shoulders. Her normally sallow cheekbones were pink and her eyes seemed to sparkle and flash more than they did in the darkness of her sitting room at home. She wore a brown suit and a blouse of creamy lace. At her throat was a cameo brooch which matched the brown of her suit. It was the first time Danny had seen her legs, the first time he had seen her out of her dressing-gown.

Danny had begun to dislike Mr Wyroslaski. He had pulled away from the handkerchief but the man's bony hand had held the back of his neck so that he couldn't. Now as Wyroslaski listened to Miss Schwartz his mouth hung open and his eyebrows were raised like pause markings, as if he did not believe what she was saying. His face was prepared for laughter even though nothing funny was being said. They were talking too much. Danny began reading the stained menu. Then Wyroslaski lowered one eyebrow and said something in a foreign language at which Miss Schwartz laughed, covering her lower face with both hands. She replied to him in the same sort of language. Danny turned the menu over but there was nothing on the back of it.

Eventually she turned to Danny and said,

'He is such a handsome boy, my archangel, isn't he? *Mein Lieber*, we all must go. Your Aunt Letty will be worried about you. Mr Wyroslaski has kindly said that he will drive you there in his car. What do you say?'

'Thank you,' said Danny.

'We'll drop you off and I'll see you in good time for the bus in the morning.'

As they rose from the table, Mr Wyroslaski flicked his hair out from his collar with his knuckled cellist's hand.

The next day on the long bus journey home, Miss Schwartz was quiet and often seemed not to be interested in or understand what Danny said to her. She did point out the freshness and greenness of everything. Hedges flashed by, fields moved, mountains turned in the distance.

'It is spring. The sap is rising, quickening in all things. Do you not feel it?'

'No,' said Danny. And they lapsed into silence again.

At the next lesson, Miss Schwartz opened the door in her familiar black dressing-gown.

'Well, Danny, have you forgiven me?'

'What for?'

'I thought you had fallen out with me. Is that not so?'

'No.'

'You did not feel neglected?'

Danny began searching through his pages for his piece. He shrugged.

'It was *your* day, Danny. It was wrong of me to enjoy it.' He set his music on the piano.

'What did you think of Mr Wyroslaski? Wasn't he . . .'

'He smiled too much,' Danny interrupted her.

'You *are* annoyed, aren't you, Danny?'

'No.'

And she touched his hair with her extended hand and her face opened in a warm smile of disbelief and delight.

After he played for her she asked,

'How did your mother like your certificate?'

'She says she's going to get Dad to frame it.'

'Tell her not to bother. There will be more. Bigger and better ones. And what's more, you can tell her I will give you extra lessons and it doesn't matter whether she can pay or not. Two a week for the price of one. How would you like that?'

Danny was not so sure, but he said yes to please her.

In July Danny's sister married. The remainder of the guests from the hotel all crowded into the McErlanes' front room after the reception. Danny's mother sat stunned and a little drunk. Her husband, Harry, was even more drunk, but had through practice learned to keep going. He was asking everybody what they would have to drink. Aunt Letty, who didn't drink, was helping him pour the whiskeys and uncork the stout. Danny sat in the corner with an orange juice in his hand which he dared not drink. Everybody that day had bought him an orange juice.

'Well, that's that,' said Harry, falling back into an armchair, his knees still bent. He waved his thumb in the direction of the corner. 'There's only one left. The shakings of the bag has yet to go.'

'It'll be a while yet, Harry,' said a neighbour, 'and he'll only go when the notion takes him. He'll not be forced.'

Harry blinked his eyes and focused on whoever had spoken. It was Red Tam.

'Tam, I hope you're not meaning anything by that remark.'

'What do you mean "meaning"?'

'About being forced. There was no forcing at today's match and well you know it.'

'The child, Harry,' warned Mrs McErlane.

'My girl is a good girl. She'd have none of that sort of filth.' Danny's father spat the last word out.

'Aye, I know. Time will tell,' said Red Tam.

'What the bloody hell do you mean, "time will tell"? If it's a fight you want, Red Tam, we'll settle it right now.' He struggled to escape from the armchair. Red Tam put up his hands and laughed.

'I'm saying, Harry, that time will prove you right. That's all. You're too jumpy, man.'

Harry was not so sure. Mrs McErlane interrupted.

'Danny is going to play the piano for us. Won't you, son? A bit of entertainment will settle us all.'

'The old Joanna,' someone shouted above the din.

'Good stuff.' A spatter of applause went round the room. Danny blushed.

'I'd wash my hands of any girl that would allow herself to be led into that sort of dirt before marriage.'

'It happens, Harry. It happens.'

'Not in my house it doesn't.'

'Look at big Maureen from Bank Street. Thirty-two years old, they say. At her age you'd think she'd have known better.'

'An animal,' said Harry, 'if ever there was one. There was

that many of them she didn't know who to blame. The beasts of the field . . .'

'Stop it, Harry. The child,' hissed Mrs McErlane. 'Go and get your music, son.' She turned in explanation to her neighbour, saying, 'He's not allowed to play without it.'

Danny lurched shyly from the corner, saying that he wouldn't, but hands grabbed him and guided him through the crowded room to the piano. He took out the music for the piece he had just been practising.

'What are you going to give us?'

Danny propped the music up, opened the lid and the room became silent, except for the noise of somebody in the kitchen washing dishes. He began to play a movement from a Haydn sonata.

'That's grand stuff,' said his father proudly through the music.

'Very highfalutin' but good. It's well done,' said Red Tam.

'He has the touch,' said Mrs McErlane. 'So his music teacher tells me. Miss Schwartz, y'know. But you'd know to listen to him yourself.'

Danny played on, the glittering phrases mounting in elegance. Letty leaned in from the kitchen and, aware that she had to be quiet, hissed,

'Harry, will you have another stout?'

'I will, aye.'

'Whisht till we hear,' said Danny's mother. Red Tam rang notes on his empty whiskey glass with a horny fingernail and waved it at Letty. The piece came to an end and Danny's fingers had barely left the keys but they were folding away his music. Everyone applauded loudly.

'What was that?' asked Red Tam.

'Haydn,' said Danny his voice barely audible.

'Grand. Do you know any Winifred Atwell tunes? Now there *is* a pianist. How she does it I just do not know. The woman must have ten fingers on each hand. Do you know "The Black and White Rag" at all?' Red Tam took a gulp of his new whiskey. 'Did you ever hear any of her, Harry?'

'Aye, she's on the wireless, isn't she?'

'You can say that again. She's never off it. The money that woman must be making.' He shook his head in disbelief. 'And her coloured, too.'

'Do you like the rock and roll, Tam?' said Mrs McErlane, winking, 'I thought it would be right up your street.'

'Indeed I do not.'

'You're right there,' Danny's father joined in, 'I can't take this classic stuff the boy is at all the time but I know for sure the rock and roll is rubbish.'

'I like *some* classic stuff,' said Tam 'Mantovani . . .'

'I like good music – something with a bit of a tune to it,' Harry went on, 'Bing's my man.' He stuck the pipe in the corner of his mouth, his eyes closed, and he began to croon, slurring the words in an American accent,

'A'm dream – ing of a wha – ite Christmas.'

'Aye,' said Tam, interrupting the song, 'that's where the money is at. This rock and roll will not last.'

'It'll not be heard of in another year's time,' agreed Harry. 'The boy there could be making money before long. There's many's the dance band would snap him up if he was older. The classical stuff is all right. It gets the hands going. Good practice, y'know. But the bands is the place where the money is.'

'Or on the wireless,' added Tam. Harry rose and stood expansive and swaying in front of the fire.

'You did well at the speaking, Harry, for one that's not used to it,' said his wife.

'Aye. At least I kept it clean. Which is more than I can say for some.'

'Uncle Bob. Wasn't that a disgrace.'

One of the others, drunker than the rest, overheard and mimicked,

'"The bride and groom have just gone upstairs to get their things together."' Half the people laughed again at the joke. Harry said,

60

'That man Bob has a mind like a sewer.'

Danny threaded his way to the door and once upstairs threw what was left of his orange down the lavatory.

They worked hard all though that summer, the boy in shirtsleeves at the piano, Miss Schwartz, despite the heat, still in her silk dressing-gown. One day Danny discovered that she wore nothing beneath it because when she bent over to point out some complexity in the score the overlap of her gown rumpled and he saw cradled there the white pear shape of one of her breasts. He pretended not to understand the notation but when she bent over again her dressing-gown was in order.

'The black marks, Danny. Pay attention to the black marks.'

He felt his knees shaky and could not concentrate to play any more.

After the lesson they would go out to the small garden and have tea beneath the apple tree, tea with no milk but a slice of lemon in it – a thing Danny had never heard of. Miss Schwartz had pointed out to him when the flowers had fallen off the tree and each week they inspected the swelling fruit. Lying back in striped deck chairs they both watched the flickering blue of the sky as it dodged between the leaves.

Miss Schwartz had resurrected from the attic an ancient wind-up gramophone on which she played records outdoors.

Danny came to know many pieces. Sometimes if there was a concert on the wireless she would open the kitchen window, turn the volume up full and point the set towards the garden. One day, during a performance of Mahler's '*Kindertotenlieder*', she said,

'You know, Danny, the reason I bought this house was because of the garden. We had one just like it when I was a girl. I was about your age when we had to leave it.'

'Where was it?'

'In Poland. A place called Praszka. I remember it as beautiful.'

'Why don't you go back?'

She laughed. 'Because I am too long away. The longer you are away the more you want to go back. And yet you realise the longer you are away the more impossible it is to return. The early monks had a phrase for it – what you suffer. If you died for God, that was simple. That was red martyrdom. If you left your country for God and lived in isolation, that was white martyrdom. To be an exile, to be cut off from your country is a terrible thing.' She smiled. 'I left, not for God, but for convenience. It was a time of fear.' She shuddered and looked up into the apple tree.

Danny sat stripped except for his shorts. He glanced up to where the music was coming from and saw himself reflected brightly in the window. His hair had grown longer and darker. Light from a spoon on the tray lying on the grass reflected into his face.

'But it is not so bad. There are compensations,' she said, smiling at him.

Many times on his way home Danny would stop off at the forge, if it was open, and listen to the blacksmith. He loved the way the man did not shave often and had black bristles on his chin like the baddies in cowboy comics. He was always joking and talking. 'Am I right or am I wrong?' was his favourite phrase. One day, sitting astride his anvil, he talked about Miss Schwartz.

'She's a rum bird, isn't she?'

Danny nodded.

'Why do you agree with me? The nod of the head is the first sign of a yes-man. Well, are you just a yes-man?'

'No,' said Danny and laughed.

'This bloody country is full of yes-men and the most of them's working class.' He dismounted from the anvil and began to rake the fire to life. 'Yes, your honour, no, your honour. Dukes and bloody linen lords squeezing us for everything we've got, setting one side against the other. Divide and conquer. It's an old ploy and the Fenians and Orangemen of this godforsaken country have fallen for it again.' He began to work the bellows himself and the centre of the fire reddened. Danny loved the colour of blue that the small flames took on when the fire was heating up. He could feel the warmth of the fire on the side of his face and his bare arm. The smith was now talking into the fire.

'But a change is coming, Danny Boy. We must be positive. Prepare the ground. Educate the people. Look to the future the way Connolly and Larkin did in 1913.'

He threw the poker down among the fire-irons with a clang and turned to Danny. His face changed and he smiled.

'You haven't a baldy notion what I'm talking about, have you?'

'No.'

'But am I right or am I wrong?'

'You're right,' was always Danny's answer.

It was about this time that Danny began to notice a change in Miss Schwartz. She became moody and did not smile or laugh as much as she used to. One day when he arrived early for his lesson, panting from running most of the mile, it was a long time before she opened the door. When she did she was thrusting a handkerchief up her sleeve and she had obviously been crying. Her eyes were heavy-lidded and red.

When she went in, she said. 'Get your breath back,' and began to water her plants from a small Japanese tea-pot, turning her back on him. She talked to the plants the way other people would talk to a pet. She said it encouraged them to grow.

'Lavish love and attention on growing things and they will not let you down.'

'What about your apple tree? Do you talk to it?'

'It hears music from the house.' She smiled weakly at her own answer.

'But I know houses . . .'

'Your piece, Danny. I want to hear it.'

Danny gave a small, knowing smile. Miss Schwartz half

reclined on the sofa at the bay window, her feet gathered beneath her. She turned to face the light and waited. Danny set his music on the chair and began to play. It was the opening movement of the Beethoven C sharp minor Sonata. She disliked calling it, 'The Moonlight'. Danny looked round to see if she had noticed, but her eyes were closed. He played on, trying to feel the music as she would have felt it. Sunlight slanted into the room and Danny thought her face looked haggard. Some of her tight hair had come adrift and hung down by her throat.

When he finished Miss Schwartz opened her eyes and they were glassy with tears.

'How beautiful, Danny,' she said in a whisper.

'You didn't notice,' he said, his feet swinging on the stool.

'What?'

'I played it without the music.'

Miss Schwartz came to him.

'How utterly superb,' she said, taking his face in her hands. She put her arms around his head and gave him a tight squeeze of joy. Danny sensed the huge softness of her breasts against his cheek, enveloping his face, the faded scent of her, the goosefleshy wedge at her throat.

'Oh Danny, how superb.' This time she held him at arm's length, watching his blushes rise. Danny tried to dismiss it.

'I practised it –

all week end,' he said.

'Oh Danny,' Miss Schwartz let a gasp out of her. 'Say that again.'

'I prac –

-tised it all week end.'

'Danny, your voice is breaking.' She put one hand over her mouth, a look of disbelief in her eyes. She sat down at the piano and asked him to sing some of the notes she played. His voice was accurate but kept flicking an octave down. She sat at the piano, her fingers poised above the keyboard, touching it but not heavily enough to depress the keys. Her head was bowed.

'The purest thing in the world is the voice of a boy before it

64

breaks,' she said, 'before he gets hair. Before he begins to think things – like that.' Her face looked the same way as when he played badly.

'But I hardly even notice it, Miss.'

'I do and that is sufficient,' she said. 'Today in the garden I will play you purity.'

The kitchen was full of a mute bustling as she made the tea. Danny carried the tray out, she the record. It was a boy soprano singing Latin. A blackbird from the ridge-tiles of the roof sang loud enough to drown certain passages. When the music was finished Danny said,

'My Mum says to tell you that I'm going to Grammar School.'

'You passed your Qualifying!' Danny nodded. 'Oh, I'm delighted. Which school?'

'Our Lady's High.'

'Hm.' She thought for a moment and then smiled. 'They don't have a music teacher as yet.'

Danny sat in the school yard eating his cheese piece, a bottle of milk in his hand. He saw Mingo coming across to him, his white hair weaving through the crowd. He had started the Grammar in September as well, but everybody knew that his father was paying for him.

'Hiya, piss face,' said Mingo. 'You still going out to that black bitch for music?' Danny looked at him but could not answer because the tacky cheese had stuck to the roof of his mouth.

'Sucker,' said Mingo. 'I don't have to go any more. Haw-haw-haw.' He spoke the laughter in words.

'Why not?'

'Because my old woman just stopped me. She was talking to Schwartzy in town and she came home and said, "That's it, no more music for you, my lad." Haw-haw-haw. McErlane the sucker still has to go.'

'It's O.K. She's not bad.'

'She has a good pair of tits on her,' said Mingo, groping the air before him. 'She likes you, McErlane. You're her pet. Does she ever let you feel her?' Danny looked at Mingo's flickering white eyelashes – he was constantly blinking behind his tinted glasses. He wanted to punch him in his foul mouth. Instead Danny said,

'I saw them one day.'

'Her tits?'

'Yeah.'

'What were they like?'

'Just ordinary.' Danny gestured with his hands.

'How did you see them?'

'She opened her dressing-gown one day and she wasn't wearing a . . . thingy.'

'Liar. I don't believe you.'

Danny shrugged and threw his crusts into the waste-basket.

'Were they nice bloopy ones?'

'Yeah.'

Danny sucked the bluish watery milk through a straw until it was finished. It made a hollow rattling sound at the bottom of the bottle. He asked Mingo,

'Are you going to music to anybody else?'

'There isn't anybody for miles, thank God.'

'I don't think I'd want to go to anybody else.'

'Aye, not if she shows you her tits, I don't blame you.'

There was a pause. Danny laced the used straw into a knot of angles.

'She shows them to more than you,' said Mingo.

'What do you mean?'

'She's a ride.'

'What's a ride?'

'Haw-haw-haw, he doesn't know.' Mingo folded up with mock laughter. 'She's going to have a baby.'

'So what?'

'So she's a ride.'

'How do you know?'

66

'My Mum says.'

'Your Mum's . . . a ride,' said Danny.

Mingo suddenly reached out and grabbed Danny by the ear, digging his nails into it shouting,

'Nobody says that about my Mum.'

Danny yelled out in pain and punched. He struck Mingo on the nose and dislodged his glasses. Mingo let go of Danny's ear and turned and ran, clutching his glasses to his chest, a trickle of blood on his white upper lip. He stopped at the far side of the playground and made a large 'up ya' sign with two fingers. It began at the ground and ended above his head. He kept doing it, jumping up and down to exaggerate the gesture. Danny turned away in disgust and slotted the empty milk bottle into the crate.

The road to Miss Schwartz's place was ankle-deep in brown scuffling leaves. The apples on the tree had become ripe and she had given Danny one. He bit into it and a section of its white flesh came away with a crack. Juice wet his chin.

'It must be the music,' he said crunching.

Now he practised with real determination, getting up with his father and doing an hour before school. He had to wait until his father went out because he said he couldn't stand the racket first thing in the morning. He did another hour in the evening before his father came in. His mother didn't seem to mind. She slept through the morning session and she would be out in the kitchen making Harry's dinner for most of the evening practice. She was glad to see the piano used so much. One evening Danny's mother came in to lay the table and stood watching him play.

'Your hair is getting darker. I thought the sun would have helped,' she said. Danny stopped playing.

'Mum,' he said, 'Miss Schwartz wants to know if you could pay her in advance for this term.'

'Oh, I don't think so. Look at the money I had to lay out for your uniform for the High.' She went to the cupboard and looked in the jar on the top shelf.

67

'No, tell her I'm sorry but I just can't do it.'

'A whole lot of her pupils are leaving.'

'Why's that?'

'I don't know,' said Danny, closing the lid of the piano.

It was shortly after this that the biscuits stopped. Miss Schwartz apologised and said that she was getting too fat. However, they still had tea together.

Danny's father, being a bus driver, got the pick of all the papers left in his bus, but the only one he would bring home was the *Daily Express*. He had a great admiration for it.

'First with everything,' he said, 'and no dirt.'

From his armchair he read a piece to Danny that said that the Russians had launched a satellite into space and that it would be possible to see it for the next few evenings if conditions were right.

'It's wonderful too,' he said nodding his head. 'At one end of the world the Russians is firing things into outer space and we still have a blacksmith in the town shoeing horses.'

'He says he knows you,' said Danny.

'Who?'

'The blacksmith.'

'When were you talking to him?' His father's voice had risen in pitch.

Danny shrugged.

'After music,' he said.

'Well, you'll just stop it. You hear me? If I catch you in that forge I'll take my belt off to you.'

The loud voice brought Danny's mother out from the kitchen. Her head was cocked to one side with curiosity and concern.

'Who's this?' she asked.

'You know who – the blacksmith. If he's pouring the same poison into your ear, son, as he's been spewing out in the pub, he's a bad influence. He'd have you into guns and God knows what. Denying religion at the top of his voice.'

'God forgive him,' said Mrs McErlane.

'Aye, and what's more he said they weren't serious in 1922 because they didn't shoot a single priest.'

'Did he say that?'

'Do you hear me, Danny, steer clear of vermin like that or you'll feel the weight of my hand.'

The next lesson Danny had he told Miss Schwartz of the satellite. She agreed that they should go out at six and try to see it.

The night was cold, black and clear as a diamond. A swirl of stars covered the sky so that it seemed impossible to put a finger between two of them. And they stood and waited, their necks craned.

'Isn't it marvellous,' Miss Schwartz said. Danny said nothing. His eye was searching for the satellite.

'Can you see it?' he asked.

When they stopped walking, the crackling underfoot ceased and the silence seemed enormous. In the frost nothing moved. Then Miss Schwartz whispered,

'Look. Look there.' It was as if she had seen an animal and to speak would frighten it.

'Where?'

'Follow my finger.'

In the darkness Danny had to get close to look along the line of her arm. He smelt her perfume and the slightest taint of her own smell, felt his face brush the texture of her clothing.

'There,' she said, 'can you see it? Like a moving star. A little brighter than the rest.'

'Oh yes. I can see it now.'

They stood in silence, close to each other, watching the pinpoint of light threading its way up the sky from the horizon. To their left was the faint orange dome of light from the town. When the satellite was directly above them it paused, or seemed to pause, and they held their breath, their faces dished to the sky. Miss Schwartz put her hand round Danny's shoulder.

'How utterly lonely,' she said. 'The immensity of it frightens me.'

They were silent for a long time, watching its descent down the other side of the sky, moving yet hardly moving. Some miles away a dog barked. A car's headlights fanned into the sky and they heard its engine as soft as breathing. Miss Schwartz said in a whisper,

'The music of the spheres. Do you hear it, Danny?'

'No. What is it?'

'It's a sort of silence,' she said and in the darkness he knew that she was smiling. Suddenly she returned to her normal voice.

'What I don't understand, Danny,' her fingers began to knead his shoulder, 'is how it stays up there. I'm very silly about these things. Why does it not fall down?'

'It's kind of suspended. Outside earth's gravity. I think the moon pulls it one way and the earth pulls the other and nobody wins — so it just stays up there. Something like that anyway. The papers say it will fall back to earth after a few months.'

'Caught between the heavens and the earth. How knowledge-able you are, Danny.'

'The science teacher told us today at school.' He began to tremble with the cold.

'Oh, but you are shivering. We must go in or your mother will be angry with me. If you catch a chill she will have my life.'

Inside Miss Schwartz made tea while Danny waited, sitting on his stool by the fire, listening to a record he had chosen himself.

'I'm glad that you picked that one,' she said when she came into the room. 'On Sunday at church I will play you your favourite.'

'Which?'

'The Bach. "*Liebster Jesu, wir sind hier*".'

'What does that mean?'

'"Jesus we are here".'

'Seems a funny thing to say. You'd think he'd know that.'

'Sometimes I wonder,' she said, approaching her tea with her mouth because it was so hot without milk or a slice of lemon.

On his way home Danny followed the wobbling yellow disc his torch made on the ground. He was not afraid of the dark but felt protected by it in some way. He noticed from a distance that light was coming from the forge. The door was open and a slice of the roadway in front of it visible. The blacksmith must have heard him because when Danny stopped outside he began to sing 'Oh Danny Boy'.

'Come in,' he shouted. From the threshold Danny refused.

'Why not?'

'My Dad says I'm not allowed.'

The blacksmith laughed and said that he had a fair idea why.

'What would he do if he caught you here?'

'Take his belt off to me.'

The man snorted and came to Danny in the doorway. He rucked up his leather apron and thrust his hands into his pockets.

'Danny,' he said and there was a long pause. 'You're coming to an age now when you've got to think. Don't accept what people tell you – even your father. Especially your father. And that includes me.'

Danny eased his hip on to a large tractor tyre propped by the door.

'Your Dad and I have very different views of things. He accepts the mess the world is in whereas I don't. We've got to change it – by force if necessary.'

'Did you see the satellite?' asked Danny. The blacksmith nodded and laughed.

'It takes the Russians. I bet the Yanks feel sickened. That's an example of what I'm talking about. Equal shares and equal opportunity leads to progress, Danny. The classless society. It'll happen in Ireland before long. There's nothing surer. Am I right or am I wrong?'

Danny smiled and said that he would have to go. The blacksmith touched him on the shoulder.

'If you want to come back here, Danny, you come. The belt shouldn't stop you. You've got to be your own man, Danny Boy.'

71

'I'll maybe see you.'

On the road Danny waited for the hammer blows so that he could walk in step but none came and he had to choose his own rhythm.

On Sunday Danny waited to hear the familiar thumping sound of Miss Schwartz taking her place in the organ loft. She was not the same religion as the McErlanes but she had told Danny that she had needed the money and that it was a chance to play regularly on the best organ for a radius of twenty miles. After mass she had taken him up several times into the loft and he had been astonished by the sense of vibration, the wheezes and puffs and clanks of the machinery which he hadn't heard from the church. He loved the power of the instrument when she opened the stops fully to clear the church.

He heard the door of the organ loft close and was surprised when he looked round to see a man. He was bald with a horse-shoe of white hair and horn-rimmed spectacles. Throughout the distribution of communion he played traditional hymns with a thumping left hand and a scatter of wrong notes. Afterwards he drove away in a white Morris Minor.

Outside on the driveway Father O'Neill talked to Danny's mother. The boy was sent on ahead while they talked. All that Sunday the house was full of whispers. Danny would come into a room and the conversation would stop. He thought Miss Schwartz must be ill.

The next day, the Monday before Christmas, when he came home from school his mother was sitting at the table writing a letter. He gathered his music and was about to go out when she called him.

'Here's a note for your music teacher.' Then she added, 'Don't be too disappointed, son.'

'What do you mean?'

'Never mind. Just you take that to your teacher and maybe she'll explain.'

On the road the wind was cold. Some hailstones had fallen and gathered into seams along the side of the road. The wind hurt the lobes of his ears and the tip of his nose.

He gave Miss Schwartz the note and she opened it jaggedly with a finger. She chinked the money into her hand, then read the letter. She looked as if she was going to cry but she stopped herself by biting her lip. Her teeth were nice and straight and white.

'Play for me,' she said.

Danny began to play the Field Nocturne he had been practising. The dark descended slowly. When he had finished she said,

'Let us not have a lesson. Let us play all the best things.'

'You didn't play the organ on Sunday. Were you sick?'

'Yes. I was indisposed.' She thought for a while, then put her hand to the back of her head and untied her hair. With a shake she let it fall darkly forward.

'I'm pregnant,' she said. Danny nodded.

'That means I'm going to have a baby.'

'Yes, I know.'

'They don't want me any more.'

'Why not? You're the best organist I've ever heard.'

'You can't have heard many. No more talk, Danny. That's enough. What are you going to play?'

'Can I have the light on?'

'No,' she said. 'Play me the Schubert. You know it well enough to play in the dark. It makes the other senses better. In the dark we are all ears, are we not?' Her voiced sounded wet, as if she had been crying.

'Which one?'

'The G flat.'

Danny began to play. Somehow he felt a sense of occasion, as if she was willing him to play better than he had ever played before. To feel, as she had so often urged him, the heart and soul of what Schubert had heard when he wrote down the music. In the dark he was aware of her slight swaying as he played.

73

Now she sat forward on the sofa, her long hair hanging like curtains on each side of the pale patch of her face. She sat like a man, her knees wide apart, her elbows resting on them. The melody, more sombre than he had played it before, flowed out over the rippling left hand. Then came the heavy base like a dross, holding the piece to earth. The right hand moved easily into the melody again, the highest note seeming never to reach high enough, pinioned by a ceiling Schubert had set on it. Like the black notes he had struck in Uncle George's room by himself creating a disturbing ache. The piece reached its full development and swung into its lovely main melody for the last time. It ended quietly, dying into a hush. Both were silent, afraid to break the spell that had come with the music. Danny heard Miss Schwartz give a sigh, a long shuddering exhalation and he too sighed. She leaned forward and switched on a small orange lamp which stood on the side table.

'Danny, you are my last pupil. They have taken all the others away from me. But I do not care about them. They are money. But you are the best. You are more than that. You are the best thing I have ever had and when they try to take you away from me . . .' She stopped and dipped her face into the handkerchief she had rolled in her hand. She looked up at him and began again.

'This is your last lesson. Your mother does not allow you to come here again.'

'Why not?' Danny's voice was high and angry. Miss Schwartz raised her shoulders and splayed out her hands.

'I think in our time together we have accomplished much, Danny. There is so much more technique that you have to learn. But your heart must be right. Without it technique is useless. Sometimes I am ungenerous and doubt others' sensitivity. It is hard to believe that someone can feel as deeply as oneself. It is difficult not to think of oneself as the centre of the universe. But I believe in yours, Danny. I see it in your eyes, in your face. Do you know what a frisson is?'

'No.'

It is a feeling that you get. Indescribable. A shivering. Your hair stands on end when you hear or read or know something that is exceptionally beautiful. Did you ever get that?'

'No.'

'Have you ever cried listening to a piece of music – not from sadness but from the sheer beauty of it? Have you ever *felt* like crying?'

'No. I don't think I have.' Danny wanted to please her but she asked the question with such a seriousness, beseeched him, that to tell a lie would have been wrong.

'I can only compare it to something which you have not yet experienced. Something you would not understand. But it will come. That is what is wrong with this world. People are like the beasts of the field. They know nothing of music or tenderness. Anyone whom music has spoken to – really spoken to – must be gentle, must be kind – could not be guilty of a cruelty.'

She stood up and was walking back and forth with her fists tight.

'*Mein Lieber*, in the light the pale people see nothing. The glare blinds them. It is easy to hurt what you cannot see. To drop bombs a million miles away.' She stopped walking and pointed her finger straight at him. 'One of your Popes had a great thing to say once. He had been listening to some music by Palestrina with Palestrina himself. He said to him, "The law, my dear Palestrina, ought to employ your music to lead hardened criminals to repentance." Do you think this,' and she hissed out the s sound, 'this town would do this to me if they had truly heard one bar of Palestrina? Listen. Listen to this.'

She stamped across the room and took out one of the books of records. She put one on and turned the volume up full and announced,

'Palestrina.'

She sat down on the sofa, rigid with anger, electricity almost sparking from her hair.

'Close your eyes,' she commanded.

Danny closed his eyes and let his hands rest on his bare knees.

The unaccompanied singing seemed to infuse the room with sanctity. The clear male voices, intricate and contrapuntal, became an abstraction. Stairs of sound ascending and yet descending at the same instant. Danny thought of what she had said, her tirade. He thought of being taken away from this room, never to be allowed back again to talk and work with Miss Schwartz. Never to be allowed to call in on the blacksmith and be talked to as if he were a man. The garden, the sunlight, the tea. Her concern for everything he did and said. The pumping of the bellows and smell of coke. Her perfume and her laugh, her plants, her music. Her bare breast. Am I right or am I wrong, *mein Lieber*? He thought of being deprived of all this, never to be allowed back to it. And he began silently in his own dark to cry.

Miss Schwartz saw the tears squeeze from his eyes and she jumped from the sofa, all her anger gone, and rushed to him. In her haste the tail of her dressing-gown caught a pot-plant and it tumbled to the floor. Black loam spilled out and the dislodged plant fell from the pot, displaying its tangled skirt of white roots. She knelt before him, her arms about his waist. She too was crying. She kissed his knees and he felt her long hair tickle his legs as she swung her head back and forth.

'You are one of us, my love.'

She continued to weep, the tears streaming down her face, wetting her chin. It was only now that Danny felt her fatness through her gown, not soft fatness, but a hard pumped-up bigness pressing against him. She held him so tightly, so closely that after a time he was unsure whether the hardness belonged to him or to her. To stop himself falling off the stool he put his hands around her neck and as she pressed her cheek to his he felt the sliding wetness of it. She smelled beautiful in the darkness of her hair. She began to move in time to the music, crushing his face to hers. He heard and felt her mouth implode small kisses on the side of his face, moving towards his mouth, but he wrenched his head to the side, not knowing what to do. They stayed like that until the record ended with a hiss and the tick-tick-tick of the over-run.

Miss Schwartz got up from her knees and straightened her dressing-gown. She pushed back her hair and sniffed loudly.

'Go, Danny. Now. At once.'

He stopped at the door, his hand on the handle. She was kneeling again, sweeping the springy black loam with her hands into a pile on the mat. She knelt on her gown so that it pulled taut over the hump of her stomach and for the first time Danny saw how big it was. Her hands, dirtied with the soil, hung useless from her wrists.

'Promise me one thing before you go,' she said. 'Find a good teacher. *Bitte, mein Lieber*. You might yet be great. Please – for me?'

Danny, unable to find the right words, nodded and left. Running in the swirling snow, the only thing he could think of was that she had not given him tea.

When he got home there was the worst row ever. Danny screamed and shouted at his mother, hardly knowing what he was saying. The answers they gave him he could not understand. They called her a slut and spoke of marriage and sin and Our Blessed Lady. He asked to be allowed back, he cried and pleaded, but his father ended it by thrashing him with his belt and threatening to take an axe to the piano.

Danny ran out into the night, down the garden, where he had built himself a hut of black tarred boards.

'Let him go, let him go,' he heard his mother scream.

The snow had lain and was thick under foot. The fields stretched white away from the white garden. Danny crawled into the darkness of his hut and squatted on the floor. He put his arms around his ankles and rested his wet cheek on his knees. He did not know how many hours it was he stayed like that.

He heard his mother coming out, her feet crunching and squeaking on the frozen snow.

'Danny,' she called, 'Danny.' She bowed down into the hut

77

and took him by the arm. He had lost his will and when she drew him out, he came. The boy walked as if palsied, stiff and angular with the cold, his mother supporting him beneath his arm. He was numb, past the shivering point.

'Come into the heat, love,' she said, 'come in from the night. Join us.'

Some Surrender

Two FIGURES move slowly up the steep angle of the Hill, waist deep in gorse and bracken. The man taking up the rear, by far the younger of the two, is dressed in anorak and climbing boots while his companion wears a light sports-jacket, collar and tie and ordinary brightly polished shoes. The older man walks with his arms swinging, leaning into the slope. Strung tightly over his shoulder is the strap of a binocular case which raps and bobs against his back. There is a spring in his step and he tends to climb the narrow path on his toes. The more bulky man behind is breathing heavily and placing his hands on his thighs and pushing against them for leverage. At this point the Hill is like a staircase, the path worn brown and notched with footholds. They come to a flat area at the top of the staircase and the younger man flops on to the grass.

'Jesus, Dad, take a break.'

'Are you serious?'

The old man is breathing normally. He stands with his back to the panorama of the city while his son gets his breath back.

'Look at that view,' says the son.

'I save it till I get to the top. Then I take it all in.'

'You're some machine. How do you keep so fit?'

'I walk a lot. I've done this climb since you were small.'

'Think I don't remember. The tears and the sore legs and the nettle stings.'

The old man smiles.

'Roy, I'm not as fit as I look. There's bits of the system not in full working order.'

'Like what?'

'When I put too much pressure on the legs I tend to blow off,' he laughs. 'Like a horse at the trot.'

The son gets to his feet.

'In that case, if you don't mind, I'll go first.'

Roy leads the way up the next section, his father speaking to him from behind.

'There's a design fault built into Man.'

'What's that?'

'Age. The teeth are beginning to go.'

'At seventy-five I'm not surprised.'

'Loosening. I've lost two big, back molars on both sides. That means their opposite numbers overgrow. Nothing to grind against. So they get sensitive. I can't eat ice-cream – or lollipops.'

The son laughs, 'I've never seen you eat an ice-cream in your life.'

'You haven't been around much lately.'

'Who's fault was that?'

The path widens and they are able to walk side by side. There is silence for a while except for Roy's breathing and the slithering noises his anorak makes with each step. The old man says, 'Would you not come and see her?'

'No.'

'I suppose I take your point. A lot of people don't get on with your mother. But there's nobody else I'd rather be with.'

'She has got to ask me back.'

'It's not off the ground you lick it – you're both stubborn.'

'I don't want to see her. Anyway, in twenty years she's hardly crossed my mind.'

'Liar.'

They come to the edge of a wood which covers most of the slope of the Cave Hill and sit down on a large stepped rock. The old man crosses his legs and Roy sits down at his feet. The day is bright but occasionally clouds pass in front of the sun. Shadows chase across the landscape.

'Remember the first time we met at the Ireland-Scotland game? Afterwards I told her. I said, "I met Roy on the terraces today," and she said, "Roy who?"'

There is a long silence. Roy says, 'I like looking into a wood like that,' he jabs his hand towards it. 'The way you see in under

81

the trees, like a colonnade. The way the birds echo.'

'I like seeing out. Being in a wood, seeing out to a field in the sun through trees.'

'You'd argue a black crow white.'

'I would – if it was.'

Roy laughs and digs into his anorak pocket and produces a camera. He opens the bellows and begins to photograph the woods again and again.

'That's a brave old-fashioned job.'

'A Leica,' says Roy with his eye to it, pressing the shutter. 'I got it in a junkshop in London. It's great for this kind of work. Feels like a favourite paintbrush.' He winds the film on with his thumb and changes the camera to the upright position. 'There's a lovely lens in it.' Roy turns and looks up at his father. From where he sits he can see the sinews taut in his neck. He raises the camera to his eye and focuses. The old man sees what he is doing and looks away into the woods.

'Don't start that nonsense.' The shutter clicks.

'Portrait of retired, famous architect on his seventy-fifth birthday.'

'Put that thing away.'

'But I've never taken any pictures of you.'

'Keep it like that.'

The old man begins to pluck moss from the rock he is sitting on and crosses his legs the other way revealing his thin white shin.

Roy closes the camera with a snap, returns it to his pocket and laughs, 'Forty-four years of age and I'm still looking up to you.' His father gives a snort. 'No, really. Even then . . .'

'When?'

'When you didn't come out on my side.'

'You must always remember that I chose your mother. I didn't choose you.'

Roy gives a sigh which is meant to be heard and stands up.

'I mean that philosophically – that you can't choose your

children. It's not to say that I wouldn't have picked you. It's a bit like "Old Maid" – you pick and then see what you've got. There's the appearance of choice.'

They begin walking again, leaving the woods behind. On the open ground the birdsong changes from a blackbird to larks. The old man stops and looks up narrowing his eyes. He says, 'What's your own son doing?'

'Still at Aberdeen, so far as I know. At least he was before Christmas.'

'What's he like?'

'Aw – Damien, he's great. I'm very fond of him – yet there's no particular reason to be. As you say, you can't choose them. Every time I see him . . . he's gauche, unsure of himself, a bit brilliant – and sometimes he makes me laugh out loud.'

'An oddly Romish name for a grandson of mine. What's he studying?'

'Law. Aberdeen has a good reputation and it's what his mother wanted him to do.'

'You and I know that doesn't count for much.'

'I didn't even have the qualifications to get in.'

'You failed because you didn't work hard enough.'

'For fucksake, Dad, don't start. We're talking about twenty-five years ago.'

'Even though we're on a mountain there's no need for language. Save it for the terraces.'

'Do you not even give me credit for doing okay now?'

'I do.'

'It doesn't seem like it. I did all my studying a generation after everybody else.'

'At a London Poly.'

'Come on Dad, you make it sound like some sort of Craft School for the Less Able.'

'No-oo, you've got me wrong. I see your postcards all over the place. Supermarkets even.'

'And there's the possibility of a book.'

'Congratulations. I didn't know.'

'There's a lot to catch up on. Photographers who get books are few and far between.'

'What's it about?'

'Belfast. Belfast people. But I wrote the text myself.'

'Are you happy with it?'

'What?'

'The book?'

'The pictures – okay. The text I'm not sure of. The best one in the whole thing is from down by the Markets. A white horse rearing up in front of the knacker's yard. You only realize afterwards, in the darkroom, that you've got it all in the frame.'

'My father was a man who knew the value of education. His ambition for me was to get a job indoors.' The old man laughs and climbs in silence for a while.

'Why did you come back, Roy? And to Dublin of all places?'

'I got an offer of sharing some darkroom space there. In London the warring parties would have seen too much of each other. I suppose that's why Belfast was out, as well. With you and Mother.'

On the exposed side of the Hill the wind is fresher and blows his father's white hair about. He keeps trying to smooth it down with his hand.

Roy clears his throat and says, 'What galls me the most is you were right.'

'Hard to admit.'

'But it was for the wrong reasons. She wasn't even a good Catholic.'

'Thank God.'

'She gave the whole thing up after a couple of years in England.'

'But I bet she insisted on sending your boy to a Roman Catholic school.' Roy nods.

'It's ingrained deep in them.'

'That's a tautology. If it's ingrained it must be deep.'

'Thank you for pointing this out to me. My life will never be the same again.'

'Religion has f . . . nothing to do with it. She and I were . . . we just didn't get on – fought like weasels in a hole. You go through the whole bit, "It's best to stay together for the sake of the boy." But when it came to a boxing match I thought I'd better go.'

'Did you ever get married?'

'After the baby was born.'

'In a Roman Catholic church?'

'It's what she wanted at the time. Very, very quiet. There were only about five of us. We went to a pub in the afternoon for our honeymoon.' Roy laughs and his father looks quizzically at him. 'We had to arrange an all-day babysitter.'

'I don't find it funny, even yet. Your mother has been known to cry if the subject is raised.'

'Come on, people who get married nowadays are the exception.'

'We're not talking about nowadays, we're talking about the mid-sixties. But that's only part of it. Your mother was more offended by . . .' The old man pauses and begins to gesture with his hands. 'You know the way you feel about Jews?'

'I don't feel anything about Jews.'

'Well, the way most people feel about them. That's what we think of Roman Catholics. There's something spooky about them. As my father said, "Neither employ them nor play with them."'

'Doesn't leave much.'

'That's the idea,' he pauses again, then says, 'Taigs.'

'Do you know what that word means?'

'Fenians. Catholics.'

'I know *that*. But it's Gaelic – the word means poet.'

'So what?'

'We use it as a term of abuse – dirty taig – and all the time it means poet.'

'You're learning too much south of the border. And none of it's good for you.'

'We lack culture. Sashes and marches.'

'Nobody ever survived on poems. Hard work and thrift. People that speak their mind – that's a culture. I'm proud to be part of it – and so should you be.'

'You don't understand.'

'Why?'

Roy laughs. 'You're an oul bigot.'

'I'm a man who knows what's right and if that's being a bigot, then I am one.'

Roy stops walking and his father looks over his shoulder at him. Roy makes a fist and shakes it in the air.

'Catholics have too many children. Their eyes are too close together. They keep coal in the bath.'

His old man grins. 'Tell me something new.'

'Let's talk about something else. This is beginning to annoy me.'

'You're aisy annoyed.'

They walk on, saying nothing. Every so often Roy glances over his shoulder at the view but the old man strides on looking neither right nor left.

Ahead of them and slightly to their right they can see Napoleon's Nose, a cliff face dropping away for several hundred feet. Set back a little from the edge is a concrete beacon which from this distance looks like a wart on the nose. When they reach it Roy stands leaning against it, panting. It is covered in graffiti, the most prominent of which is a red 'No Surrender'. His father stands beside him shaking his head.

'Can you imagine carrying a spray can the whole way up here just to do that?'

'Shows Ulster determination, I suppose.'

His father goes over to the edge. A crow flaps across the space beneath him.

'You're high up when you can look down on the birds.'

'Careful,' says Roy. 'Don't stand so near the edge. In your condition one fart would propel you over.' Roy stands at a safe distance and takes out his camera. He snaps the panorama, moving a little to the right each time. The blue Lough lies like a wedge between the Holywood hills at the far side and the grey mass of the city at his feet and to his right. Spires and factory chimneys poke up in equal numbers. Soccer pitches appear as green squares with staples for goalposts.

The old man shouts over the wind. 'You could read registration plates in Carnmoney on a day like that.'

'But who'd want to be in Carnmoney?'

'Good one, Roy.' He laughs and comes over to his son who is crouching, threading a new film into his camera. He clicks the back shut and takes three quick exposures of his feet, each time winding on with a flick of his thumb.

He looks up at his father and says, 'This was the place the United Irishmen took an oath to overthrow the English. They were all Prods as well.'

'History, Roy. It's not the way things are now.' He plucks up the knees of his trousers and sits down on the plinth of the beacon. 'It's never been worse.'

'The design fault here is the border.'

'What do you mean?'

'I think we should at least consider the island being one country.'

'Roy, please.' He shakes his head as if to rid himself of the idea, then goes on, 'The British Government are on the same side as the terrorists now. They're beating us with the stick *and* the bloody carrot. God knows where we'll be in ten years time.'

'I'd like to see a new slogan, SOME SURRENDER.'

'Never.'

'When Ireland score a try at Lansdowne Road, father – don't tell me you've no feeling for it.'

'Peripheral. That's all peripheral. What matters is our identity. We've been here from the sixteenth century.'

'A minute ago you dismissed history.' Roy reaches out and

punches his father on the shoulder. The old man smiles. Roy says, 'History in Ireland is what the other side have done to you. People have got to stop killing each other and talk.'

'I read a good quote in Sunday's paper. Let me get it right. "For evil to flourish all that need happen . . ."'

'"Is that good men do nothing." That was Burke. We must read the same paper.'

'That's how the Civil Rights and the IRA got a foothold. The good men of Ulster sat back and did nothing.'

'Rubbish. The IRA probably say exactly the same thing.'

'What do you mean?'

'They see the Prods and the Brits as an evil force. Reagan used it as an excuse to bomb Libya. It *sounds* like a good phrase . . . but . . . good and evil are very personal – like false teeth, they don't transfer easily.'

'But there must be standards. Rules.'

'That's the Catholic way. Do you want me to get you an introduction?'

'Catch yourself on.'

His father takes out the binoculars and rests his elbows on his knees to scan the distance.

'I have to do it like this. Shaky hands.'

'Let's have a look.'

'In a minute.'

When the old man looks through the glasses his mouth opens. He focuses and swings farther to the right.

'They're clearing the site,' he says and passes the binoculars to Roy.

'What's this?'

'You can see the lorries and the JCBs. Over there, towards the Shore Road.' Roy raises the binoculars and finds where his father is pointing.

'That was the multi-storey block they demolished? I saw it on the News,' he says, without taking the glasses from his eyes. 'It was pretty spectacular coming down. Slow motion Wallop!'

'Lagan Point. It was one of mine.'

'I didn't know that.'

'There's a lot to catch up on.'

Roy lowers the binoculars.

His father smiles. 'The people that lived in it had a better name for it. No Point.' The old man grunts and rises to his feet. He stands with his hands joined behind his back looking down on the city.

'I got a prize for it, too. There was a plaque on the wall at the front door. It occurred to me to salvage it but the ironies were too obvious.' He begins to rock backwards and forwards on his feet. 'The other two I built are due to come down over the next couple of years. Just as soon as they can get the people housed.'

'Jesus.'

'That's almost the complete works.'

Roy looks at his taut back and asks, 'Is it structural?'

'It's everything.' The old man lifts his shoulders, then drops them. 'The whole idea came from Morocco or somewhere. A steel skeleton with cladding. But nobody took into account the Belfast climate. The continual rain got into the bolts no matter how well they were sealed. Shortcuts were taken. At the time we were looking for cheap housing for a lot of people. Quickly. It seemed to be the answer.'

'I took some of the pictures for this book in Divis Flats. They're pretty terrible – the Flats, not the pictures. Nobody should be asked to live in such conditions.'

'Divis is not mine.' He leans back against the concrete and looks at the sky. 'The principle of living stacked is a perfectly sound one. Look what van der Rohe did in Chicago. And Le Corbusier. What they hadn't reckoned with was the Belfast working-class.'

'Bollicks, Dad. You can't shift the blame that way.'

'I suppose not. But the concept works with a different population. Put security on the door, good maintenance and fill the place with pensioners. Bob's your uncle.'

'That's like saying Northern Ireland would be fine without the extremists. You must take account of what is. Would you like to live in one?'

'We're living in sheltered housing at the moment . . .'

'Have you sold the house?'

'Three years ago.'

'God – after the matches I thought you were going back home.' Roy shakes his head. 'That's really thrown me. I pictured you going back to mother in our house. The place I knew.' He shakes his head again. 'Why should that worry me?'

'Best thing we ever did – to get rid of that barracks. Your mother wasn't up to it and it was expensive to heat.'

'I can't think of you anywhere else.'

'We've moved into this sheltered place. It's fine. You get your shopping done – if anyone takes ill you just press the buzzer. I have a bit of a garden, my "defensible space", which keeps me amused. If you came up I could give you some broccoli.'

'And I'd get to meet Mother.' The old man shrugs his shoulders again.

'I was *never* keen on talking to her. When she'd take me into town to get shoes or something I kept thinking, "What'll I talk about – I don't know what to say." At the age of twelve I talked to my mother on the bus *about the weather*. Because I felt I had to say something.'

The old man laughed a little, nodding.

'You're not the only one.'

'I remember on one of these jaunts she bought me a treat of currant squares. When we came out of the shop I was so delighted I swung the bag round and the weight of the things tore through the bottom and they ended up all over the wet street.'

'Aw poor Roy!'

'If it had happened to me as a parent I'd have bought another bagful, but not Mother.'

'Maybe at the time we couldn't afford it.'

'Aw come on! She was training me in thrift.'

'No bad thing, if it was true.' The old man paused. 'Did you ever feel that about me?'

'What?'

'Having to make up things to say.'

'No. You always seemed to be busy. I had to fight to get talking to you. Listening to you with Charlie Burgess or Billy Muir I used to be amazed at the stories you could tell. Why didn't you tell them to me? All you'd talk to me about was filling the coal-scuttle and school. And just when it was getting interesting Mother would always say, "I think Roy should be in bed."'

'Why're we able to talk now?'

'God knows. I suppose . . . I don't know. There was a gap – for a long time – and it couldn't have been worse.'

'And here we are again.'

'Yeah, here we are again. But I'll forego the broccoli, if you don't mind. Broccoli as Trojan horse. Speaking of gifts . . .'

Roy puts his hand in another of his anorak pockets and takes out a small wrapped package. 'Happy birthday,' he says.

The old man is genuinely surprised.

'I was going to give it to you when we reached the top.'

'Well, we're here – so what's different?' His father begins to unpick the sellotape then gives up and tears off the wrapping paper. 'It seems like . . . after what you've just told me . . . like a kind of consolation prize.'

'Damn the bit.'

It is a silver hip-flask. He weighs it in his hand, then shakes it close to his ear listening to the tiny glugging noise.

'It's full.'

'For the terraces.'

The old man unscrews the cap and sniffs.

'Is there water in it?'

'Come on, Dad. I've been to three matches with you.'

The old man puts the flask to his mouth and tips it up. Afterwards he makes a face. Roy says, 'It's hall-marked.'

'I didn't know they could do that with whisky. Thanks, I'm

delighted with this. How did you remember?'

Roy laughs.

'We made a date – after the Scotland game. You said why don't you drive to Belfast and we'll climb the Hill on my birthday.'

'That's right. Of course.' His father taps his temple. 'When's the next one?'

'Saturday three weeks. Against the English.'

'I'll be there.' He clenches his fist and shakes it at the sky. With his other hand he offers Roy the hip-flask.

'No thanks, I'll stick to the beer. I've never liked the taste of whisky.'

'That's what has you the shape you are.'

Roy rummages in his anorak and takes out a can of beer. He jerks at the ring pull. A small explosion of beer sprays over his father who jumps sideways. Roy laughs and apologizes.

'I forgot it would be all shook up.' He takes a hanky from his pocket and reaches towards his father. The old man ducks away.

'It's clean.' Roy dabs at the beads of beer. 'Wait – it's all over your tie.'

'Your mother'll accuse me of smelling like a brewery when I go in.'

'She'd be right.' Roy sits down to finish what is left of his can. 'For once.'

His father looks away in another direction.

'Would you not come back with me?'

Roy sighs and shakes his head.

'What would be the harm?'

'You're making it out to be a big thing,' says Roy. 'It's not. I'm not keen on talking to her – that's all.'

'But you might come round to it – some day?'

'Who knows?'

His father folds the torn wrapping paper and puts it in his pocket. Roy says, 'More thrift.'

'No. I'm anti-litter as well as everything else.' He takes up the binoculars again and looks towards the Lough.

'The constructive thing to get into these days is demolition.' He lowers the glasses and his head turns slowly from left to right. 'When I die bury me here for the view.' There is a long silence between them. Roy breaks it by laughing.

'Sure thing,' he says.

The two men go back the way they came.

'That's when you know your age.'

'What?' says Roy.

'When going down is harder than coming up.' Roy goes in front and offers his hand as they come down the steep, stepped part of the path. The old man ignores it and instead leans his weight on Roy's shoulder. Guiding him between two rocks the son puts his hand on his father's back and is startled to feel his shoulder-blades, the shape of butterfly wings, through the thin material of his jacket.

Eels

THE OLD WOMAN sat playing solitaire, hearing the quiet click of her wedding-ring on the polished table top each time she laid her hand flat to study the ranks of cards. They were never right. Never worked out. A crucial king face down, buried – and the game was lost. She realised how futile it was – not only this particular game but the activity of playing solitaire, and yet she could not stop herself, so she dealt the cards again. They flipped down silently, cushioned as they slid on the shine of the wood. She was reluctant to cheat. She played maybe six times before she gave up, put the cards away and sat gnawing her thumbnail. Perhaps later, left alone, it would come out.

She moved to the kitchen and took her magnesia, not bothering with the spoon but slugging the blue bottle back, hearing the white liquid tilt thickly. She swallowed hard, holding her thrapple. She stopped breathing through her nose so as not to taste, and held her mouth open. She walked to the bedroom, still breathing through her mouth until she saw herself in the mirror with crescents of white at the sides of her open lips. When she closed her teeth she heard and felt the sand of the magnesia grate between them. Her skin was loose and wrinkled, hanging about the bones she knew to be beneath her face. There were crows' feet at the corners of her eyes. With one finger she pressed down beneath her eye, baring its red sickle. They watered too much when the weather was cold. She wiped the white from the sides of her mouth with a tissue and began dressing, putting on several layers against the cold, with her old cardigan on top. She combed her white hair back from her forehead and looked at the number of hairs snagged on the comb. She removed them and with a fidget of her fingers dropped them into the waste-paper basket.

She remembered as a girl at the cottage combing her hair in spring sunshine and each day taking the dark hairs from the comb and dropping them out of the window with the same fidget of her fingers. A winter gale blew down a thrushes' nest into the garden and it was lined and snug with the black sheen of her own hair. For ages she kept it but it fell apart eventually, what with drying out and all the handling it got as she showed it to the children in class.

She lifted her raffia basket and put into it the magnesia, the pack of cards and a handful of tea-bags. In the hall she put on her heavy overcoat. The driveway to the house had not been made up, even though the house had been occupied for more than three years. It was rutted with tracks which had frozen over. She stopped to try one with the pressure of her toe, to see how heavy the frost had been. The slow ovals of bubbles separated and moved away from her toe. They returned again when she removed her weight but the ice did not break. She shuffled, afraid of falling, the ice crisping beneath her feet. Above her she saw the moon in its last phase shining at midday.

The air was bitterly cold. She had a pain in her throat which she experienced as a lump every time she swallowed. She had to chew what little she ate thoroughly or she felt it would not go past the lump. Everyone accused her of eating like a bird. Everyone said that she must see a doctor. But she knew without a doctor telling her that she would not see another winter. In September her son Brian had offered to buy her a heavy coat but she had refused, saying that she wouldn't get the wear out of it.

On the tarmac road she walked with a firmer step. There was no need to look up yet. She knew the bend, the precise gap in the hedge where she could see the lough. First she had to pass the school. The old school had been different, shaped like a church, built of white stone. But still, the new one had good toilets – better than the ones that she as a monitress had had to share with the whole school. It had got so bad that she eventually learned to hold on for the whole of the day.

The sound of the master's voice rang out impatiently as she passed, shouting a page number again and again. She smiled and anticipated the gap in the hedge. The shoulder of the hill sloped down and she raised her eyes to look at the lough. It was there, a flat bar almost to the horizon, the colour of aluminium. She stopped and stared.

Round the next turn was the cottage, set by itself with its back to the lough. No one saw her. Not that it would really matter. She let herself in the front door with her own key and hung her coat on the hall-stand beside a coat of her son's. He never wore it because he went everywhere in the car. He had got fat with lack of exercise and the modern things that Bernadette fed him. Spaghettis and curries that made the old woman's gorge rise to smell them.

In the kitchen she felt the heat on her face. She opened the door of the Rayburn so that she could see the fire and its red glow. She sank into the armchair and extended her feet to warm her shins before putting the kettle on.

From where she sat she could see the lough framed between the net curtains of the back window. When she had moved house it hadn't really occurred to her that she would miss it but the first morning when she woke she had glanced towards the window and been aware of the difference – like passing a mirror when she had had her hair cut. Then with each waking morning the loss grew. She did not become used to the field at the back. It had a drab sameness. The lough was never the same, changing from minute to minute. Now it was the colour of pewter. Through all the years she had spent in this cottage the lough was a presence. She would stand drying dishes, her eyes fixed on it but not seeing it. Making the beds, she knew it was there behind her.

Suddenly the phone rang, startling her. She looked at it, willing it to stop. She began to count the rings. At ten they should have stopped but they went on. Insistently. When they did stop they left a faint trembling echo in the silence.

She moved to fill the kettle. What if it had been an accident? At Brian's place anything could happen to him. She remembered a Saturday in Cookstown when she missed the bus and had to go round to the garage to get a lift. Brian lay in dungarees beneath a jacked-up car, speaking out to her. She hated the whole place. It was like a dark hangar, full of the smell of diesel and the echoes of dropped spanners. Rain came in through a broken sky-light and stayed in round droplets on the oily concrete. A mechanic, whistling tunelessly, started a car and revved it until she thought her head would burst. She hated the fact that Brian owned this place, but what was worse was the fact that he had bought it with money earned from fishing. Always the men of her family had fished for eels.

The kettle began a tiny rattle on the range and she took a tea-bag from her basket and put it in a cup. When the water boiled she poured it, watching it colour from yellow to mahogany. She removed the plump tea-bag with a spoon and dropped it hissing into the range. The tea clouded with the little milk she added to it.

The eels had become profitable a couple of years before her husband Hugh had died. A co-op had been formed and the prices soared. Within the space of a couple of months cracked lino was thrown out and carpet appeared in its place. They changed their van for a new car − not second-hand new. But they had worked hard for it, snatching sleep at all hours of the day and night. Often she had seen Hugh making up the lines by the light of the head-lamps − four hundred droppers with hooks off each section of line, four lines in all, while she, with her back breaking, stooped, a torch in one hand, pulling the small slippery hawsers of worms from the night ground to bait every one of them.

One night she had taken a step to the side and stood on something that made her whole head reel, something taut and soft at the same time − something living. An eel. Eels. An *ahh* of revulsion followed by 'Mother of God'. She remembered the words exactly and remembered the hair of her head being alive and rising from her scalp. She had stepped back but another squirmed under her heel. Her torch picked out the silent writhing procession, crossing the land from one water to another. Out of the depths, into the depths. Glistening like a snail's trail. Shuddering at the memory, she almost spilled her tea.

She turned on the transistor and changed the wavelength from Radio One to the local station for the news. She heard without listening, staring at the lough. Accidents, killings. The lough will claim a victim every year, was what they said. It was strange that, because on the lough there were no real storms. The water became brown and fretted when the wind got up. Even so, there were windy nights when the men were out fishing that she worried, seeing the water see-saw in the toilet bowl. Last year Hugh had died in his bed, thank God. The cat died about the same time. Both were ill for long enough.

Only once in her life had she gone out with them in the boat. When she had asked, Hugh had laughed and scorned the idea but she had said that all her life she had been cooking for them and she was curious to know what they did. Besides, now that they had a cooker that could switch *itself* on there was no reason why she shouldn't. Every time Hugh looked at her – a spectator sitting in the prow of the boat with her arms folded – he shook his head in disbelief saying to Brian, 'As odd as two left feet.' And she knew it was a compliment. It was an open boat with an outboard and in the middle sat an oil-drum with a kitchen knife blade sharpened to a razor's edge protruding above the rim, like an Indian's feather. As the men lifted the lines, if there was an eel on, they walloped it into the drum, the blade slicing the line as they did so. She had felt a strange admiration for her husband and her son as they became involved in their work. They were so deft yet so unaware of her watching their deftness. She wanted to reach out and touch them but she knew she could not touch the thing that awed her, knew they would mock her if she tried to put it into words. She watched the writhe of brown and yellow eels build up inside the drum, intricate, ceaselessly moving, aware that each one had swallowed a hook. She was too soft, they all said. They had ridiculed her when, drowning a bagful of kittens, they caught her warming the water in the bucket to take the chill off it.

She finished her tea, swallowing hard, and while she remembered she returned the pointer on the transistor to Radio One and switched it off. It would be the kind of thing that Bernadette would notice. Always she had to leave the place exactly as she found it. One day when she had been on one of her 'visits' she had seen a young man crouching outside the garden gate at the back. She was not afraid but curious. As an excuse she had hung out a dish-towel and asked him what he was doing.

'I'm a student – of a sort. I'm looking at rocks.'

He had a bag over his shoulder and a hammer in his hand. She offered him a cup of tea and he accepted. He was young and full of an enthusiasm for learning that her own son lacked. But he had tried to talk down to her, using simple words to explain the geological research he was engaged in. She told him curtly that she had been a teacher.

'The latest theory,' he said, 'is that the continents are moving. These vast countries can move vast distances. But it takes a vast time.'

'I'm vastly impressed,' she said. 'More tea?'

He held out his cup by the handle and she filled it. His skin was pale and he had not shaved for several days, but his eyes were keen.

'Can you imagine it,' he said, 'that South America and Africa were once joined together? And now they are thousands of miles apart? The evidence is in the rocks. Think of the power.

He set down his cup and slid one hand heavily over the other.

'Yes,' she said.

As they talked the boy smoked a lot of cigarettes, each time offering her one, which she refused. She asked him if he was married and he told her that he was engaged to a girl from Cookstown. After he graduated they would get married. To her surprise the old woman did not know her name or any of her connection when he said it. It was a changed place, Cookstown.

After he had gone she brought in the dish-towel and flapped it in front of the open window to clear the house of smoke. Bernadette had a sharp nose, which she wrinkled at any smell.

She also detested the way her daughter-in-law held her shoulders high as she worked about the house – the clipped way she spoke, as if to say, 'I'll talk to you but I have my work to get on with.' Old before her years, that one. The house was perfect anyway, without chick nor child to untidy it. One of the things that had annoyed her most was the speed with which Bernadette had redecorated the cottage when they had moved out to the new bungalow. She couldn't have lived with the walls as they were, she said, giving that little shrug of her spiky shoulders.

The old woman moved to the table at the window and began a game of solitaire. The lough had become the colour of lead. She looked at the sky, now overcast. The snap-up roller blind was stuck all over with long-legged midges. They came in clouds in the summer and, like a smell, couldn't be kept out by shutting doors or windows. She dealt quickly, the cards making a flacking noise as they came off the deck. Solitaire annoyed Bernadette. She thought it a waste of time. The old woman *knew* it was. All her life she had wanted to halt the time passing but she never felt like that until *afterwards*. She was either too busy or too tired to capture and hold the moment. Brian was now married and loosened his trousers after a meal. How long ago was it that she had taken his two ankles between the trident of her fingers to position him on his nappy? Or used egg-white to stiffen and hold in place the flap of hair that fell over his eyes before he had his first communion photograph taken? Or nudged him in his stained suit to the bedroom and let him lean his head on her shoulder while she fumbled at the laces of his shoes and became white with anger and fear that he had driven the van home in such a condition? Like everyone else, she had applauded at his wedding.

Jack on queen and she was stuck. There was nothing else to move and she pulled the cards towards her with a sigh of exasperation. She rose to go to the bathroom. As she climbed the stairs she put a hand on each thigh and pushed. There was a time when she could have bounded up them two at a time.

In the bathroom the toilet-roll was olive green and went almost black in the bowl. She wandered the bedrooms, not recognising them as her own. The neatness, the colours. The view from the window had not changed. This was the room where she had given birth to Brian. The only detail she remembered from that night was the crackling of newspaper beneath her. To this day she couldn't bear to sit on a newspaper, even if it was beneath the cushion.

Downstairs she made another cup of tea and ate a dry biscuit, massaging it past her thrapple the way she had seen the vet help pills down the cat's throat. She found that it went down easier if she put her head back in the chair . . .

She woke in panic. It was dark and the rain was rattling against the window. For a moment she did not know where she was, thought the cottage was her own again. She switched on the table lamp and looked at the clock – a quarter past five. She began to gather her stuff. She washed the cup and returned it to its hook. She hadn't realised that it had been so late. As quickly as she was able she damped down the fire with slack and closed it up. Some spilled from the shovel on to the lino with a rattle and she cursed herself for her carelessness. She swept it in beneath the range.

Outside it was moonless dark and still raining but the cold of the morning had disappeared. The cottage was silent after the echoing slam of the door except for the gurgling of water in the gratings.

Behind the hill she saw the white fan of a car's headlights, then the electric glare as it broke the horizon. She watched it come towards the cottage. It slowed down and indicated before the lane end. Quickly she slipped through the gap in the hedge into the field. The car splashed and bounced through the pot-holes up the track. Unable to crouch much, the old woman put her neck forward and lowered her head. They must have left early. The cottage flooded with light. She heard Bernadette's voice, complaining as usual, say,

'You don't expect me to carry this weight, do you?'

The front door banged shut. The old woman stood in the field trembling.

'And what makes you so different?' she said. They were the first words she had spoken since Tuesday and they made the bones of her head vibrate. The moon was in its last phase and she felt the rain on the backs of her hands. Her tremble turned to nausea and panic and she shuddered. On such a night the eels would be moving through the grass. Her hair became live. She had seen Hugh's finger once when bitten by an eel, the bone like mother-of-pearl through the wound. Tensing the arches of her feet, she stepped awkwardly through the gap in the hedge. In the lane she kept to the side, avoiding the pot-holes. Somewhere a procession of eels would be writhing towards the lough. Out of the depths, into the depths. She turned her head and looked to see the water. She saw nothing but blackness, an infinity rising unbroken in an arch above her head.

Now as she looked at the cottage backed by darkness with its yellow windows reflected in the puddles, and in the knowledge that somewhere not too far away the earth was alive with eels – at that moment she knew her life was over. It hadn't come out. Not the way she wanted. She was aware of the lump in her throat and knew that her eyes were full of water. Beneath her feet continents were moving. She put her head down into the slanting rain and began the slow walk to the bungalow, her coat unbuttoned.

More than just the Disease

As HE UNPACKED his case Neil kept hearing his mother's voice. *Be tidy at all times, then no one can surprise you.* This was a strange house he'd come to, set in the middle of a steep terraced garden. Everything in it seemed of an unusual design; the wardrobe in which he hung his good jacket was of black lacquer with a yellow inlay of exotic birds. *A little too ornate for my taste – vulgar almost.* And pictures – there were pictures hanging everywhere, portraits, landscapes, sketches. *Dust gatherers.* The last things in his case were some comics and he laid them with his ironed and folded pyjamas on the pillow of the bottom bunk and went to join the others.

They were all sitting in the growing dark of the large front room, Michael drinking hot chocolate, Anne his sister with her legs flopped over the arm of the chair, Dr Middleton squeaking slowly back and forth in the rocking-chair while his wife moved around preparing to go out.

'Now, boys, you must be in bed by ten thirty at the latest. Anne can sit up until we come back if she wants. We'll not be far away and if anything does happen you can phone "The Seaview".' She spent some time looking in an ornamental jug for a pen to write down the number. 'I can find nothing in this house yet.'

'We don't need Anne to babysit,' said Michael. 'We're perfectly capable of looking after ourselves. Isn't that right Neil?' Neil nodded. He didn't like Michael involving him in an argument with the rest of the family. He had to have the tact of a guest; sit on the fence yet remain Michael's friend.

'Can we not stay up as late as Anne?' asked Michael.

'Anne is fifteen years of age. Please, Michael, it's been a long day. Off to bed.'

'But Mama, Neil and I. . .'

'Michael.' The voice came from the darkness of the rocking-chair and had enough threat in it to stop Michael. The two boys got up and went to their bedroom.

Neil lifted his pyjamas and went to the bathroom. He dressed for bed buttoning the jacket right up to his neck and went back with his clothes draped over his arm. Michael was half-dressed.

'That was quick,' he said. He bent his thin arms, flexing his biceps. 'I only wear pyjama bottoms. Steve McQueen, he-man,' and he thumped his chest before climbing to the top bunk. They lay and talked and talked – about their first year at the school, how lucky they had been to have been put in the same form, who they hated most. The Crow with his black gown and beaky nose, the Moon with his pallid round face, wee Hamish with his almost mad preoccupation with ruling red lines. Once Neil had awkwardly ruled a line which showed the two bumps of his fingers protruding beyond the ruler and wee Hamish had pounced on it.

'What are these bumps? Is this a drawing of a camel, boy?' Everybody except Neil had laughed and if there was one thing he couldn't abide it was to be laughed at. A voice whispered that it was a drawing of his girlfriend's chest.

Neil talked about the Scholarship examination and the day he got his results. When he saw the fat envelope on the mat he knew his life would change – if you got the thin envelope you had failed, a fat one with coloured forms meant that you had passed. What Neil did not say was that his mother had cried, kneeling in the hallway hugging and kissing him. He had never seen anyone cry with happiness before and it worried him a bit. Nor did he repeat what she had said with her eyes shining. *Now you'll be at school with the sons of doctors and lawyers.*

Anne opened the door and hissed into the dark.

'You've got to stop talking right now. Get to sleep.' She was in a cotton nightdress which became almost transparent with the light of the hallway behind her. Neil saw her curved shape outlined to its margins. He wanted her to stay there but she slammed the door.

After that they whispered and had a farting competition. They heard Michael's father and mother come in, make tea and go to bed. It was ages before either of them slept. All the time Neil was in agonies with his itch but he did not want to scratch in case Michael should feel the shaking communicated to the top bunk.

In the morning Neil was first awake and tiptoed to the bathroom with all his clothes to get dressed. He took off his pyjama jacket and looked at himself in the mirror. Every morning he hoped that it would have miraculously disappeared overnight but it was still there crawling all over his chest and shoulders: his psoriasis – a redness with an edge as irregular as a map and the skin flaking and scumming off the top. Its pattern changed from week to week but only once had it appeared above his collar line. That week his mother had kept him off school. He turned his back on the mirror and put on a shirt, buttoning it up to the neck. He wondered if he should wear a tie to breakfast but his mother's voice had nothing to say on the subject.

Breakfast wasn't a meal like in his own house when he and his mother sat down at table and had cereal and tea and toast with sometimes a boiled egg. Here people just arrived and poured themselves cornflakes and went off to various parts of the room, or even the house, to eat them. The only still figure was the doctor himself. He sat at the corner of the table reading the *Scotsman* and drinking coffee. He wore blue running shoes and no socks and had a T-shirt on. Except for his receding M-shaped hairline he did not look at all like a doctor. In Edinburgh anytime Neil had seen him he wore a dark suit and a spotted bow-tie.

Anne came in. '*Guten Morgen, mein Papa*. Hello Neil.' She was bright and washed with her yellow hair in a knot on the top of her head. Neil thought she was the most beautiful girl he had ever seen up close. She wore a pair of denims cut down to shorts so that there were frayed fringes about her thighs. She also had what his mother called *a figure*. She ate her cornflakes noisily and the doctor did not even raise his eyes from the paper. *Close*

108

your mouth when you're eating, please. Others have to live with you.

'Some performance last night, eh Neil?' she said.

'Pardon?'

'Daddy, they talked till all hours.'

Her father turned a page of the paper and his hand groped out like a blind man's to find his coffee.

'Sorry,' said Neil.

'I'm only joking,' said Anne and smiled at him. He blushed because she looked directly into his eyes and smiled at him as if she liked him. He stumbled to his feet.

'Thank you for the breakfast,' he said to the room in general and went outside to the garden where Michael was sitting on the steps.

'Where did you get to? You didn't even excuse yourself from the table,' said Neil.

'I wasn't at the table, small Fry,' said Michael. He was throwing pea-sized stones into an ornamental pond at a lower level.

'One minute you were there and the next you were gone.'

'I thought it was going to get heavy.'

'What?'

'I know the signs. The way the old man reads the paper. Coming in late last night.'

'Oh.'

Neil lifted a handful of multi-coloured gravel and fed the pieces singly into his other hand and lobbed them at the pool. They made a nice plip noise.

'Watch it,' said Michael. He stilled Neil's throwing arm with his hand. 'Here comes Mrs Wan.'

'Who's she?'

An old woman in a bottle-green cardigan and baggy mouse-coloured trousers came stepping one step at a time down towards them. She wore a puce-coloured hat like a turban and, although it was high summer, a pair of men's leather gloves.

'Good morning, boys,' she said. Her voice was the most superior thing Neil had ever heard, even more so than his elocution teacher's. 'And how are you this year, Benjamin?'

'Fine. This is my friend Neil Fry.' Neil stood up and nodded. She was holding secateurs and a flat wooden basket. He knew that she would find it awkward to shake hands so he did not offer his.

'How do you do? What do you think of my garden, young man?'

'It's very good. Tidy.'

'Let's hope it remains that way throughout your stay,' she said and continued her sideways stepping down until she reached the compost heap at the bottom beyond the ornamental pool.

'Who is she?' asked Neil.

'She owns the house. Lets it to us for the whole of the summer.'

'But where does she live when you're here?'

'Up the back in a caravan. She's got ninety million cats.' Mrs Wan's puce turban threaded in and out of the flowers as she weeded and pruned. It was a dull overcast day and the wind was moving the brightly-coloured rose blooms.

'Fancy a swim?' asked Michael.

'Too cold. Anyway I told you I can't swim.'

'You don't have to swim. Just horse around. It's great.'

'Naw.'

Michael threw his whole handful of gravel chirping into the pond and went up the steps to the house.

That afternoon the shelf of cloud moved inland and the sky over the Atlantic became blue. The wind dropped and Dr Middleton observed that the mare's-tails were a good sign., The whole family went down the hundred yards to the beach, each one carrying something – a basket, a deckchair, a lilo.

'Where else in the world but Scotland would we have the beach to ourselves on a day like this?' said Mrs Middleton. The doctor agreed with a grunt. Michael got stripped to his swimming trunks and they taught Neil to play boule in the hard sand near the water. The balls were of bright grooved steel and he enjoyed trying to lob them different ways until he finally copied the doctor who showed him how to put back-spin on them. Anne wore a turquoise bikini and kept hooking her fingers beneath the elastic of her pants and snapping them out to cover more of her bottom. She did this every time she bent to pick up her boule and Neil came to watch for it. When they stopped playing Michael and his sister ran off to leap about in the breakers – large curling walls, glass-green, which nearly knocked them off their feet. From where he stood Neil could only hear their cries faintly. He went and sat down with the doctor and his wife.

'Do you not like the water?' she asked. She was lying on a sunbed, gleaming with suntan oil. She had her dress rucked up beyond her knees and her shoulder straps loosened.

'No. It's too cold.'

'The only place *I'll* ever swim again is the Med,' said the doctor.

'Sissy,' said his wife, without opening her eyes. Neil lay down and tried to think of a better reason for not swimming. His mother had one friend who occasionally phoned for her to go to the Commonwealth Pool. When she really didn't feel like it there was only one excuse that seemed to work.

At tea Michael took a perverse pleasure out of telling him again and again how warm the water was and Anne innocently agreed with him.

The next day was scorching hot. Even at breakfast time they could see the heat corrugating the air above the slabbed part of the garden.

'You *must* come in for a swim today, Fry. I'm boiled already,' said Michael.

'The forecast is twenty-one degrees,' said the doctor from behind his paper. Anne whistled in appreciation.

Neil's thighs were sticking to the plastic of his chair. He said, 'My mother forgot to pack my swimming trunks. I looked yesterday.'

Mrs Middleton, in a flowing orange dressing-gown, spoke over her shoulder from the sink. 'Borrow a pair of Michael's.' Before he could stop her she had gone off with wet hands in search of extra swimming trunks.

'Couldn't be simpler,' she said, setting a navy blue pair with white side panels on the table in front of Neil.

'I'll get mine,' said Michael and dashed to his room. Anne sat opposite Neil on the Formica kitchen bench-top swinging her legs. She coaxed him to come swimming, again looking into his eyes. He looked down and away from them.

'Come on, Neil. Michael's not much fun in the water.'

'The fact is,' said Neil, 'I've got my period.'

There was a long silence and a slight rustle of the *Scotsman* as Dr Middleton looked over the top of it. Then Anne half-slid, half-vaulted off the bench and ran out. Neil heard her make funny snorts in her nose.

'That's too bad,' said the doctor and got up and went out of the room shutting the door behind him. Neil heard Anne's voice and her father's, then he heard the bedroom door shut. He folded his swimming trunks and set them on the sideboard. Mrs Middleton gave a series of little coughs and smiled at him.

'Can I help you with the dishes?' he asked. There was something not right.

'Are you sure you're well enough?' she said smiling. Neil nodded and began to lift the cups from various places in the room. She washed and he dried with a slow thoroughness.

'Neil, nobody is going to force you to swim. So you can feel quite safe.'

Michael came in with his swimming gear in a roll under his arm.

'Ready, small Fry?'

'Michael, could I have a word? Neil, could you leave those bathing trunks back in Michael's wardrobe?'

On the beach the boys lay down on the sand. Michael hadn't

spoken since they left the house. He walked in front, he picked the spot, he lay down and Neil followed him. The sun was hot and again they had the beach to themselves. Neil picked up a handful of sand and examined it as he spilled it out slowly.

'I bet you there's at least one speck of gold on this beach,' he said.

'That's a bloody stupid thing to say.'

'I'll bet you there is.'

Michael rolled over turning his back. 'I can pick them.'

'What?'

'I can really pick them.'

'What do you mean?'

'I might as well have asked a girl to come away on holiday.' Neil's fist bunched in the sand.

'What's the use of somebody who won't go in for a dip?'

'I can't, that's all.'

'My Mum says you must have.a very special reason. What is it, Fry?'

Neil opened his hand and some of the damp, deeper sand remained in little segments where he had clenched it. He was almost sure Anne had laughed.

'I'm not telling you.'

'Useless bloody Mama's boy,' said Michael. He got up flinging a handful of sand at Neil and ran down to the water. Some of the sand went into Neil's eyes, making him cry. He knuckled them clear and blinked, watching Michael jump, his elbows up, as each glass wave rolled at him belly-high.

Neil shouted hopelessly towards the sea. 'That's the last time I'm getting you into the pictures.'

He walked back towards the house. He had been here a night, a day and a morning. It would be a whole week before he could get home. Right now he felt he *was* a Mama's boy. He just wanted to climb the stair and be with her behind the closed door of their house. This had been the first time in his life he had been away from her and, although he had been reluctant because of this very thing, she had insisted that he could not turn down an invitation from the doctor's family. *It will teach you how to conduct yourself in good society.*

At lunch time Michael did not speak to him but made up salad rolls and took them on to the patio. Anne and her father had gone into the village on bicycles. Neil sat at the table chewing his roll with difficulty and staring in front of him. *If there is one thing I cannot abide it's a milk bottle on the table.* Mrs Middleton was the only one left for him to talk to.

'We met Mrs Wan this morning,' he said.

'Oh did you? She's a rum bird – feeding all those cats.'

'How many has she?'

'I don't know. They're never all together at the same time. She's a Duchess, you know?'

'A real one?'

'Yes. I can't remember her title – from somewhere in England. She married some Oriental and lived in the Far East. Africa too for a time. When he died she came home. Look.' She waved her hand at all the bric-à-brac. 'Look at this.' She went to a glass-fronted cabinet and took out what looked like a lace ball. It was made of ivory and inside was another ball with just as intricately carved mandarins and elephants and palm leaves, with another one inside that again.

'The question is how did they carve the one inside. It's all one piece.'

Neil turned it over in his hands marvelling at the mystery. He handed it carefully back.

'You wouldn't want to play boule with that,' he said.

'Isn't it exquisitely delicate?'

He nodded and said, 'Thank you for the lunch. It was very nourishing.'

He wandered outside in the garden and sat for a while by the pool. It was hot and the air was full of the noise of insects and bees moving in and out the flowers. He went down to the beach and saw that his friend Michael had joined up with some other boys to play cricket. He sat down out of sight of them at the side of a sand-dune. He lay back and closed his eyes. They had laughed at him in school when he said he didn't know what l.b.w. meant. He had been given a free cricket bat but there was hardly a mark on it because he couldn't seem to hit the ball. It was so hard and came at him so fast that he was more interested in getting out of its way than playing any fancy strokes. Scholarship boys were officially known as foundationers but the boys called them 'fundies' or 'fundaments'. When he asked what it meant somebody told him to look it up in a dictionary. 'Part of body on which one sits; buttocks; anus.'

He lifted his head and listened. At first he thought it was the noise of a distant seagull but it came again and he knew it wasn't. He looked up to the top of the sand-dune and saw a kitten, its tiny black tail upright and quivering.

'Pshhh-wshhh.'

He climbed the sand and lifted it. It miaowed thinly. He stroked its head and back and felt the frail fish bones of its ribs. It purred and he carried it back to the house. He climbed the steps behind the kitchen and saw a caravan screened by a thick hedge. The door was open and he had to hold it steady with his knee before he could knock on it.

'Come in,' Mrs Wan's voice called. Neil stepped up into the van. After the bright sunlight it was gloomy inside. It smelt of old and cat. He saw Mrs Wan sitting along one wall with her feet up.

'I found this and thought maybe it was yours,' said Neil handing the cat over to her. She scolded it.

'You little monkey,' she said and smiled at Neil. 'This cat is a black sheep. He's always wandering off. Thank you, young man. It was very kind of you to take the trouble to return him.'

'It was no trouble.'

She was dressed as she had been the day before except for the gloves. Her hands were old and her fingers bristled with rings. She waved at him as he turned to go.

'Just a minute. Would you like something to drink – as a reward?' She stood up and rattled in a cupboard above the sink.

115

'I think some tonic water is all I can offer you. Will that do?' She didn't give him a clean glass but just rinsed one for a moment under the thin trickle from the swan-neck tap at the tiny sink. She chased three cats away from the covered bench seat and waved him to sit down. Because the glass was not very clean the bubbles adhered to its sides. He saw that nothing was clean as he looked about the place. There were several tins of Kit-e-Kat opened on the draining-board and a silver fork encrusted with the stuff lay beside them. There were saucers all over the floor with milk which had evaporated in the heat leaving yellow rings. Everything was untidy. He set his glass between a pile of magazines and a marmalade pot on the table. She asked him his name and about his school and where he lived and about his father. Neil knew that his mother would call her nosey but he thought that she seemed interested in all his answers. She listened intently, blinking and staring at him with her face slightly turned as if she had a deaf ear.

'My father died a long time ago,' he said.

'And your mother?'

'She's alive.'

'And what does she do for a living?'

'She works in the cinema.'

'Oh how interesting. Is she an actress?'

'No. She just works there. With a torch. She gets me in free – for films that are suitable for me. Sometimes I take my friend Michael with me.'

'Is that the boy below?'

'Yes.'

'I thought his name was Benjamin. But how marvellous that you can see all these films free.' She clapped her ringed hands together and seemed genuinely excited. 'I used to love the cinema. The cartoons were my favourite. And the newsreels. I'll bet you're very popular when a good picture comes to town.'

'Yes I am,' said Neil and smiled and sipped his tonic.

'Let's go outside and talk. It's a shame to waste such a day in here.' Neil offered his arm as she lowered herself from the step to the ground.

'What a polite young man.'

'That's my mother's fault.'

They sat on the deckchairs facing the sun and she lit a cigarette, holding it between her jewelled fingers. Her face was brown and criss-crossed with wrinkles.

'Why aren't you in swimming on such a day?' she asked.

Neil hesitated, then heard himself say, 'I can't. I've got a disease.'

'What is it?'

Again he paused but this old woman seemed to demand the truth.

'A thing – on my chest.'

'Let me see?' she said and leaned forward. He was amazed to find himself unbuttoning his shirt and showing her his mark. In the sunlight it didn't look so red. She scrutinized it and hummed, pursing her mouth and biting her lower lip.

'Why does it stop you bathing?'

Neil shrugged and began to button up when she stopped him.

'Let the sun at it. I'm sure it can do no harm.' He left his shirt lying open. 'When I was in Africa I worked with lepers.'

'Lepers?'

'Yes. So the sight of you doesn't worry me,' she said. 'Watch that you don't suffer from more than just the disease.'

'I don't understand.'

'It's bad enough having it without being shy about it as well.'

'Have you got leprosy now?'

'No. It's not as contagious as everybody says.'

Neil finished his tonic and lay back in the chair. The sun was bright and hot on his chest. He listened to Mrs Wan talking about leprosy, of how the lepers lost their fingers and toes, not because of the disease but because they had lost all feeling in them and they broke and damaged them without knowing. Eventually they got gangrene. Almost all the horrible things of leprosy, she said, were secondary. Suddenly he heard Michael's voice.

'Mrs Wan, Mum says could you tell her where . . . ' his voice tailed off seeing Neil's chest, ' . . . the cheese grater is?'

'Do you know, I think I brought it up here.' She got up and stepped slowly into the caravan. Neil closed over his shirt and began to button it. Neither boy said a word.

At tea Michael spoke to him as if they were friends again and in bed that night it was Neil's suggestion that they go for a swim.

'Now? Are you mad?'

'They say it's warmer at night.'

'Yeah and we could make dummies in the beds like Clint Eastwood.'

'They don't *have* to look like Clint Eastwood.' They both laughed quiet sneezing laughs.

After one o'clock they dropped out of the window and ran to the beach. For almost half an hour in the pale darkness Neil thrashed and shivered. Eventually he sat down to wait in the warmer shallows, feeling the withdrawing sea hollow the sand around him. Further out, Michael whooped and rode the breakers like a shadow against their whiteness.

End of Season

THE ELDER Miss Bradley walked to the end of the small pier and stood listening to the sea thumping in from below. White horses flecked the bay and the wind was strong enough to make her avert her face from its direction. She was convinced that the summer was over. A week back at school and already the first gale of winter. On this exposed coast with no trees autumn did not exist.

She liked to come here on her way home, particularly on windy days. It rinsed the experience of school from her. She did not stand long – a minute, perhaps two, facing into the wind with her eyes closed. Then she turned on her heel and walked slowly, leaning back into the wind, trying not to let its strength fluster her or make her movements awkward.

The briefcase was heavy with jotters and she wished she had brought the car. The school was only three-quarters of a mile from the house but each day she debated whether or not she should walk the distance for the good of her health. It would not do to have two invalids in the one house.

The family home was one of a terrace of cream-painted houses, set back from the road behind long, well-kept gardens. Some of the houses still had little gibbets overhanging the pavement with 'Bed & Breakfast' signs swinging in the wind. As she walked up the path she faintly heard her sister, Kathleen, laughing and thought it odd – a feeling which increased when she opened the front door and smelt tobacco smoke. In the front room a man sat in her armchair beside the bookcase, with his back to the light, talking.

'Ah Mary, there you are,' said her sister. The man stood up politely.

'You remember' Mr Maguire?'

'Eh . . . yes, indeed.'

In his hand Mr Maguire held their old guest book. He sat down again and opened it so quickly that he must have had his finger in the place. 'I was just looking at when we were here last.' He passed the book to Mary. She found Mr and Mrs Maguire whose stay was dated July 1958.

'We were on our honeymoon,' he said. 'We had only booked one night but we stayed a week.' The man had a distinct Belfast accent.

'Mr Maguire thought we were still a guest house,' said Kathleen.

'Oh no. We stopped that a long time ago.' Mary flicked to the last entry in the book. 'In 1971.' She set it on the sideboard and, rubbing her hands, moved closer to the fire.

'It's like January,' she said. 'Is the kettle on?'

Her sister asked Mr Maguire if he would have more tea.

'I wouldn't say no.' He handed over his empty cup and saucer and Kathleen rattled it on to the tray with her own. She elbowed her way out of the door to the kitchen, leaving Mary and the stranger in silence.

'Are you looking for a place to stay?' Mary asked.

'Yes. I decided to treat myself to a holiday. It's years since I've gone anywhere.'

'Have you tried any of the other guest houses?'

'No. This is where I wanted to come.'

'It was nice of you to remember us.'

'It's funny how well you remember good times, holidays,' he said. 'I'm sure you don't remember us. We would have been one couple in a crowded summer.'

'Yes, sometimes it's difficult. But I rarely forget a face. Names, yes.'

Mary sat down on the rug in a delicate side-saddle posture and shivered. From her low position she could see the man's immaculately polished shoes. Her mother had always told her a man's footwear was the key to his character. 'Beware of some-one with dirty shoes,' she had said. 'Even worse is the man who has polished his shoes but neglected to do his heels. But worst of all is the man with black polish stains on his socks. It's the ultimate sloth.' Mary looked up at him but his face was in

shadow because his back was to the grey light from the window.
He wore an open-necked shirt, a pair of trousers too light for
his age and a blue sweater with a small emblem of a red jaguar
on it.

'And Mrs Maguire?'

'My wife died last December.'

'Oh I'm sorry.'

'She had been ill for a long time. It was a merciful release.'

'Oh I am sorry,' she said. 'What brings you back to this part
of the world?' He hesitated before answering.

'I wanted to see Spanish Point. Where the galleon went down.
The Girona.'

'Yes, I walk out there frequently myself. There's nothing
much. Rocks, sea.'

'I was at an exhibition in the museum – of the stuff they
brought up – and I thought I'd just like to look at the place.
Imagine it a bit.'

Kathleen's voice called loudly from the kitchen. Mary
excused herself and went out.

'He wants to stay for a couple of nights,' whispered'
Kathleen. 'I told him I'd have to ask you. What do you think?'

'How do you feel about it? Can you cope?'

'Yes, I don't mind. The money would come in handy.' Mary
was about to go back to the other room when her sister held her
by the arm.

'But listen to this,' Kathleen laughed and wheezed. 'We had
been talking about books. He tells me he reads a lot – as a matter of fact he's book mad – and when I came in with the tea I
said "Do you like Earl Grey?" and he says, "I don't know.
What did he write?" Isn't that marvellous?' Mary smiled and
nodded while Kathleen giggled uncontrollably, saying to herself, 'Stop it Kathleen,' and slapping the back of her wrist. She
straightened her face and set out some more biscuits on a plate.
Then she burst out laughing again.

'He kept talking about the eedgit, at one stage.'

'The what?'

'The book "The Eedgit". One of the big Russians. He meant *The Idiot*.'

'Oh,' said Mary.

'Really, Kathleen, control yourself.' Her sister again straightened her face and picked up the tray. Mary opened the door for her.

'It'll be something for me to do,' Kathleen whispered over her shoulder as she led the way into the other room.

'That'll be fine, Mr Maguire,' she said. 'If you'll give me a minute I'll fix up your room for you.' He edged forward in his seat and made a vague gesture as if to assist Kathleen with the tray.

'Thank you very much,' he said and smiled up at the two sisters. 'I'll try and cause as little disruption as possible.' Mary sat on the rug again to be near the fire. Mr Maguire sipped from his cup holding his saucer close to his chest.

'Why did you stop the bed and breakfast?' he asked.

'Several reasons,' said Kathleen. 'Me for one. My asthma was getting intolerable. It's really a nervous condition with me. The very thought of summer would bring on an attack. Then there was the Troubles, of course. After 'sixty-nine people just stopped coming. Now we call this place the last resort.'

'When we were here the place was full of Scotch.'

'Yes, and the same ones came back year after year. But after the Troubles started nobody would risk it. Then Mary got a job teaching when the new school was built.'

'And mother died,' said Mary.

'Oh did she? I never saw her. We just heard her – upstairs.'

'She was very demanding,' said Kathleen, 'and I was in no position to cope with her. It was she really who insisted that we keep the place open. All her life she had a great fear of ending up in the poor-house. She was the one who had the bright idea of extending out the back just before the slump. We're still paying the mortgage.'

Mr Maguire set his cup and saucer on the hearth. 'Do you mind if I smoke a pipe?' He addressed Mary who turned to her sister.

'Kathleen?'

'I like the smell of pipe-smoke. It's cigarettes I can't stand.'

Mr Maguire took out a small pipe and a yellow plastic pouch. He filled the pipe as he listened to Kathleen talk about the old days when the house was full of guests. Mary watched him press the tobacco into the bowl with his index finger. When he struck the match he whirled his hand in a little circle to attenuate the flare before holding the match to his pipe. The triangular flame gave little leaps as he held it over the bowl and drew air through it, his lips popping quietly. Throughout the whole operation he continued to nod and say 'hm-hm' to Kathleen's talk.

'You'll just have to take us as we are,' she was saying, 'not being officially open and all that. I'll give you a key and you can come and go as you like.'

'Thank you,' said Mr Maguire, striking another match.

'And breakfast. Would you like a fry in the morning?'

'Yes, please. It's the only time I ever do have the big fry. I wouldn't think I was on holiday if I didn't. Do you still bake your own wheaten bread?'

'No. My asthma. The flour can sometimes go for it. Let me get you an ashtray,' said Kathleen, jumping up. Mr Maguire sat with a tiny bouquet of dead matches between his fingers. 'Did you ever think of selling?'

Kathleen laughed and Mary smiled down at the fire.

'We tried for three years,' said Kathleen. 'Would you want to buy it? The ads were costing us so much that we had to take it off the market.'

When the tea was finished Kathleen showed him up to his room, talking constantly, even over her shoulder on the stairs. Mary followed them, her hands tucked into opposite sleeves, like a nun. The bed was stripped to its mattress of blue and white stripes. Mr Maguire set his bag by the window.

124

'I'll put the electric blanket on to air the bed for you,' said Kathleen.

'Thank you,' he said. 'You get a great view from this window.' Mary stared over his shoulder at the metallic sea. His face in the light was sallow and worn, with vertical creases down each side of his mouth and his forehead corrugated into wrinkles as he spoke. He wouldn't win any prizes for his looks but somehow his face suited him. He gave the impression of being an ex-sportsman, wiry and tough, sufficiently tall to have developed a slight stoop of the shoulders. He had enough hair to make her wonder whether or not it was a toupee. If it was it was a very convincing one.

'Where's a good place to eat now?'

'The Royal do a nice meal,' said Kathleen.

'The Royal?'

'Is that too expensive?'

'It was in my day.'

Kathleen lifted the foot of the bed and eased it out from the wall.

'Try the Croft Kitchen,' she said. 'I think they're still open. What little season there is, is over.' Seeing him hesitate she added, 'It's on High Street opposite what used to be the Amusements.' She stepped out on to the landing. 'The bathroom is second on your right. The light switch is on the outside.'

'Yes, I remember.'

'I'll just get some bed-linen.' Kathleen hurried off.

'She's excited,' said Mary, her voice lowered. Mr Maguire smiled and nodded. His voice was as quiet as hers.

'On our honeymoon,' he said, 'my wife went to the bathroom . . .' Mary withdrew her hands from her sleeves and straightened a picture, 'and someone turned out the light on her. She was terrified. She heard a footstep, then the light went out, then breathing. The poor woman sat for half the night in the dark before she had the courage to come out. I was sound asleep, of course.'

'How awful,' said Mary.

Kathleen strode in, the fresh bed-linen pressed between her arms like a white accordion. 'Right, there's work to be done,' she said, dumping them on the bed.

That night even though she felt tired and had gone to bed early Mary could not sleep. She heard Mr Maguire come in at a reasonable hour. Apart from a little throat-clearing he himself was quiet but she heard everything he did – the popping of the wash-hand basin in her own room as he used his, the flush of the toilet from the end of the corridor, through the wall the creaking of his bed as he got into it. It seemed hours before she heard the snap of his bedside light being switched off and she wondered what book it was that kept him reading so late.

She woke several times and each time was wet with perspiration, so much so that she was afraid she had had an accident. She felt like the shamelessly vulgar girl on the calendar which hung above the cash desk in the garage, emerging from the waves in a dripping white chemise which concealed nothing. Her condition was becoming worse instead of better. At times in front of her classes she felt as if there was a hole in her head and she was being filled from top to toe, like a hot-water bottle. Some months ago Kathleen had become alarmed seeing her sister steady herself with her knuckles on the kitchen table, her face red and wet with perspiration.

'What's wrong?'

Mary had simply said that her ovaries were closing down. The inner woman was giving up the ghost, but not without a struggle. She showered twice a day now – when she got up in the morning and before her evening meal. She refused to go to the doctor because, she said, the condition was normal. The *Home Encyclopedia of Medicine* told her all she wanted to know. Letters in women's magazines frequently dealt with the subject, in some cases in embarrassing detail. It was a sign of the times when you bought a perfectly middle-of-the-road woman's magazine and were frightened to open the pages because of what

126

you might read: sex mixed in with the knitting patterns; among the recipes, orgasms and homosexuality and God knows what. She was embarrassed, not on her own behalf but for the teenagers in her classes. Magazines like the ones she bought would inevitably be going into all their homes. Each time her eyes flinched away from reading such an article she blushed for the destruction of her pupils' innocence. As for some of the daily papers, she wouldn't give them house-room.

Mr Maguire cleared his throat and she heard the twang of him turning in his seldom-used bed.

During the last class of the day Mary stood staring, not out, but at the window. On this the leeward side of the school, the glass was covered with rain droplets which trembled at each gust of wind. Behind her a fourth-year class worked quietly at a translation exercise. She was proud of her reputation for having the most disciplined classes in the school. She knew the pupils disliked her for it but it was something they would thank her for in later life.

At ten to four she saw Mr Maguire walking out of town with his hands clasped behind his back and his head down into the wind. When she eventually got out of school he was standing smiling at the gate.

'I thought it must be that time,' he said, 'and I was just passing.' He offered to carry her bag but she said that it was light enough. They began walking into the fine drizzle.

'What a day that was. Do you have children, Mr Maguire?'

'No, my wife was never a well woman. It would have been too much to ask.' Again she was struck by the coarseness of his accent. His face relaxed and he smiled. 'Where did all the books come from in your house?' he asked.

'That was my father mostly. He was Headmaster of the local Primary. He was interested in all sorts of things. Nature study, science, history. We were always used to books in the house.'

'Lucky. I had to do all the work myself. At a very late stage. Imagine sitting your A-levels for the first time at fifty.'

'Is that what you did?'

'I'm afraid so.'

'I admire that.'

Mr Maguire shrugged shyly.

'Not everybody does. My wife used to make fun of me. But she had a very hard time. She was in a lot of pain and couldn't understand. I think she was jealous of the time I spent reading. She thought it was a hobby or a pastime or something like that. She couldn't have been further from the truth.' Seeing Mary change her briefcase from her right to her left hand Mr Maguire insisted that he carry it. She reluctantly let him take it.

He continued talking. 'When you find out about real education you can never leave it alone. I don't mean A-levels and things like that – you are just proving something to yourself with them – but books, ideas, feelings. Everything to do with up here.' He tapped his temple. 'And here.' He tapped the middle of his chest.

Mary asked, 'What do you like to read then?'

'The classics. Fiction. Good stuff.'

The wind tugged at his hair, blowing it into various partings. It was definitely not a toupee.

'I sometimes stop here and walk to the end.' She pointed to the pier, its back arched against the running sea. Occasionally a wave broke over it and spray slapped down on the concrete. Some boys with school-bags were running the gauntlet along the pier.

'They'll get soaked, or worse,' said Mr Maguire.

'That's nothing. This summer I saw them ride off the end on a bicycle. They had it tied to one of the bollards so's they could pull it up each time. I couldn't watch. It gave me the funniest feeling. I had to go away in the end.'

When they got back to the house Mr Maguire set her briefcase in the hall, nodded to her and climbed the stairs. Mary went to the kitchen and sat on a stool beside the Rayburn drying out as the kettle boiled.

'Where's our guest?' asked Kathleen.

'Upstairs.'

'He's a strange fish. But nice.'

'Yes, you and he certainly seem to get along,' said Mary. Kathleen rolled her eyes to heaven.

Mary laughed and said, 'He walks like the Duke of Edinburgh.' She stood up and did an imitation backwards and forwards across the kitchen, her hands joined behind her back, her head forward like a tortoise.

Kathleen giggled, saying, 'I was making his bed today and do you know what he's reading? Or at least has lying on his bedside table.'

'I've no idea.'

'A book of English verse.'

'Why not?'

'It doesn't tally somehow. Him and poetry. And do you know – he's brought a full shoe-polishing kit with him. Brushes, tins, cloths, the lot. Mother would have been so pleased.'

'You shouldn't nosey.'

'I couldn't help seeing them. I had to move them out of the way to make the bed.'

'What's wrong with being careful about your appearance?'

'Nothing. But it does seem a bit extravagant.'

Kathleen heard Mr Maguire's footsteps on the landing and bounded to the kitchen door.

'There's a cup of tea in the pot, Mr Maguire,' she called.

When he came in Mary smelt soap off his hands as he reached in front of her for his cup.

'Well, how was your day?' asked Kathleen.

'The rain drove me home,' he smiled. His hair was dark and neatly parted, as if he had used hair-oil. 'You see how I call it home already.' Kathleen offered him a biscuit but he refused.

'How was your meal in the Croft Kitchen last night?'

'It was closed.'

'Where did you eat then?'

'The café on the front. It was good. Reasonable too.'

129

'Eucch, what a place,' Kathleen shuddered. 'All those sauce bottles on the tables. They're encrusted.'

'No, it was fine, really.'

'Look, we don't eat extravagantly ourselves but you're welcome to join us this evening.'

'Ah now that wouldn't be fair.'

'We're just having mince and carrots. It's no bother to set a place for an extra one.' Mr Maguire hesitated. He looked at Mary who was staring into her cup. She raised her eyes to him.

'Why don't you stay?' she said.

'Only on one condition. You must charge me extra.'

'That's settled then,' said Kathleen. 'We can haggle about the price later.'

'It's very kind of you. Both of you.'

Mr Maguire appeared at dinner time wearing a tie but no jacket. Mary sat opposite him, the tails of hair at her neck still damp from the shower, while Kathleen served and talked.

'There's a whist drive tonight in the hall, Mr Maguire. Guests are very welcome.'

'I'm sorry,' said Mr Maguire, 'I was never any good at card games – especially whist. Partners depending on you to play the right card. I played once or twice and at the finish up my shins were black and blue.'

'I *have* to go,' said Kathleen. 'I'm organizing a table. Mary, will you run me up? I have all those cups and saucers and things.' Mary nodded.

'Can you not drive?'

'No, I'm too nervous. But Mary is very good, runs me everywhere.'

Kathleen took on the responsibility of the silences and when one occurred she talked, mostly to Mr Maguire.

'What do you do?'

'At the moment, nothing. I've just been made redundant. One of the three million.'

130

'Oh that's too bad.'

'Yes, when I got my redundancy money I said to heck, I'll treat myself to a holiday.'

'You were just right,' said Kathleen. 'You can't take it with you.'

'There'll be none of it left to take with me.'

Both sisters smiled. Mr Maguire looked at Mary and she felt obliged to speak.

'What did you work at?'

'In a big warehouse. Spare parts for cars.'

'Oh I see,' said Mary.

'I'd been there for most of my life.'

'Then you know a bit about cars?'

'A bit.'

'It's just that mine is not going properly.'

'What is it?'

'A Fiat.'

'No, I mean what is the problem?'

'It seems to have no power, sluggish.'

'I could have a look at it tomorrow.'

Kathleen interrupted. 'But I thought you were going tomorrow?'

'Would you mind if I stayed the weekend? I have no real reason to rush back.'

'Certainly,' said Kathleen. 'Especially if you can fix the car.'

'Thank you.' Mr Maguire had cleared his plate in a matter of minutes. Kathleen offered him second helpings.

'It's the sea air,' he said. 'Gives you an appetite. This is what I cook mostly for myself because it's easy.' Then he seemed embarrassed. 'I'm sorry. This tastes a hundred times better than my efforts. I just mean that it doesn't take much looking after on the stove.'

'I gather you don't like cooking?'

'No. At home I do a standard menu. The boiled egg. The mince. When you're on your own food doesn't seem as interesting. I find it hard enough to get through a whole loaf without

131

it going bluemould.' He laughed. 'I eat watching the news with my plate on my knees. Rarely set a table.'

'Is there any chance you'll get another job?'

'I doubt it. The car trade is in a bad way and it's the only one I know. I'm fifty-six now. Prospects poor.' He shrugged. Mary looked at his hands. They were big and red, making toys of his knife and fork. The nail of his thumb was opaque like a hazelnut.

'I don't really want a job,' he said. 'Now I'll have time to do what I want.'

'What's that?'

'Read. Dig my plot. I'm going to do this Open University thing. On television. I've just enrolled but it doesn't start until next January. I paid the fees out of my redundancy.'

'You make the dole sound like a good thing.'

'I've always been keen. If there's a WEA class on the go, I'm your man. History, English, Philosophy – there was a Botany year but I couldn't make head nor tail of it. Anything and everything, I'm a dabbler.'

Kathleen got out of the car at the church hall balancing a cardboard box full of trembling cups. She slammed the door with her heel.

'Hey, just you be careful with that Mr Maguire, Mary,' she said through the driver's window.

'He's a bit down-market for me, dear.' Mary laughed. 'Besides it's you he fancies.'

'Will you pick me up?'

Mary nodded.

On her way back she was irritated again by the lack of energy in the engine. On the hill of the High Street it seemed barely to have sufficient power to pull her up. She thought about Mr Maguire.

'Thank God it's Friday,' she said aloud.

She had kicked off her shoes and was just sitting down to look at the paper when there was a quiet rap on the door. Mr Maguire stood there with a light bulb in his hand.

'I'm sorry to trouble you,' he said, 'but my reading light has gone and I wondered if you had a spare one?' Mary, in stockinged feet, climbed on to a stool and produced a new sixty watt bulb from a high cupboard. She exchanged bulbs with him and for some reason felt foolish. He stood for a moment with the cardboard package in his hands.

'Is it raining?' he asked.

'No, not now.'

He moved the piece of card that held the bulb in place against the corrugations of the package, rippling it.

'Are you busy this evening?' he asked. Mary hesitated.

'No.'

'Would you like to go somewhere for a drink perhaps?'

'I don't like going into pubs.'

'The hotel – we could go to the Royal, just for a while. An orange juice, if you like.'

Mary was now swinging the dead bulb by its tiny pins between her finger and thumb. 'It's Friday,' she said. 'Why not?'

Mr Maguire smiled. 'In about half an hour then?'

'Yes.'

He turned quickly, holding up the new light bulb in a gesture of thanks. For a ridiculous moment she expected it to light as if he was some kind of statue.

She closed the door and, out of habit, before she threw the used bulb in the waste-paper basket she shook it close to her ear. There was no tinkling sound. She switched off the standard lamp and removed the hot bulb with a serviette. Mr Maguire's bulb lit when she switched it on.

In the hotel lounge after the first sip of her sherry she took a tissue from her handbag and wiped the red crescent stain of her lower lip from the rim of the glass. Mr Maguire was drinking Guinness. She sat on the edge of her seat, her shoulders back.

Her mother had always chivvied her about 'bearing'. One day as they walked to church she had prodded Mary between the shoulder-blades with the point of her umbrella.

'If you want to keep your bosoms separate – don't slouch.' She could feel the ferrule to this very day. And yet now, without being told, she did everything her mother had asked of her.

'Relax,' said Mr Maguire. Muzak took away from the early evening hush.

'I'm not used to places like this. I've only been here at weddings.'

'It's a nice place.'

'The word'll be out on Monday that Miss Bradley was seen boozing with a man.'

Mr Maguire laughed.

'What do you teach?'

'German and a little French.'

'Have you been to Germany?'

'No, but I taught for a year in a German-speaking part of Switzerland. In a beautiful place called Kandersteg.'

'I've never been abroad. Never in anything bigger than a rowing-boat. And if you ever hear of me being killed in a plane crash you'll know it fell on me.'

'It was up in the mountains. A typical Swiss village with cuckoo-clock houses and snow when you looked up. The children were so well behaved it was a dream to teach there.'

Mr Maguire took out his pipe and lit it. By his face and the tilt of his head he was still listening to her.

'It was like a holiday really – it's funny how you remember the good things so vividly.'

'Maybe it's because there's so few of them,' he said. 'I remember my honeymoon as if it was yesterday. This town, your house. It was a cold summer. I sat with you by the Rayburn and we talked to the wee small hours.

'We did?'

'Well, once, maybe twice. And then one night I remember

134

you were going to a dance. You were in your stockinged feet frantically looking for your shoes. You left a wake of scent behind you.' Mary laughed, covering her mouth with her hand. Mr Maguire drew large rings around himself with his arms. 'You were out to here with petticoats. The dress was white with green flecks in it.'

'That's right, that's right. I remember that one. Parsley Sauce we used to call it. Those were the days when you had so few dresses you gave them names.' She rolled her eyes to heaven. It was as if he had produced an old photograph of her. 'Isn't it awful that I remember the dress but I've no recollection whatsoever of you.' Suddenly her face straightened in mock disapproval. 'And you noticed all this on your honeymoon?'

'You have no control over what you notice.'

'And where was your wife when you were sitting talking to me – to the wee small hours?'

'She was ill even then. She always went to bed early. I'm a night-owl myself.'

'Oh dear me,' she said. 'What a thing to remember – old Parsley Sauce.' Mr Maguire bought more drinks and Mary began to feel relaxed and warm.

'I'm glad we're here,' she said. 'This is nice.'

Some ex-pupils of hers came in and sat at the bar. They nodded and smirked towards the corner where she sat.

Mr Maguire asked her about what books she read and she told him she was an escapist reader. Four or five library books a week she got through. Anything, just so long as it didn't make too many demands on her. And of course nothing which would disturb. None of that embarrassing nonsense. It was hard to avoid nowadays. Library books should have warnings on the covers – be graded like films. Kathleen was different – she went in for the more heavy-weight stuff.

Mr Maguire said that unless a book was making him puzzle and think he would throw it away. He had read more first chapters than anybody else in the world. With regard to the embarrassing stuff, if it was not written for pornographic reasons he could accept it. It was a part of life the same as any other.

Mary refused another sherry saying that her head was already light, but insisted on buying Mr Maguire another bottle of Guinness, provided he wanted a third. After all, he was on the dole and she was working. When she returned with the poured glass Mr Maguire said, 'Books should not be a means of escape.'

'Why not? We're surrounded by depressing things. Who wants to read about them? When I read I prefer to be transported.' Suddenly she put her hand over her mouth in horror. 'Kathleen!' she said. 'I promised to pick up Kathleen. What time is it?'

All the lights were out in the church hall and Kathleen was pacing up and down. Mr Maguire carried her box of cups for her as Mary apologized for being late. For once Kathleen was quiet. The only sound coming from the back seat was the whine of her inhaler. In the house she slammed doors.

'There are some left-over sandwiches there,' she said.

As Mary made the tea she dropped a spoon twice and giggled. She felt very silly and likable but was aware of herself hurrying to get back to the other room where Kathleen and Mr Maguire were alone.

The next morning she slept late and was wakened by the constant revving of an engine. She looked out and saw Mr Maguire in a navy boiler suit beneath the open bonnet of her car, tinkering. Before going downstairs in her dressing-gown she freshened up and made herself look presentable. Mr Maguire came in, his oily hands aloft, and washed at the kitchen sink. Kathleen, also in her dressing-gown, offered him a cup of tea from the pot.

'I think you should see a big improvement,' he said. 'When did you last have it serviced?'

'Goodness,' said Mary. 'I can't really remember.'

'I reset your points, put in three new plugs . . . '

'I know nothing about it. You might as well be talking Double

Dutch.' Mr Maguire shook his head in disbelief and sat down at the table.

'You look very smart,' said Kathleen, looking at his boiler suit.

'I always carry this in the boot. I've been caught before, changing a wheel on a wet night.'

'But it's so clean.'

Mr Maguire nodded and turned to Mary.

'Would you like to try her out?'

'Let me get dressed first. Kathleen, would you like to come for a run?'

'No, I've things to do.' She said it with an echo of the previous night's bitterness still in her voice.

'Very well, suit yourself.'

They drove towards Spanish Point. Mary was delighted with the change in the car – it even sounded different. She said so to Mr Maguire, now back in his casual wear. She herself wore trousers – a thing she never did on teaching days. Mr Maguire said, 'The thing that really fascinated me about this wreck was a ring they found. Gold, with an inscription round the inside. *No tengo mas que dar te.*' With his Belfast accent his attempt at pronunciation was comical.

Mary smiled. 'More Double Dutch.'

'It's Spanish. It means, "I have nothing more to give thee".'

'That's nice.' She changed down through the gears as they came up behind a tractor.

'I thought it very moving – to see it after all those years. What I wondered was this. Was he taking it back as a present for a loved one in Spain or had somebody given it to *him* as he sailed away with the Armada? It makes a big difference.'

'Yes, I suppose it does.' Mary indicated and passed the tractor, giving a little wave over her shoulder.

'That's Jim McLelland,' she said.

137

They walked awkwardly on a beach of apple-sized stones, hearing them clunk hollowly beneath their feet. Mary had to extend her arms for balance and once or twice almost had to clutch at Mr Maguire.

'This is silly,' she said. They halted and looked across at Spanish Point. Now that the rumble of stones had stopped it was very quiet.

'Mary.' Hearing him use her name for the first time she looked up startled.

'Yes?'

'You're a remarkable woman,' he said. 'I told you that I came on holiday to see this place.' He nodded to the black rocks jutting out into the sea. 'That's not the whole truth.' Mary began to feel frightened, alone on a beach with this man she hardly knew. She picked up a stone and moved it from hand to hand. It was the tone of his voice that scared her. He was weighing his words, not looking at her.

'I had a memory of this town that was sacred in a way. And over the last couple of days I realize that it is partly your fault – I don't mean fault. I mean you're part of what's good about it.' Still he didn't look at her but continued to stare out to sea. Mary could think of nothing, afraid of what he would say next.

'I had forgotten about you, but not completely. Can you imagine how surprised I was when you were still here?'

'I've no idea.' She couldn't prevent the sarcasm in her voice. But he seemed not to notice. She threw the stone with a clatter at her feet and rubbed her hands together to clean them.

'I think we'd better be getting back,' she said. They turned and began to walk towards the car.

'I'm sorry. I hope I haven't overstepped the mark.'

'I'm not sure what you mean.'

'These past few days have been very real for me. You turn out to be . . . ' he paused, 'better than I remembered. You have a kind of calm which I envy. A stillness inside.' Mary smiled at him and walked round to the driver's door.

'You don't know me at all,' she said, 'if you think I'm calm

138

and still. I'm shaking like a leaf with the kind of things you're saying.'

'I'll just say one more – and that'll be the end of it. I'd like you to think about the idea of marrying me.'

She turned to him, her eyes wide and her mouth dropping open. She laughed. 'Are you serious?'

Mr Maguire smiled slightly as he stared at her, his brow creased with wrinkles. 'Yes, I am.'

'I don't even know your first name.'

'Anthony.'

'You don't look like an Anthony, if you don't mind me saying so.'

'You don't have to say anything. All I want you to do is give it some thought.'

Mary turned on the engine, indicated left and did a U-turn to the right but stalled midway. She tried to switch on the engine again.

'What have you done to this machine?' she said.

'Would you like me to drive?'

Mary agreed and he drove her home in the most embarrassing silence she had ever known.

Mr Maguire climbed the stairs. Mary went straight to the kitchen where she heard Kathleen singing.

'Well?' said Kathleen. 'Big improvement?'

Mary sat down on the stool by the Rayburn. She said, 'Make me a cup of tea. I need it badly.'

'What's wrong? Did it break down?'

Mary began to laugh. 'You'll never believe this.' Her sister turned from filling the kettle. 'But I've just been proposed to.'

'What? Who?' Her voice was a screech. Mary hushed her and rolled her eyes to the ceiling as Mr Maguire closed a door. 'I don't believe you. You'll find out then if it's a real toupee.'

'It's not funny,' said Mary, still laughing. 'I was there.'

'What did you tell him?'

'I said I'd think about it.'

As Kathleen made the tea her shoulders shook.

'You'd end up keeping the shine on his wee shoes. And the crease in his boiler suit. Mother would be pleased.' She wiped her eyes and gave her sister a cup.

'You're not seriously thinking about it?'

'No, but . . . '

'But what?'

'It's just that I've never really been asked.'

'You have so. Twice. You told me.'

'But they were ludicrous.'

'And this one isn't?'

'There's something gentlemanly about him.'

'A gentleman of leisure. He's on the dole, Mary.' Kathleen grinned again. 'Did he go down on one knee?'

'Don't be silly.'

Later that afternoon when the laughter had worn off and Mr Maguire had gone for a walk Kathleen said, 'And what would become of me?'

'For goodness' sake Kathleen, I only said I would consider it.'

'I don't think I'll be able to manage on my own. Financially.'

'Kathleen! Will you excuse me. I'd like to make up my own mind on this one.'

Mary went to her bedroom and sat looking at herself in the dressing-table mirror. A hot flush came over her and she watched her face redden, like an adolescent blushing. She flinched at the thought of a kiss from Mr Maguire. And yet he would make a good companion. Eccentric, yes – but basically a good man. In so far as she knew him. Pinpoints of sweat gleamed on her forehead and upper lip. She pulled a tissue from the box on the dressing-table and dabbed herself dry, then she lay down on the bed. Perhaps she should stall him. Write letters for a period. That way things would not be complicated by his physical presence. By that time, with any luck, these fits would have passed and she would have returned to normality. Stall him. That was the answer. He would enjoy writing to her. It would give him a chance to quote poetry. For some reason Kandersteg came into her mind and with a little thrill she thought of going there on her honeymoon. In July just as soon as the school holidays had started. She would have to do all the translation for Mr Maguire. They could call and see if Herr Hauptmann was still alive and they could relive their days at the school while poor Mr Maguire would have to stare out the window at the beautiful view: the grey clouds of mist that moved against the almost black of the forest; the cleanness, the tidiness of their streets; the precision with which the trains came and went, not to the minute, but to the second; Herr Hauptmann's hazel-coloured eyes as he listened to her.

At dinner Kathleen, activated by nervousness, talked non-stop until she left the room to make the coffee. Mr Maguire nodded his head as if it had become a reflex to the torrent of words and one that he could not stop even when she had left the room. He whispered to Mary, 'Kathleen's problem is that she hasn't heard of the paragraph.' He said that he would like to settle his bill as he would be leaving first thing after Mass in the morning when the roads would be relatively traffic free.

Mary said, 'It might be nice if we walked up to the hotel later. I'd like to make my position clear.'

'Yes, that would help.'

'About eight?'

After Mr Maguire had excused himself Mary said to her sister, 'I'm going for a walk with him later.'

'It makes no difference to me. I have to go to the church to do the flowers.'

'Oh that's right. It's Saturday . . . ' Kathleen began to stack the cups on to the tray with a snatching movement.

'Have you made up your mind how you're going to tell him?'

'I'm not sure,' said Mary. 'I'm not even sure *what* I'm going to tell him.'

'Don't allow me to influence you one way or the other. You

can do whatever you like. All I hope is that you won't do something you'll regret for the rest of your life. And if you go traipsing off with him I'll need some help with the mortgage.'

'There's no question of that.' Mary was aware that her voice had risen. 'You can be sure that I'll be sensible about it. If I've waited this long ... ' Kathleen carried the tray out to the kitchen and set it on the draining-board with a crash.

At eight o'clock they both left their rooms. Mr Maguire, his shoes burnished, wearing a tie and jacket, walked like the Duke of Edinburgh, one hand holding the other by the wrist behind his back. The night was windless and at intervals between the glare of the street lights they could see stars. Mary was conscious of her heels clicking on the paving stones and was relieved when she came to the softer tarmac footpath where she could walk with more dignity.

Mr Maguire cleared his throat and asked, 'Well, did you think about what . . . ?'

'Yes, but don't talk about it now. Talk about something else.' Mr Maguire nodded in agreement and looked up at the sky for inspiration.

'What is it that makes your life worthwhile?'

'I don't know.' She laughed nervously and tried to give an answer. 'What a strange question. I suppose I help children to learn something – the rudiments of another language. And I help Kathleen who cannot work . . . '

'I don't mean worthwhile to others. But to yourself.'

'Sometimes, Mr Maguire, you say the oddest things. I'm sorry, I don't see the difference.'

'Take it from another angle. What makes you really angry?'

She felt her shoulder brush against his as they walked. 'The kind of thing that's been going on in this country. Killings, bombings . . . '

'If you were to give one good reason to stop someone blowing your head off tonight, what would it be?'

'I've jotters to correct for Monday.' Mr Maguire laughed.

142

'Well there's that and children and love and Kathleen . . . '

'And?'

'And I've dresses I've only worn once or twice. And the sea. And the occasional laugh in the staffroom. Just everything.'

'You would be part of the reason I would give.'

There was a long pause and Mary said, 'Thank you. That's very nice of you. But as I say I'd prefer to wait until we were settled inside before we have our little talk.' Mr Maguire shrugged and smiled. Mary veered off to look in Madge's Fashions which was still lit up. There was a single old-fashioned window model with painted brown hair instead of a wig. White flakes showed where the paint had chipped, particularly at the red fingernails.

'They've changed this dress since yesterday,' said Mary. 'I like that one better.' She joined Mr Maguire in the middle of the pavement still looking back over her shoulder.

They sat at the same table as the prevous night and Mr Maguire bought the same drinks.

'They'll be calling me a regular next,' said Mary, as he slipped into the seat beside her. 'Well now. I think . . . First of all let me say that I find it extremely difficult to talk in a situation like this. I'm out of my depth.' She tried not to sound like she was introducing a lesson, but what she said was full of considered pauses. She spoke as quietly as she could, yet distinctly. 'You are an interesting man, good – as far as I know you – but these are not reasons,' she paused yet again, 'for anybody to get married. It has happened so quickly that there is an element of foolishness in it. And that's not me.'

'It's me,' said Mr Maguire, laughing.

'There are so many things. I'm not a free agent. Kathleen has got to be considered.'

'She can fairly talk.'

'Yes, sometimes it's like living with the radio on. She never expects an answer.'

'Do you love her?'

143

'I suppose I must. When you live with someone day in, day out, the trivial things become the most important.' She sipped her sherry and felt the glass tremble between her fingertips. 'And there are other things which frighten me. I don't think I'm that sort of person.' Mr Maguire looked at her but she was unable to hold his eye and her gaze returned to her sherry glass.

'My wife was in poor health for many, many years – so that aspect of it should not worry you. I am in the habit of – not. I would respect your wishes. Although I miss someone at my back now when I fall asleep.' Mary thought of herself slippery with sweat lying awake making sure to keep space between herself and Mr Maguire's slow breathing body.

'I can't believe this is happening to me.' She laughed and turned to face him, her hands joined firmly in her lap. 'My answer is – in the kindest possible way – no. But why don't you write to me? Why don't you come and stay with us for longer next year? Writing would be a way of getting to know each other?'

'Your answer is no – for now?'

'Yes,' said Mary. 'I mean it's ridiculous at our age.'

'I don't see why. Could I come at Christmas?'

She thought of herself and Kathleen in new dresses, full of turkey and sprouts and mince pies, dozing in armchairs and watching television for most of the day. The Christmas programmes were always the best of the year.

'No. Not Christmas.'

'Easter then?'

'Write to me and we'll see.'

Mr Maguire smiled and shrugged as if he had lost a bet.

'You've kind of taken the wind out of my sails,' he said.

The next morning when she got up Mr Maguire had gone. Kathleen had called him early and given him his breakfast.

When he had paid his bill she had deducted a fair amount for the servicing of the car.

144

After Mass, surrounded by the reality of the Sunday papers, Mary thought how silly the whole thing had been. The more she thought about the encounter the more distasteful it became. She resolved to answer his first letter out of politeness but, she said firmly to herself, that would be the finish of it.

On Monday she was feeling down and allowed herself the luxury of a lesson, taught to four different levels throughout the day, in which she talked about Kandersteg, its cuckoo-clock houses and the good Herr Hauptmann.

Words the Happy Say

AFTER HE HAD cleared the breakfast things he guided the crumbs to the edge of the table with a damp cloth and wiped them into his cupped and withered hand. He took out his board and laid it on the cleaned surface. Some people liked to work at a tilt but he had always preferred it flat in front of him. From his back window on the third floor he could hear the children moving along the driveway into the primary school. Because it was summer and the large lime tree, sandwiched between the blackened gable ends, was in full leaf, he could see them only from the waist down. He noticed the boys with rumpled socks and dirty shoes always walked together. Girls, neat in white ankle-socks, would hop-scotch and skip past in a different group. If he stood on tiptoe at the window he could see down into the small backyard but he no longer bothered to get up from his work for the diversion of seeing the new girl downstairs getting a shovel of coal.

He arranged his inks and distilled water and set his porcelain mixing-dish in the middle. Each shallow oval indentation shone with a miniature reflection of the window. He looked at the page he had been working on the previous day and his mouth puckered in distaste. He was unhappy that he had started the thing in English Roundhand and thought of going back again and beginning in Chancery.

'We, the Management and Staff of V.R. Wilson & Sons Bakery Ltd, wish to offer our heartfelt thanks and sincere gratitude to MR VERNON WILSON for all he has done in the forty-two years he has been head of V.R. WILSON SONS BAKERY LTD . . .'

He worked quietly for an hour getting the Indian ink part finished, listening to the soft, pulled scratch of the pen, forming each letter in a perfect flow of black and at the perfect angle.

He was always impatient to rub out the horizontal pencil guidelines but took the precaution of making and drinking a cup of coffee before he did so. A page could be ruined that way. The rubber across damp ink could make a crow's wing of a down-stroke. He settled to drawing in pencil the embellishments to the opening W, then painted a lemon surround with tendrils of vermilion. He had to paint quickly and surely to avoid patch-iness – a double layer of colour.

Suddenly he lifted his head and listened. There was a hesitant knock on the lower door. He rinsed his brush in the jam jar with a ringing sound and went down the short flight of stairs. He opened the door and saw a woman standing there.

'Are you the man that writes the things?' she asked. He nodded. 'I hope I'm not disturbing you.'

'No.' He felt he had to invite her in. He went up the stairs behind her and when they came to the landing she was unsure of where to go. To show her the way he went into his kitchen in front of her but realized that he should have let her go first for the sake of manners. She stood holding her basket not know-ing what to do.

'Sit down,' he said and sat with his back to the table and waited.

'You do that lovely writing?' she said again. He smiled and agreed. 'I saw it in the church. That thing you did – for the people who gave money for the stained glass window.'

'The list of subscribers?'

'Do you do anything? I mean, not just religious things?'

'Yes.'

She was a woman about the same age as himself, maybe younger. Her whole appearance was tired – drab grey raincoat, a pale oval showing just inside her knee where she had a hole in her tights, her shoes scuffed and unpolished. She looked down into her basket.

'How much would . . . ?' She seemed nervous. 'Would you do a poem?'

'Yes.'

'How much?'

'It depends on how long it is. Whether you want it framed or not. What kind of paper.'

'It's very short.' She took a woman's magazine from her basket and flicked through it looking for the page. She leafed backwards and forwards unable to find it.

'Ah, here it's.' She folded the magazine at the right page and gave it to him. 'It's only four lines.' He glanced at the page and saw the poem framed in a black box.

'I could do that very reasonable,' he said. The corners of her mouth twitched into a relieved smile. 'Five pounds.' It was obviously too much for her because the smile disappeared and she set her hand on the arm of the chair as if she was about to stand up.

'That would be framed and all,' he added.

'Maybe some time again.' She kept looking into her basket.

'On the best paper.'

'What about cheaper paper?'

'Four pounds?'

Still the woman hesitated.

'That's still a pound a line. I didn't think it would be as much as that.'

'Any less and it'd be a favour,' he said. Already he was out of pocket. He stood up to end the bargaining. Again she looked down into her raffia basket. He saw two tins of cat food at the bottom.

'All right,' she said. 'Four pounds. How soon will it be done?'

'The end of the week. Call on Friday.'

She seemed pleased and nervous that she had made a decision.

After he had shown her out he read the poem.

> The words the happy say
> Are paltry melody

But those the silent feel
Are beautiful –

It was by E. Dickinson. He looked at the date on the magazine and saw that it was over three years old. He closed it and set it on the shelf. It was like the woman herself, dog-eared and a bit tatty. She'd had nice eyes but her skin had been slack and almost a grey colour as if she'd been ill. Yet there had been something about her which had made him lower his price. He was not used to bargaining – most of his jobs came in the post from a small advertising agency. What they couldn't be bothered to do in Letraset they passed on to him. But the work was not regular and he couldn't rely on it – unlike the diplomas he did each year for the teacher training college.

Two days later when he wrote out the poem he was dissatisfied with it and scrapped it. For the second attempt he wrote it on one of his most expensive papers and further surprised himself by using his precious gold leaf. He hated working with the stuff, held between its protective sheets, thin as grease on tea. It curled and twitched even when he brought the heat of his fingertips near it. Yet on the finished page it looked spectacular.

On the Friday he found that, instead of working in the morning, he was tidying the flat. It was not until late evening that he heard her at the door. He turned down the volume of the radio and went to answer it. She sat down when invited and placed her hands on her lap. Her appearance had improved. She wore a mauve print summer dress, a white Arran cardigan and carried a shoulder bag, which made her seem younger. The weak sun, squared by shadows from the crossbars of the window, lit the back wall of the room behind her.

'I'm sorry,' he said, 'it's not finished.' Her mouth opened slightly in disappointment. 'I didn't know whether you wanted the name on it or not.'

'What name?'

He held out the magazine and pointed to the name beneath

151

the poem with his bad hand. It was as if he were pointing round a corner.

'E. Dickinson.'

The woman thought for a moment then nodded. 'Put it on.' She seemed quite definite. He folded the protective paper back from his work and reached for a pen.

'Can I see it?' she asked. He handed her the written poem and watched her face.

'Aw here,' she said. 'Aw here now.' Then she spoke the poem, more to herself than to him. As she read he watched her eyes switching back and forth across the lines.

'Lovely,' she said. 'Just lovely.' He was unsure whether she was praising his work or the poem. She handed it carefully back and he turned to the table to write the name.

'Can I watch?'

'Sure thing.'

She came, almost on tiptoe, to his shoulder and watched him dip the pen and angle the spade-like nib. As he wrote, his tongue peeped out from the corner of his mouth. When he had finished he blew on the page, tilting it to the light to see if it had dried.

'Where did you learn – all this?' she asked.

'I taught myself. Just picked it up.' He stood and went over to the shelf and took down a book. 'From things like . . . this Book of Hours.'

'Ours?'

He smiled and passed it to her. She smiled too, realizing her mistake when she read the title. She opened it gingerly. The pictures were interleaved with tissue paper which slithered in the draught she made turning the pages. Each tissue bore a faint mirror image of the drawing it protected. The book was an awkward size so she sat down and laid it across her knees. She looked at the pure colours, the intricacy of the work.

'This must have taken you years,' she said.

'I didn't do it.' He smiled. 'It's a printed book.'

'Oh.' She turned another page. He stood feeling idle in front of her.

'Would you like some tea?'

She looked up and hesitated.

'It's no bother,' he said. 'I've got milk.'

'All right. That would be nice.'

He put the kettle on and set out his mug and a cup and saucer for her. The crockery rattled loudly in the silence. The kettle seemed to take ages to boil. He asked her how she had known who he was and where he lived. She said that the priest had told her after she had admired the framed list of names in the church.

When he handed her the cup and saucer she set the book carefully to one side.

'It would be just like me to spill something on it.'

He sat down opposite her. The sound of the contact between her cup and saucer made him feel nervous.

'Do you like doing this work?'

'Yes, it suits me fine. I don't have to leave the house.'

'You're like myself,' she nodded in agreement. 'Once I've the one or two bits of shopping done, I stay put. I hate the city. Always have since the day and hour I moved here. And it's getting worse. You used to be able to have a chat in Dunlop's till they changed it into a supermarket. How can you talk to the check-out girl with a queue hopping behind you?'

'You haven't lost your accent.'

'And please God I never will.'

He finished his tea and stood up. He inserted the finished poem into its frame and began to tape up the back of it. He was conscious of her watching the awkward guiding movements of his bad hand.

'It's the quiet I miss the most,' she said. 'In the country you can hear small things.'

'Would you go back?'

'Like a shot.'

'Maybe some day you will.'

She smiled at this.

With an awl he made two holes in the wood frame and began

153

to insert the screws. He said, 'You have a cat?'

'Yes. How did you know?'

He explained about seeing the cat food in her basket.

'It thinks it's a lion,' she said. 'We have a yard at the back with pot plants and it lies flat like it's in the jungle and his tail puffs up.' He laughed at her. She went on, 'What I like about cats is the way they ignore you. There's no telling what way they feel. If I want to be popular all I have to do is rattle the tin-opener and he's all over me, purring and sharpening his back on my shins.'

'What do you call it?'

'Monroe. My husband thought that one up – not my idea at all. At first we called it Marilyn until we found out it was a boy. Then we had it neutered because of the smell. We used to go a lot to the pictures.' After a pause she added, 'He's dead now God rest him.'

'Who?'

'My husband.' She set her saucer on the floor between her feet and held the cup in both hands. The sunlight on the wall behind her had changed from yellow to rose until it finally disappeared, yet the room seemed to hold on to some of the light. 'Since I got the TV there's no need to go out. All the good movies come up there.' She looked around the darkening room.

'I prefer the radio,' he said. 'It means I can work at the same time. Or look at the fire.'

He got to his feet and asked her if she felt chilly. Even though she said no, he lit the fire. The firelighter blazed in a yellow flame a few inches above the coal until it caught. It made a pleasant whirring noise.

'I couldn't be without the TV,' she said. 'It's like having another person in the house.' He smiled at her and began sweeping the hearth.

'Am I keeping you back?' she said suddenly.

'No. No. Not at all,' he said. 'It's not often anybody comes in.'

'Especially me,' she said. As the coals of the fire began to redden and burn without the help of the firelighter she talked about her childhood in the country: of making shadow pictures of monsters on the wall with a candle; of her elder sister scaring the wits out of her with stories of the devil at dances. She told of ringworm and of the woolly balaclava she had to wear to cover her bald patches; of sheep ticks and how the only way you could get them out of your skin was to burn their backsides with a hot spent match and then pluck them out while their minds were on other things. He listened to her shudder at the memory, but it was obvious from her voice that she loved it all.

When she waited for him to tell something of himself he shied away and asked her if she would like some more tea. He did tell her that he had never known his father and that his mother had died asking what time it was. Famous last words. What time is it? When he said this she held back her laughter until he laughed.

'What time *is* it?' she asked. He squinted through the gloom in the direction of the clock on the shelf and told her.

'What? I must go,' she said. But she did not get up.

'I've given you a bit of picture cord.' He hung the framed text on his finger for her to see. 'Although it's very light.'

'Light verse,' she said and laughed. He handed her his work and she held it at arm's length to admire it. He switched on the Anglepoise for her and it seemed very bright after the slow increase of dusk.

'It must be great to be an artist,' she said.

He pooh-poohed the idea saying that he couldn't draw to save his life. He said he was an artisan and added, seeing her blank look, 'A man with one skill.'

She set the picture down and opened her shoulder bag.

'Four pounds you said?' She took her purse from the bag and looked up at him, waiting for confirmation of the price.

'It doesn't matter,' he said. 'This one is free.'

'What?'

'I enjoyed doing it.'

'I wouldn't dream of it. Here,' she said and set the four pound notes on the table. He picked them up and offered them back to her. She took them and set them on the mantelpiece out of his reach.

'It's a lovely job of work. You must be paid.' She was now bustling, returning her purse to her bag, straightening her cardigan. She seemed embarrassed and he wished he had just taken the money without any fuss.

'I am very pleased with it,' she said. 'It was kind of you to offer. But no, thank you. And now I'll be off.'

He hesitated for a moment, then said, 'Let me wrap it for you.' He looked in a cupboard and found some brown paper he had saved. She sat down again to wait. He wrapped her magazine and the picture together, sellotaping down the triangular folds he had made.

A summer insect flew into the metal dome of the Anglepoise and knocked around like a tiny knuckle. She said in admiration that he was very good with his hands. He was aware of her embarrassment in the silence which followed. He held on to the parcel when he was finished and tried to think of something to say. He asked her if she had ever worked at anything. She said that for some years before she had married she had worked in a sewing-machine factory – years which had bored her stiff. He asked her if she had any children but she replied that they had not been blessed in that way. Her husband had worked with an X-ray machine before they knew the damage it could do. She averted her eyes and he did not know what to say. Eventually she stood up.

'You have more than one skill,' she said, looking at the neatness of the finished parcel. 'Thank you very much for the tea – and everything.' She stretched out to shake hands but it was an awkward clasping rather than a handshake, with his left hand in her right.

'I'll show you out,' he said, turning on the landing light. They went down the lino-covered stairs.

'Maybe I'll see you again – some time in church,' she said, looking up over her shoulder at him.

He nodded. 'Maybe. I eh . . . '

She waited for what he was going to say but he reached past her and opened the Yale lock. Sounds of children playing below echoed up the stair-well. She left smiling, clutching beneath her arm the parcel of her poem.

Upstairs again he sat down in front of the illuminated address for the bakery firm but did not begin to work. He stayed like that for a long time then punched the table hard with the knuckles of his fist so that the radio at his elbow bounced and gave a static crackle. It had been on all this time. He turned up the volume and filled the flat with the noise of voices he could not put a face to.

Across the Street

ON SUMMER EVENINGS she used to practise the flute in front of a music-stand with the window open. She played with verve, her elbows high, her body moving to the tempo of the music. Every time she stopped she flicked her shoulder-length hair with her hand and, with a little backward-shaking motion of her head to make sure it was out of her way, she would begin again. In the pauses of her playing Mr Keogh could hear the slow hooting of pigeons.

From his window on the opposite side of the street he would sit on his favourite chair, a round-backed carver which supported his aching back, and watch her. He fitted the chair the way an egg fits an egg-cup. His fat hand would rest on the top of his blackthorn stick and when she had finished a piece he would knock its ferrule on the floor between his splayed feet in appreciation.

'The girl done well – the girl done very well,' he would say. Once Mrs O'Hagan, the landlady, had come the whole way up the stairs to see what he wanted.

'Me? Nothing. I'm just at one of my concerts.'

'You might have been having a heart attack,' she said and slammed the door. 'You'll cry wolf once too often,' he heard her shout from the landing.

If the afternoon was sunny he would come down the stairs stepping carefully sideways one at a time and sit with Mrs O'Hagan at the front doorway. The houses were terraced and each was separated from the street by a tiny area of garden just wide enough for Mr Keogh to stretch out his legs. Most of the other houses had privet hedges and a patch of mud or weeds but Mrs O'Hagan's had white iron railings and was flag-stoned. Window-boxes and a half barrel, painted white, bloomed with azalias, nasturtiums and begonias. There was also a little windmill with a doll figure of a man in a red waistcoat supposedly turning the handle every time the wind blew.

'It's a bit like the tail wagging the dog,' Mr Keogh had said, pointing his pipe at it. When he smoked in this garden Mrs O'Hagan insisted that he bring out an ashtray for his spent matches. Once he had struck a match on the cement between the bricks and she had looked at him in such a way that he knew never to attempt it again.

She always sat on a canvas chair and knitted while he used the more substantial wooden chair from the hallway. She knitted jumpers and pullovers and cardigans for the church bazaars at great speed. Mr Keogh noticed that she never looked at her hands while she was working but could keep the street and everything that moved in it in view. Sometimes he read the paper but in bright sunlight the tiny newsprint and the whiteness of the paper created such a glare that it hurt his eyes.

'There's your little concert artiste,' said Mrs O'Hagan. Mr Keogh looked up and saw the girl coming from Mrs Payne's door on the opposite side of the street. She wore a long kaftan and, putting her head down, walked quickly along the street. Away from her music-stand she seemed round-shouldered.

'She can fairly tootle,' said Mr Keogh.

'Aye, she's always in a hurry somewhere.'

After lunch, if it was not raining, Mr Keogh liked to walk the quarter mile to Queen Alexandra Gardens. He would sit on the first vacant bench inside the gate to recover his breath. One day he saw his flautist. She lay back with her face tilted and the undersides of her arms turned awkwardly out to catch the sun. Her eyes were closed. The weight of Mr Keogh descending at the far end of the seat made her look round.

'That's the weather, eh?' he said. She smiled a kind of wan grin which stopped abruptly, then went back to her sunbathing. A little later when he was breathing normally he said, 'You play the flute very well.'

'How do you know that?' The girl sat up and looked at him.

'I live opposite you.'

'I didn't know you could hear.'

161

'It's like everything else,' said Mr Keogh. 'There's not much you can do in this world without people getting to know.'

She shrugged and assumed her former position, feet thrust out, neck resting on the back of the bench. He noticed that when he moved she bounced slightly at the other end of the seat. He tried to keep still. He cleared his throat and asked, 'Are you working?'

'Does it look like it?'

In the silence that followed Mr Keogh took his pipe from his pocket and lit up. What little wind there was carried the smoke to the girl.

'What a good smell,' she said without opening her eyes. Mr Keogh smiled and puffed little clouds into the air. He closed down the silver lid and sat back. The girl jigged at the other end of the bench. She sat forward and scrabbled in her bag, produced a cigarette and lit it. She did this with the same urgency as she walked – as she played the flute.

'I used to play,' he said.

'The flute?'

'The cornet. In a band.'

'Oh.'

'A police band.'

One of the old march tunes went through his head and he began tapping his foot to it. He didn't whistle but clicked his tongue. The girl got up and walked away with short quick steps, her head down. She disappeared behind a clump of laurel bushes. Later, when he was leaving the park, he saw her sitting alone on a bench, her wrists still turned to the sun.

That evening in the twilight he watched her. She had switched on the light in her room with its massive white paper ball of a shade. She played a melody, some phrases of which reminded him of a tune he knew from County Roscommon. Often he had heard a flute played in the band hut and always was conscious of the spit and blow and breathiness of it. But now from across the street it was a pure sound, filtered by dis-

162

tance, melodic only. Her playing suddenly stopped and she made frantic flapping motions with her hands. She came forward, closed the window and pulled the curtains. Moths. Drawn by the light. Mr Keogh did not like them himself. If there was a moth, or worse a daddy-longlegs, in the room he could not sleep until it was dispatched with a firm rap from a rolled newspaper.

Mr Keogh groped his way from the chair to the bed and turned on his light. He toed off his shoes and flexed his feet. Slip-on shoes were the boon of his old age. For years he had made do with the kind of police boots he had worn in the force. Morning and night he had nearly burst blood vessels trying to tie and untie them. Now in the mornings he just put his socks on while lying in bed, swung his feet out and, with a little wiggling pressure, would insert them into his shoes, while his eyes stared straight ahead crinkling in a smile at the ease of it all. At one time he had been glad of the big boots, had even added steel tips to them so that they would make more noise. The last thing in the world he wanted was to confront and grapple with a surprised burglar. Give them plenty of time to run. That way nobody got hurt, especially him.

It was funny how the size of the feet never changed after a certain age. For as long as he could remember he had taken size eleven while the waistband of his trousers had doubled. His mother had made him wear shoes to school but he had preferred to take them off and hide them in the ditch until he was coming home. He did not want to be any different from the rest of the boys. When he did get home the first thing he would do would be to take the shoes off. His mother praised him for not scuffing them until she found out his trick, then she beat him with a strap for letting the family down in front of the teacher.

A thing they'd learned in the Force for an emergency birth was to ask the woman what size of shoes she took. The bigger the feet the easier the birth.

In his pyjamas he rolled on to the bed and into the depression his body had made in the down mattress. He slept, when he ever did sleep, propped on pillows because of his hernia. The doctor had said there was a gap in him somewhere but Mr Keogh had refused to allow an exploratory operation to find out where. A lump you could find, a gap was a different kettle of fish. The nearer he slept to the upright position the less it bothered him.

He turned out the bedside lamp and watched the sliver of light coming through the girl's curtains which had not been drawn exactly. Occasionally he saw her shadow fall on them as she moved around but she passed the slit of light so quickly that he could get no sense of her. She could have been naked for all he knew.

'What's that you're up to?' said Mr Keogh.

'Doily mats.'

The little man in the red waistcoat did not move, the day was so still. Mr Keogh wore a floppy straw hat to protect his baldness from the burning sun. He had had it since the days he dug a vegetable plot by the Waterworks. The cat had settled herself in the small square of shadow beneath Mrs O'Hagan's chair.

'What about the knitting needles?'

'This is crochet.'

Mr Keogh nodded and tilted his hat farther over his face. Mrs O'Hagan looked up at him, her hands still whirling.

'It's just a different way of tying knots,' she said. 'That's all knitting is when you come to think of it.'

Mr Keogh wiped the sweat from his forehead where the rim of his hat made contact.

'You look like you're melting,' said Mrs O'Hagan. He looked across at the shadowed side of the street. Up at his flautist's window. She was there for a moment. Next thing he knew she was skipping across the road towards him. There was something very different about her. It was her hair. She stopped at the gate.

'Can I have a light?' She held up her cigarette.

'Sure thing.' Mr Keogh leaned his bulk in the chair to get at his pocket and took out a box of Swan matches. She came through the gate and nodded to Mrs O'Hagan. Mr Keogh's fat fingers probed the box and some of the matches fell to the ground. The girl stooped to lift them. She struck one on the tiled path, lit her cigarette and tossed the match away. Mrs O'Hagan followed its direction with her eyes. Mr Keogh offered her a little sprig of matches in case she should need them later but she refused them.

'You've had your hair done,' he said.

'Yes.' The girl reached up and touched it as if she couldn't believe. It was done in an Afro style, a halo frizzed out round her face. 'I need something to keep me going.' She laughed and it was the first time Mr Keogh had seen her do so. He saw too much of her gums.

'Have a seat,' said Mr Keogh. He was struggling to rise from his chair but the girl put out a hand and touched him lightly. 'I'll sit on the step.' She sat down and drew her knees up to her chin. She was wearing a loose white summer skirt which she held behind her knees to keep herself decent. She was in her bare feet and Mr Keogh noticed that they were big and tendony. It was as if they were painted brown. Her arms were also deeply tanned.

'Do you like it?'

'Yes.' Mr Keogh put his head to one side. 'It makes you look like a dandelion clock.' He inhaled and blew out in her direction saying, 'One o'clock, two o'clock.' She held her springy curled hair with both hands as if to keep it from blowing away and laughed again.

She tilted her face up to the sun and sighed, 'You certainly picked the right side of the street to live on.'

'I can never see', said Mrs O'Hagan 'why people want to smoke in heat like this. In the winter I can understand it.'

Mr Keogh took out his pipe and began to fill it from his pouch. Mrs O'Hagan looked away from him to the girl.

'What's your name, dear?'

'Una.'

Mrs O'Hagan repeated the name as if she had never heard it before. The girl raised the cigarette to her mouth and Mr Keogh noticed how closely bitten her nails were, little half moons embedded on the ends of her fingers, the skin bulbous around them.

'I'm Mrs O'Hagan and this is Mr Keogh from County Roscommon.'

'We've met.'·

'So I gather.'

Mr Keogh lit his pipe with two matches held together. Just as he was about to set them on the arm of his chair Mrs O'Hagan got up and said, 'I'll get you both an ashtray.' She disappeared into the darkness of the hallway, stepping over the girl's feet.

Between puffs Mr Keogh said, 'Do you play the flute just for fun?'

She nodded.

'With anybody else?'

She shook her head.

'I used to play in a band,' he said. 'We had the best of crack. The paradiddles and the flam-paradiddles.'

'In the name of God what are they?' said Mrs O'Hagan, coming back with an ashtray, a Present from Bundoran. The girl immediately tapped the ash from her cigarette into it.

'They're part and parcel of the whole thing,' said Mr Keogh.

'I play music for the music,' Una said, 'but I can never play it well enough to please myself.' She spoke rapidly, her eyes staring, inhaling her cigarette deeply and taking little bites of the smoke as she let it out. A different girl entirely from the one he had met in the Gardens. 'If I could play as well as I want I would be overcome and then I couldn't go on.'

'We had to march *and* play at the same time. To get the notes right *and* the feet. No time for sentiment there, eh?'

'Maybe that's why I don't like brass bands,' said Una. There was a long silence. Mrs O'Hagan's hands still zigzagged around her half-made doily.

166

'Where are you from?'

'Tyrone-among-the-bushes. Near Omagh.' Una said it as if she was tired answering the question.

'And what are you working at?'

'I'm not. I was slung out of University two years ago and I've applied for jobs until I'm sick.'

'Would you not be far better off at home if you have no job to go to?'

The girl gave a snort as if that was the stupidest thing imaginable. She stubbed out her cigarette and turned to Mr Keogh.

'You're the first policeman I've ever talked to. It gives me a funny feeling.'

'Why?'

'I don't know.'

'It was a long time ago.'

'I just don't like cops – usually.' She smiled at him and he adjusted his sunhat so as to see her better.

'Do you – did you not find that people were very wary of you?'

'No – and maybe, yes. Most of my friends tended to be in the Force.'

'That's what I mean.'

'We tended to be outside things.'

'Like football grounds.' They both laughed.

Mrs O'Hagan rose from her chair and said, 'Cup of tea Mr Keogh?' He nodded. 'And you?'

'Yes, please.'

When Mrs O'Hagan had passed, the girl propped her bare feet high on the jamb of the door and clutched her dress to the undersides of her thighs.

'Mr Keogh from County Roscommon' she said quietly and began to gnaw the side of her thumb-nail.

'I hated it. But then what else could I do?'

The girl shrugged and switched to gnawing her index finger.

'It's a pity you didn't come from County Mayo.'

'Why?'

'Mr Keogh from the County Mayo sounds better.'

'I wouldn't be seen dead coming from there.' He adjusted his hat to let some air in underneath, then he sighed, 'Una from Omagh.'

Mrs O'Hagan came out with a tray, lifting it exaggeratedly high to clear the girl's head as she sat on the step. They had tea and talked and Una borrowed two more matches and smoked two more cigarettes one after the other. Then she was away as quickly as she had come, skipping on her big bare feet across the hot street.

The conversation with the girl that day had disturbed him. He rarely thought of his days in the police now. Before going to bed he opened his cupboard and had a cup from the brandy bottle left over from Christmas. As a policeman he had been timid and useless. The only way he had survived was to hide behind the formulae of words they had taught him. If he got the words right, that combined with his awesome size and weight – in those days he was sixteen stones of muscle – would generally be enough to make people come quietly. But every time he arrested someone his knees would shake.

In drinking to forget he constantly remembered. He knew there were more important and awful things which had happened to him but one in particular stuck out. It was in Belfast shortly after he'd arrived. He had been called to a house where a man was threatening to commit suicide and he'd been met by a trembling neighbour.

'He's up in his room,' she said.

When he'd gone up and opened the bedroom door there was an old man, the sinews standing out on his neck, sitting naked on the bed with a cut-throat razor in one hand and his balls clutched in the other. There were pigeons perched along the iron bedstead, cooing and burbling. The place was white with birdshit, dressing-table, drawers, wardrobe.

'I'm gonna cut them off,' the old man had screamed. The

window was wide open and the pigeons came and went with a clattering of wings.

'Suit yourself,' Keogh had said and had begun to move gently towards him. He had taken the razor from him and had intended to wrap him in the quilt but it was so congealed it had come off the bed stiff in the shape of a rectangle. He had taken a coat from the wardrobe, the shoulders of which were streaked with white.

Mr Keogh poured himself another cupful of brandy and wondered why that memory, more than all the others, frightened him so much.

He saw the girl Una several more times and each time she had changed. Once she was so excited and in such a hurry going to an interview for a job that she rushed past him giving the last part of the information walking backwards. The next time, in the supermarket, when he asked her about the job she barely acknowledged his presence and walked past him with a single item elongating her string bag. Her hair had lost some of its bushiness and had begun to lie on each side of a middle parting. She had cold sores on her upper lip which made her mouth look swollen and ugly. But from a distance it was not noticeable – like the spit and breathy sounds. Perhaps this was the reason she stopped playing the flute. Nevertheless Mr Keogh continued to watch her moving about her room. As winter approached it got dark earlier and she would turn on her light at about six. She did not bother to pull the curtains and Mr Keogh would sit in his chair and look across the street at her as she did her ironing or sat reading a magazine. Once she dodged into the room wearing only her underwear but by the time he had straightened up in the seat she was away. It wasn't that he wanted a peep-show, to be part of her privacy was enough. It gave him as much pleasure to watch her ironing as it did to see her half-dressed.

Then one night she did what he was doing and he worried for her. He had come into his room and without turning on his light looked across at her window. The place was in darkness. He sat down in his chair and waited. Staring in the darkness he thought he saw her shape sitting in the window and he felt his eyes were playing tricks on him. It must have been half an hour later when the shape moved away and it was her. After a minute she came back and sat again for the rest of the evening, just a pale smudge of a face staring down into the street. How many girls of nineteen years of age pass a Saturday night like this?

He drew his curtains and went to bed feeling heavier than ever before. He was wakened by what sounded like the slamming of a car door in the street. The luminous hands of his alarm clock said half past one. A blue light flashed a wedge on and off against the ceiling. He pulled himself from the hollow of his bed and bunching the waist of his pyjama trousers with one hand parted the curtains a little more with the other. An ambulance sat outside, its rear doors open. Farther down the street, a police car. A neighbour had come into the street to see what was happening. The door of Una's house was open. Mr Keogh put on his shoes and overcoat, took his stick and went down the stairs sideways one at a time as quickly as he dared. In the street he talked to the neighbour but he knew as little as himself. Their breath hung in the air like steam. Mr Keogh ventured up the pathway then into the lighted hall.

'Hello?'

'Hello?' The landlady's weak voice answered back.

'What's wrong?' Mrs Payne came into the hallway. She was in her dressing-gown holding tightly on to her elbows. Her face was white. A police officer stood by the kitchen door writing something down on his pad. She rolled her eyes up at the ceiling. Heavy footsteps thumped about making the pendant light tremble.

'The wee girl. She took a bath and . . .' She drew her finger across one of her wrists. 'If I hadn't needed the toilet she'd have been there till the morning.' Her mouth wobbled, about to cry. She leaned against the wall for support.

'Is she dead?'

'I don't know. I'm not sure.'

The thumping from up the stairs increased and an ambulance man appeared carrying one end of a stretcher. Mr Keogh and Mrs Payne had to back out of the hallway to let them pass. Through the fanlight Mr Keogh saw the struggle the men had to get down the narrow stairs. On the stretcher between them was a roll of silver paper with Una's blonde hair frizzed out of it at the top. What they were carrying looked like some awful wedding buttonhole. The silver paper glittered in the street lights as the men angled the stretcher into the ambulance. Her face was as white as a candle. A voice crackled from a radio in the police car. Mrs Payne stood with both hands over her mouth. The doors slammed shut and the ambulance took off in silence and at speed with its blue light flashing. The police officer came out of the house and they drove off after the ambulance.

He went in to see if Mrs Payne was all right. She was trembling and crying.

'Sit down, sit down.' She sat and rubbed her eyes and nose with the sleeve of her dressing-gown. 'Is there anything I can do?'

'Mr Keogh,' she said, her voice still not steady. 'You'll have seen things like this before. Would you check the bathroom for me? I couldn't. I just couldn't face it.' And she began to cry again.

Mr Keogh climbed the stairs as if his whole body was made of lead.

Back in his room Mr Keogh sat down on the bed until his breathing returned to normal. He listened and could faintly hear Mrs O'Hagan's rhythmic snoring. He tried to toe off his shoes but without socks the soles of his feet had stuck. Grunting with effort he reached down and pushed them off. The alarm clock said ten past three. He got to his feet and poured himself a half cup of brandy and drank it quickly. He poured himself another and sat down. The ambulance men had let the bath out. He knew that the water would have looked like wine. But they hadn't taken time to clean up. Liver-coloured clots had smeared the white enamel and these Mr Keogh had hosed away with the shower attachment. The razor-blade he threw in the waste basket. Her clothes, the kaftan and blouse, had been neatly folded on the bathroom chair. Her Dr Scholls stood hen-toed beneath it. The brandy warmed him and fumed in his chest. He held his head between his hands and prayed to God that she wasn't dead. If he had ever married and had children she would have been the age of his grandchild. He drank off the second cup, closing his eyes. Whether she was dead or not, the fact remained that she didn't want to live. If it had been him, he could have understood it. Except that they would never have been able to lift him out of the bath. He snorted a kind of laugh and got off the bed to pour himself another drink. He took off his overcoat and hung it on the hook behind the door. She must have been suffering in her mind. He wondered why it had so affected him – he had seen much worse things. A mush of head after a shotgun suicide, parts of a child under a tram. He couldn't say it was because he knew her, because he didn't really. Was it guilt because he had intruded on her privacy by watching her. The brandy was beginning to make his lips numb. He rolled into his bed, propped himself up on his pillows and took the brandy in sips. It was not having the effect he wanted. Instead of consoling him he was becoming more and more depressed. He remembered her at the window with her elbows high and the mellow flute sounds coming across to his room.

'It's like everything else,' he said aloud. He turned to the clock and asked, 'What time is it?' A quarter to four. Fuck it anyway. What's the difference between a paradiddle and a flam-paradiddle? A flam? Very few of the drummers he had actually liked. They were a breed apart. Why? Why? Why did she do it? She had so much going for her.

'Jesus Christ the night,' he said and rolled out of bed. The floor seesawed beneath him and he had to hold on to the armchair. He established where the wall cupboard was, reached out and grasped the handles. He opened both doors and began to look through the contents stacked inside. He knelt down in case he fell down and allowed his eyes to explore the contents. A tea-tray and Phillips Stik-a-Sole advertisement were in the way and he threw them out. But when he pulled them some other stuff fell down with a crash.

Behind a wireless with a cloth and fretwork front he found the small black case. He took it out and skimmed a beard of dust from the top of it with his hand. He blew on it as well but the dust was stuck. He stood up and fell back on the bed. He opened the catches and lifted the lid. It was so long since he had seen it. The silver shine of it had gone – it looked dull like pot aluminium.

'Stop. Stop everything.' He lay across the bed and had another drink from the cup on his bedside table. He turned back to the cornet and picked it out of its purple plush. He hawed on it and tried to rub it with the sleeve of his pyjamas. The valves were a bit stiff, but what comfort to get his little finger into that hook. It felt right. It balanced. He raised it to his lips and only then realized that the mouthpiece wasn't fitted. Fuck it. In the purple plush there were three. He selected his favourite and slotted it into the tube. He wiggled the valves up and down with his fingers trying to free them. A march came into his head and his foot began tapping to it. He cleared his throat, thought better of it and had another drink of brandy, then raised the cornet to his lips. What came out sounded like a fart.

'Who did that?' he said and laughed. He raised the instrument again and this time it was better. He got the tune and it was loud and clear. He knew it so well he couldn't remember the name of it. He didn't tap his bare foot but stamped it up and down to the rhythm of the march. He found he was short of puff very quickly.

'What else?' he said. Occasionally they used to have jazz sessions after band practice and Brian Goodall would sing. He began to play, hearing the voice, knowing the words. His foot stamped to the slow beat and his heel hurt and the notes, now harsh, rang out.

With a crash his bedroom door burst open and Mrs O'Hagan stood there in her nightdress.

'In the name of God Mr Keogh what are you up to?' He smiled and turned slowly to face her.

'A late hour,' he said and laughed.

'Do you know what time it is? Some of us have to be up for Mass in the morning.'

'Sorry. But that wee girl across the street . . . ' It came out slurred. Mrs O'Hagan sniffed the air and looked at the almost empty brandy bottle.

'If this ever happens again, Mr Keogh, you can find yourself another place to live.' She slammed the door as hard as she could.

'The boy done bad – the boy done very bad,' he said and rolled over on to the bed. He fell asleep almost immediately.

At midday he woke up with his head pounding and the track of the cornet, like a relief map of his innards, exact even to the gap, imprinted in his side where he had slept on it.

The Great Profundo

THE RIVER WAS so full after the recent rains that the uprights of the bridge became like prows and for a time I was under the impression that the bridge, with myself on it, was moving rapidly forward. So absorbed was I in this illusion that I accepted the sound as part of it. It was high pitched and sentimental, sometimes submerged beneath the noise of the traffic, sometimes rising above it, full of quaverings and glissandi. My curiosity was aroused to see what instrument could make such a noise. Others must have been similarly drawn because a crowd of about fifty or sixty people had gathered in a ring on the left bank of the river – women shoppers, men with children on their shoulders, young fellows elbowing each other for a better position. In the centre stood a tall man speaking loudly and waving his arms. I edged forward and was forced to stand on tiptoe. Still I could not trace the source of the music which at that moment suddenly stopped. Now everyone's attention was directed at the man in the centre whose eyes blazed as he shouted. He walked the cobblestones on bare feet, spinning on his heel now and again to take in the whole circle of the crowd. On the ground in front of him was a long, black case. With a flourish he undid the latches and flung open the lid. Inside was red plush but I could see little else from my position at the back.

'It is not for nothing that I am called the Great Profundo,' shouted the man. He wore a scarlet shirt, with the sleeves rolled up and the neck open, but his trousers looked shabby above his bare ankles. They bulged at the knees and were banded with permanent wrinkles at his groin. His hair was long and grey, shoulder length, but the front of his head was bald so that his face seemed elongated, the shape of an egg. He was not a well-looking man.

'What you will see here today may not amaze you, but I'll

176

lay a shilling to a pound that none of you will do it. All I ask is your undivided attention.'

I noticed a figure sitting by the balustrade of the river who seemed to be taking no interest in the proceedings. He must have been the source of the earlier music because in his hand he had a violinist's bow and, between his knees, a saw. The handle rested on the ground and the teeth of the saw pointed at his chest. He was muttering to himself as he began to pack these implements into a large holdall.

'I want you to look closely at what I am about to show you.' The Great Profundo stooped to his case and produced three swords. Épées. Rubbing together their metal cup hand-guards made a distinctive hollow shearing sound. He threw one to be passed around the crowd while he clashed and scissored the other two for everyone to hear.

'Test it, ladies and gentlemen. Check that it's not like one of these daggers they use on stage. The ones where the blade slips up into the handle. There are no tricks here, citizens; what you are about to see is genuine. Genuine bedouin.'

After much to-do he swallowed the three épées (they were thin with buttons at their ends no bigger than match-heads) and staggered around the ring, his arms akimbo, the three silvery cups protruding from his mouth. The audience was impressed. They applauded loudly and goaded him on to do something even more daring.

Next he produced what looked like a cheap imitation of a sword – the kind of thing a film extra, well away from the camera, would carry. It had a broad flat aluminium blade and a cruciform handle of some cheap brassy metal. He produced a twin for it and handed them both around the crowd while he cavorted on the cobblestones shouting interminably about his lack of trickery and the genuineness of what he was about to perform.

'While I want your undivided attention, I would like you all to keep an eye out for the Law. They do not approve. They'll turn a blind eye to trumpet players, tumblers and card-sharpers, but when it comes to the idea of a man putting himself into mortal danger on the public highway they have a very different attitude.'

The crowd immediately turned their heads and looked up and down the river-bank.

'You're okay,' shouted a woman.

'On you go.'

He took back both the swords from the crowd and held them to his chest. He straddled his legs, balancing himself, and put his egg-shaped head back, opening his mouth with an elaborate and painful slowness. I felt like saying, 'Get on with it. Skip the palaver.' The man swallowed both the swords, walked around the ring, staring skywards, then hand over hand extracted them to the applause of the crowd.

'And now, ladies and gentlemen,' the man shouted in a voice that heralded the finale of his act, glancing over his shoulder to check that the Law, as he called them, were not to be seen, 'I will perform something which will be beyond your imagination.'

He reached into his black case and produced a sword – a long and heavy Claymore. He tried to flex it, putting all his weight on it with the sole of his bare foot, but was unable to; then with a mighty two-handed sweep he swung it at the cobblestones. It rang and sparks flew. He balanced it on its point. The blade alone reached to his receding hairline. He stood there letting the crowd take in the length of the sword he was about to swallow. He spread his arms. The spectators became silent and the noise of the traffic on the bridge was audible. He lifted it with feigned effort, balanced the blade for a moment on his chin, then lowered it hand over hand down his throat. To the hilt. When it was fully inserted the crowd cheered. Planting his bare feet, like someone in a dream, his head at right-angles to his body, I could hear even from my position at the back the harsh rasps of the performer's breath escaping past the obstruction in his throat as he moved round the ring of people.

This time I was impressed. There was no physical way he

could have swallowed that last sword – it would have had to come out of his toes. There was a trick somewhere but I joined in the applause as he withdrew the six-foot sword from his throat. At this point I felt someone push me, and the small man whom I had seen pack away his saw elbowed his way into the middle and extended his hat to begin collecting. My money was in one of my inner pockets and it would have meant unbuttoning my overcoat.

'No change,' I said.

'It's not change we want,' said the saw-player and forced his way past me. As the crowd dispersed I hung around. The Great Profundo was packing his equipment into his case. After each item he would sweep back his long hair and straighten up. The saw-player was raking through the hat, taking out the coins of the highest denomination and arranging them into columns on the balustrade. The Great Profundo sat down to put on his boots.

'Excuse me, gentlemen,' I said, dropping some coins into the hat. 'I am a student at the University and I couldn't help seeing your act. Very interesting indeed.'

'Thank you,' said Profundo. After all the shouting his voice sounded soft, 'It's nice to get praise from a man with certificates.'

'Not yet, not yet. I'm still an undergraduate. I tell you I'm a student, not for any particular reason, but because I want to make a proposition to you.' The Great Profundo looked up from his lace tying. I noticed he did not wear socks. 'I am the treasurer of a society in the University which, once or twice a year, uses live entertainment. Would either, or both, of you gentlemen be interested in performing for us?'

'How much?' asked the saw-player from the balustrade.

'We can afford only a small fee. But you may take up a collection at the actual function.'

'If they gave as much as you did just now, there'd be no point,' said the man counting the money.

'What would the University want to look at the likes of us

179

for?' the Great Profundo said, smiling at the thought.

'Our society certainly would. It's called the "Eccentrics Genuine Club". We meet every month and have a few pints, sometimes entertainment.'

This was not the whole truth. We had met twice that year, and on both occasions the entertainment had been female strippers.

'Who?' asked the saw-player.

'Musicians. The occasional singer. That kind of thing.'

'We'll think about it,' said the Great Profundo. He wrote out his address and I said I would contact him after the next committee meeting.

As I walked away from them I heard the saw-player say, 'Eight pounds, some odds.'

'If my mother was alive, Jimmy, she'd be proud of me. Going to the University.' The Great Profundo laughed and stamped his boot on the ground.

The committee of the Eccentrics Genuine Club was delighted with the idea and even suggested a more generous sum of money than they had given to each of the strippers. However, divided between two entertainers, it still wasn't enough. I made a speech in which I said that if they valued their reputation for eccentricity – haw-haw – they would fork out a little more. A saw-player and a sword-swallower on University territory! What a coup! Who could refuse, no matter what the cost? The committee eventually approved, somewhat reluctantly, twice the sum given to the strippers. And they had no objection to a collection being taken on the night of the performance.

With this news and the idea of interviewing him for the University newspaper, I drove to the Great Profundo's. It was a part of the city where walls were daubed with slogans and topped with broken glass. I parked and locked the car. Then, seeing some children playing on a burst sofa on the pavement, I checked each door-handle and took my tape-recorder with me. It was an expensive one – the type professional broadcasters use

– which my father had bought me when I'd expressed an interest in journalism.

There was a selection of names on bits of paper beneath the doorbells of the tenement. The name on the bell of 14c was Frankie Taylor. I rang it and waited. Papers and dust swirled in the corners. A window opened and the man himself leaned out.

'Remember me?' I shouted. The figure at the window nodded and waved me up. The stone stairway smelled badly of cooked food. The Great Profundo was on the landing, waiting barefoot, when I reached the fourth floor.

'Yes, I remember,' he said and shook hands. 'The student. Those stairs knacker the best of us.' He led me, breathing heavily, into the flat and offered me a chair which I declined. Would he be free – would he and the saw-player be free – on the evening of the thirteenth of next month? The sword-swallower shrugged and said that it was very likely. He sat down in his armchair and folded his knees up to his chest. Then he sprang up again and asked me if I would like a cup of coffee. I refused politely. I offered to write down the date and time of the meeting but Profundo assured me that they would be there. He sat down again and began to finger his toes.

'Would you like a beer?'

'What kind?'

He jumped off the chair and said, 'I'll see what I've left. I didn't know you'd be coming.' He opened a cupboard and closed it again, then left the room. I went over to the window to check that my car was still in one piece.

Profundo came back with three cans of lager held together by plastic loops.

'Tennent's. From Christmas,' he said. He jerked one free and handed it over and took another himself 'Don't be worrying about the car. It's safe enough down there. The neighbours will keep an eye on it.'

I took the seat he had previously offered and said, 'There's another thing I'd wanted to ask you. I work for a student

181

newspaper, *Rostrum*, and I was wondering how you would feel about giving an interview some time.'

'Me?' I applied pressure to the ring-pull and the can snapped open. From the triangular hole the lager was fizzy and tepid. 'Why me? What could I tell you?'

'Our readers are interested in a lot of things. I'm sure with the life you've led it couldn't fail.'

'Aww here now . . . ' He laughed and looked down at his feet. Without Jimmy, the saw-player, he seemed defenceless. He was a shy man, unable to look me in the eye. His voice was quiet, conversational – not strident like he had been by the river-bank.

'If it's of any help to you . . . in your studies, like . . . Oh would you like a glass?'

'No thanks,' I said. 'Are you busy? Would you mind doing it now?'

'Do I look busy?' he said spreading his hands. I set up my machine, took a slug from the can and began my interview. (*See Appendix.*)

The bar in the students' Union was hired for the night of the thirteenth and a low platform stage erected against one wall. In my role as treasurer I was obliged to be around so another of the members of the Eccentrics Genuine was sent in his car to pick up the pair of performers. There was a splendid turn-out – everyone in formal evening wear – and I was pleased at the thought of covering expenses from the door money alone. After that, what we made on new membership and the bar was profit. I myself was responsible for about forty new members that night: part of the rugby club, friends from the Young Conservatives, Engineers, Medics and, most extraordinary of all, some people from a recently formed Society of Train-spotters.

The entertainment was due to begin at nine o'clock and for about an hour and a half before that the bar was pandemonium. I have never seen students drink so much – even the Eccentrics Genuine. As early as eight o'clock they all began clapping and singing 'Why are we waiting?' But it was all very good-humoured.

At a quarter to nine I was informed of the arrival of the artists and went to welcome them. They were both standing in the corridor outside. The Great Profundo shook hands warmly. Jimmy nodded and said to me, 'Is there anywhere we can change, get the gear sorted?'

'Pardon?'

'Like a dressing-room?'

'No. No I'm sorry. I hadn't thought you would need one – what with the street and all that.'

'Street is street and indoors is indoors.'

'It's okay, this'll do,' said Profundo. He began stripping off his checked shirt and getting into his scarlet one. He had a surprisingly hairy chest. 'You go ahead, Jimmy, warm them up.' Jimmy continued grumbling and got out his bow and saw. Profundo edged past him and took a look through the glass doors.

'A full house, by the look of it.' Then he stopped. 'Is there no women in there?'

'Not in the Eccentrics Genuine,' I said. 'It's one of the Club rules.'

'We're not *that* eccentric,' said another member of the Committee. 'We know how to enjoy ourselves.'

I slipped in at the back to listen to Jimmy's performance. The melody he played was the same one I had heard that day on the bridge but within the confines of the hall it sounded different, more sentimental. The notes soared and trembled and swooped. One member of the audience, just to my left, took out a white handkerchief and pretended to mop his eyes. In playing the saw there is a great deal of vibrato required to give the notes texture. The player's left hand quivers as the saw changes pitch.

'He's got Parkinson's disease,' shouted one of the new Medic members. But apart from that he was listened to attentively and applauded when he finished his selection.

Afterwards there was a great dash for the bar. Everyone considered it an interval and I had to hold back the Great Profundo until the crowd was settled again, which took some considerable time. While he waited patiently I pointed out to him that the floor was awash with beer, which might be awkward for him in his bare feet.

'And now, gentlemen of the Eccentrics Genuine Club, it is my great pleasure to introduce to you the one and only, the great, the profound, the Great Profundo . . . ' I gave him such a buildup in the old music-hall manner that the audience were on their feet applauding as he made his entrance. He ran, carrying his black case on his shoulders, and took a jump up on to the stage. For a man of his age he was almost lithe. His movements as he opened his box of tricks were sweeping and athletic.

On my first encounter with him I had not noticed that his patter, which he began almost immediately he reached the stage, was so juvenile. He had not tailored his talk for such an audience as the Eccentrics Genuine. They laughed politely at some of his jokes. When he inserted the three épées and held his arms out wide for approval there was a kind of ironic cheer. His act lacked music and somebody began a drum-roll on one of the tables. This was taken up throughout the room until the bar throbbed with noise. Some others began to imitate a fanfare of trumpets. When he inserted the two aluminium film-extra swords someone said, not loudly, but loudly enough, 'He's naive. He'd swallow anything.' There was a great deal of laughter at this, suppressed at first in snorts and shoulder-shaking, but which finally burst out and echoed round the bar. He silenced them by taking out the Claymore. There was a small three-legged stool beside him, on which Jimmy had sat to play his saw, and the Great Profundo, with gritted teeth, swung the broadsword and imbedded the blade a full inch into it. He had to put his foot on the stool and tug with all his might to free it and this occasioned yet more laughter. He stood the point of the sword on the small stage to let them see the length of it in relation to his height. A voice said, 'If you stuck it up your arse we'd be impressed.'

And yet he went on. He did his hand over hand lowering of the blade into the depths of himself to the accompaniment of drumming on the tables. When it was fully inserted, he spread his arms, put his head back and paraded the stage. Some of the crowd were impressed because they cheered and clapped but others kept laughing, maybe because they were drunk, maybe at a previous joke. Then the tragedy happened.

The crowd could see it coming because they suddenly quietened. With his head back the Great Profundo took one or two paces forward and stepped off the edge of the platform. He came down heavily on his right foot which slipped on the wet floor. He managed to remain upright but uttered a kind of deep groan or retch which everyone in the audience heard. He stood there, not moving, for several seconds, then he withdrew the sword and made his exit. Some of the crowd stood and applauded, others made straight for the bar. Jimmy tussled among them with a yellow plastic bucket to take up a collection.

Afterwards in the corridor I apologized for the behaviour and handed over the cheque to the Great Profundo.

'It's both on the one. I didn't know Jimmy's second name so I made it all out to Frankie Taylor.'

'Thanks.' In the corridor lights Profundo's face looked grey.

'I'll take it,' said Jimmy. 'Your audience is a bunch of shit.'

'I think we may have opened the bar too early. I'm sorry.'

'You're right there. All the fuckin money's going over the counter. They gave three pounds. I haven't seen pennies in a bucket for twenty years.'

Before putting the Claymore back in its case Frankie wiped its blade with a small damp cloth. Against the whiteness I saw specks of red.

'Will you not have a drink?' I said. 'On the house.'

They refused. They were in a hurry to leave.

When I rang the bell of 14c it was Jimmy who put his head out of the window and called me up. The door was ajar when I reached the fourth floor. Jimmy was searching for something in a cupboard. He barely looked up at me.

'Where's the man himself?' I said.

'Did you not hear? He's in hospital.'

'What?'

'He was pishing black for a week before he went to see about it. Must have been bleeding inside.'

'Is it serious?'

'They don't know whether he'll do or not. If you saw the colour of him you wouldn't hold out much hope.'

Jimmy continued to rummage among the clothes and papers. He lifted a black brassiere and looked at it.

'Where the hell did he get all the women's stuff?' he muttered, more to himself than to me. 'What did you want to see him about?'

'Just to say hello. And to tell him the article will be in the next issue.'

'A lot of good that'll do him.'

He held a pullover up to his chest, saw the holes in the sleeves and threw it back into the cupboard.

'I also wanted to return something I'd borrowed.'

'What?'

'To do with the article.'

'I'll give it to him.'

'I'd prefer to hold on to it, if you don't mind.'

'Suit yourself,' he said and closed the cupboard door. 'But the man'll be dead before the week's out.'

APPENDIX
THE GREAT PROFUNDO — SWORD-SWALLOWER
(*Rostrum* vol. 37, no. 18)

The interviewer deliberated long and hard about whether or not to include certain parts of the following material but felt justified in doing so because it is the truth. Once a writer, be he novelist, critic or journalist, fails to report the world AS HE SEES IT then he has failed in his craft.

The interviewer visited the subject at his home in Lower Coyle Street. The apartments were small and sparsely furnished with little regard for order or taste. It was a sparseness which derived not from asceticism but poverty. During the interview the subject was, at first, nervous – particularly about speaking in the presence of a tape-recorder – then, when he forgot about it, animated. Throughout the subject was barefoot and fiddled continually with his toes.

INTERVIEWER: Could you tell us something about how you became involved in such an odd profession?

PROFUNDO: Is it on now? Okay. Right. Oh God, I don't know. I was always interested in circuses and things. It was about the only entertainment we ever got where I was brought up.

INTERVIEWER: Where was that?

PROFUNDO: In the country – a village about thirty miles south of here. The circus would come through about twice a year. In the summer and maybe at Christmas. I just loved the whole thing. The smell of the animals – the laugh you had when they crapped in the ring. Some of those people! One minute you'd see them collecting money at the door, the next they'd be up on a trapeze. No safety-net, either. Anyway, I was about sixteen at the time and they'd organized a speed-drinking contest. I didn't want to win in case my mother found out – she was very wary of the drink – but I could pour a pint down like that. (*He mimics the action.*) Like down a funnel. I have no thrapple, y'see. It was a fire-eater who told me this – I thought I was just normal. He took me under his wing and got me at the sword-swallowing.

INTERVIEWER: Did you join the circus?

PROFUNDO: Not that year, but I did the next. That was the year they had the six-legged calf. It's a thing I don't like – the way they use freaks. I don't mean the wee midgets and all that – they earn good money and they can't work at much else. But I remember paying to go into a tent to see this beast. It was just deformed, that's all. Two half-bent extra legs sticking out its behind. I felt sorry for it – and a bit sick. But I said nothing. They took me on as a roustabout. I tried all kinds of things at the beginning. Acrobat – anything anybody would teach me.

(*At this point the subject demonstrated a one-armed horizontal handstand on the edge of the table. The sight brought to mind the paintings of Chagall where peasants float above their world with no visible means of suspension. This physical activity seemed to banish his nervousness and he warmed to his theme.*)

That's not good for me at my age. It's why I concentrate on swords now. Doesn't take as much out of you.

INTERVIEWER: Do you still enjoy it?

PROFUNDO: It's hard graft in all weathers and lately I've begun to have my doubts. But if I gave it up what could I do? How'd I pass the day? One of my main difficulties is that I'm not good with an audience. There's guys can come out and have a crowd eating out of their hand right away with a few jokes. That's hooring. All the time they're saying, 'Like me, like me for myself. It doesn't matter what my act is, I want you to like *me*.' If your act is no good, what's the point. It's the reason *you* are out there instead of one of them. People love to think they could do it – with a bit of practice. That's what's behind the oldest trick in the circus. Somebody asks for a volunteer and grabs a woman from the audience. He throws her around – on a horse or a trapeze or a trampoline – and we get flashes of her knickers, and all the time she's holding on to her handbag. You'd be amazed at how many people fall for it. But it's a plant. I loved playing that part – sitting up on the benches pretending you were the little old lady.

INTERVIEWER: And when did you begin to major in the sword-swallowing?

PROFUNDO: Oh that must have been thirty years ago. It was a good act – then. Not the way you saw it the other day. (*Laughs*) In those days I had STYLE. A rig-out like one of those bull-fighters, gold braid on scarlet, epaulettes, the long black hair

and a voice that'd lift the tent. And the swords. D'you see those
things I've got now? Rubbish – except for the Claymore.

INTERVIEWER: What happened to the good ones?

PROFUNDO: I'm sure they ended up in the pawn. But it wasn't
me put them there. D'you know the way I hand them round for
the people to test? Well there's some cities I've been in – I'll
not mention their names – when I handed them round they
never came back. Somebody buggered off with them. But times
were very hard just after the war. I don't really blame people.
You deserve all you get handing expensive items like that into
a crowd. But some of them were real beauties. I collected them
all over Europe.

INTERVIEWER: I didn't realize you'd been that far afield.

PROFUNDO: After the war in France was the best. People had
seen such desperate things. They wanted to be amused,
entertained.

INTERVIEWER: But there couldn't have been a lot of money
about – just after the war.

PROFUNDO: Whose talking about money? I'm talking about
when it was best to be in front of an audience. They appreciated
me. I had fans. Artists came to draw me.

INTERVIEWER: Artists?

PROFUNDO: Well, one artist – but he came time and time
again. I didn't know who he was at the time – a small man with
a white beard and glasses. He didn't talk much – just drew all
the time.

(*At this point the subject sprang from his seat and rummaged beneath his
bed and produced a dog-eared folder from a suitcase. It contained
newspaper cippings and photographs of himself and in a cellophane
envelope a signed drawing by Matisse.*) (*See Illustration.*)

What do you think of that, eh?

INTERVIEWER: This must be worth thousands.

PROFUNDO: I know it's valuable but I wouldn't sell it. Not at
all. I didn't much like it at the beginning – I mean it's just . . .

But I got to like it the more I looked at it. He did about thirty of me. Somebody tells me there's one hanging in New York somewhere.

INTERVIEWER: Do you think I could borrow it to reproduce with the article?

PROFUNDO: Sure. But I'd like to have it back.

INTERVIEWER: Of course. Why don't you frame it and put it on the wall.

PROFUNDO: You'd just get used to it then. This way I see it once every couple of years – when somebody calls. Then it's fresh. Far better under the bed. The last time it was out was to show to Jimmy. He didn't think much of it.

INTERVIEWER: I was going to ask you about him. Where does he fit in?

PROFUNDO: I met Jimmy a couple of years ago when I came back to work this place. The hardest thing about street work is gathering a crowd. He does that for me. The sound of that bloody saw attracts them from miles away and they all stand about listening. Once they're all there I go straight into the routine. We split the proceeds. Jimmy has a good money head on him.

INTERVIEWER: I'd say so.

(The subject offered his last can of lager which was refused. He went to the kitchen to get two glasses in order to share it. In his absence the interviewer noticed that the subject had, in his rummagings in one of the cupboards, disturbed a box, which on closer inspection was seen to contain a variety of ladies' underwear. The interviewer in all innocence asked the following question when the subject returned.)

INTERVIEWER: Do you have family? Daughters?

PROFUNDO: No? I'm by myself here.

(The subject then realized that the question was brought about by the contents of the box. He seemed embarrassed.)

Oh that. You weren't meant to see those. Is that machine of yours still going?

INTERVIEWER: No. I've switched it off now. I hope you're not offended by this question, but are you homosexual?

PROFUNDO: No, I'm not offended and no, I'm not a homosexual. I've been in love with many women in my time. Sometimes I like to imagine myself as one. Wearing their clothes is a kind of tribute to them. It does no one any harm.

INTERVIEWER: (*After an awkward silence*) And how do you see the future?

PROFUNDO: I wait for it to come and then look at it (*laughs*).

INTERVIEWER: And lastly what about trade secrets? Can you tell any?

PROFUNDO: There aren't any to tell. You'd better switch your machine on again. Okay? Trade secrets. I used to keep the blades very clean – wipe them down with spirit. But there's as many germs on the bread that goes into your stomach, so after a while I stopped that.

INTERVIEWER: But *how* on earth do you swallow that big one?

PROFUNDO: The Claymore? The same way as all the others. It's a craft. I can't explain it. I once worked with a man who could eat light bulbs, pins and needles, but I could never do that kind of thing. My talent is different.

INTERVIEWER: Thank you.

Glossary: reading the text

Father and Son

3 *to tie a blood knot*   special knot used by fishermen. Also traditionally used to show family ties or relationships.

Toome   village in Ulster, Northern Ireland.

4 *valium*   tranquiliser, a drug used to calm someone.

6 *threshold*   doorway, the entrance to the house.

---

1   After reading the story carefully, share ideas about what happened to the son in England.

2   Why, at the end, has he been shot?

3   For whom do you have more sympathy, the son or the father? Be prepared to give reasons.

A Time to Dance

10 *Mothercare*   shop specialising in goods for babies and children.

In the Gardens avoiding distant uniforms   in Princes Street Gardens, keeping out of sight of policemen. The Gardens are in Edinburgh, where Bernard Mac Laverty taught for some time.

Opticludes   patch worn over an eye to allow it to recover, or to induce the other to function properly, independently.

11 *Ah ken*   (slang) 'I know', or 'Yes'.

12 *In Lent there were the Black Babies*   the period before Easter observed as a time of fasting and self denial; a time for charitable causes.

Portobello beach   beach close to Edinburgh.

Skiving   truanting.

13 *Saughton*   prison in Edinburgh.

Children's Panel   committee empowered to review the cases of particular children who are 'at risk'.

14 *one o'clock gun*   gun located in Edinburgh castle which goes off each day at precisely one o'clock.

17 *Adidas bag*   expensive sports bag.

21 *school phobia*   abnormal fear of school, a recognised medical condition.

R K   Religious Knowledge.

---

1   Why do you think Nelson truants from school?

2   Do you think he realises what his mother does to earn money?

3   What is your opinion of Mrs Skelly as a mother? Think also about what you've learned about her background.

4   How helpful and sympathetic are the school staff?

5   What do you think will become of Nelson in the future?

The Beginnings of a Sin

24 *surplice*   loose, wide sleeved garment worn by priests, clothing the body down to the knees.

gutties   cheap canvas shoes.

altar-boys   boys serving as attendants to the priest.

Miss Grant, the housekeeper   the woman who was employed to run Father Lynch's house and domestic arrangements.

Mass   the celebration of the Eucharist; when Christ's last supper is commemorated by offering the bread and wine to God.

vestry   room attached to the church where robes or sacred items are kept.

amice   piece of white linen worn by priests around the neck and shoulders under the *alb*, which also covers the sleeves.

cincture   a kind of belt.

chasuble   cloak, an outer sleeveless garment worn by priests when celebrating Mass.

feasts of the martyrs   celebrations for those who died because of their religious beliefs.

25 *trumphery*   useless or worthless garments.

ballot tickets   tickets for drawing lots; now called raffle tickets.

26 *soda farls on a griddle*   oatcakes on a flat iron plate.

said the Family Rosary   series of prayers counted on a string of beads.

27 *Sacred Mysteries*   rituals or celebrations of significance to religious believers.

Lourdes   French town, a special place of pilgrimage for Roman Catholics because a peasant girl had visions there of the Virgin Mary.

28 *in awe of the Blessed Sacrament*   in admiration of the celebration of Mass.

National Health round ones   spectacles available free under a national government scheme.

Parochial House   house given to the priest by the parish or community.

33 *Carnegie*   rich manufacturer, born in Scotland, who gave financial assistance for the education of the poor.

breviary   book of prayers recited daily by priests.

Consecration   a part of the Mass when the bread and wine are offered to God.

elevate the white disc of the host   a thin circle of bread representing Christ.

34 *genuflect*   to bow down, as if to worship.

---

1   What do we, the readers, find out about Father Lynch? Do you think Colum finally realises this too? Find evidence in the story to support your answers.

2   Why does Colum not tell his mother the truth about the glasses? Would you have done so?

3   Would you describe the wad of pound notes as a gift, a payment or a bribe?

Remote

1 To whom does the old woman post the letter?

2 Why do you think she does so?

3 Why does Christmas day, especially, hold some significance for her?

My Dear Palestrina

43 *Palestrina* (1526?–1594) Italian composer. His work was mostly choral and religious in nature.

44 *Schwartz* German word meaning black.

45 *Auf wiedersehen* (German) goodbye.

47 *Rilke* (1875–1926) Austrian/German romantic poet.

51 *colander* dish with holes in the bottom for removing water from food.

52 *celandine* flower called after the Greek word for swallow. The plant was believed to parallel the migration of swallows.

pianola mechanical piano; the keys are played by air pressure from bellows through holes in a paper roll.

Cantabile should be performed as if singing.

55 *mein Lieber* (German) my pet, my sweet.

Wunderkind (German) child who is very gifted in his or her field.

63 *Fenians and Orangemen* Catholics and Protestants.

Connolly and Larkin socialists who organised unskilled Irish workers into trade unions.

65 *Grammar School* selective secondary school for children who have passed certain qualifying examinations.

76 *sanctity* holiness.

loam soil, compost.

77 *slut* an immoral woman.

Our Blessed Lady the Virgin Mary.

1 Why does Danny grow to like Miss Schwartz?

2 What is your opinion of her?

3 Was his family right or wrong to forbid his return to her house?

4 Why is Danny so desolate at the end?

Some Surrender

81 *Cave Hill*   well-known hill in Belfast.

82 *colonnade*   set of evenly spaced columns or tree trunks.

83 *Romish*   Catholic.

84 *tautology*   repetition of words which have similar meaning.

86 *Sashes and marches*   Orange Order (Protestant) marches and celebrations of King William of Orange.

No Surrender   slogan used by militant Protestants, meaning that control of Ulster would not be relinquished to Ireland.

87 *Prods*   Protestants.

Lansdowne Road   rugby ground in Dublin.

Peripheral   unimportant.

88 *Burke*   (1729–1797) British statesman who believed in greater democracy.

89 *van der Rohe, Le Corbusier*   famous twentieth-century architects.

90 *thrift*   being cautious about spending money.

1 Why has Roy decided to meet his father again?

2 What has happened in his past life to divide both his and his father's family?

3 Does this meeting really suggest some surrender?

Eels

96 *solitaire*   card game, sometimes called Patience. The object is to lay out the cards in various combinations until the whole pack is used up.

magnesia   laxative medicine.

thrapple   throat.

97 *lough*   lake, or a bay.

monitress   teacher's assistant who would later train to be a teacher.

99 *co-op*   cooperative business: ownership and profits are shared by a number of people.

hawsers   ropes.

02 *in such a condition*   drunk.

03 *slack*   small pieces of coal and ash.

---

1   Why does the old woman visit her former home, now her son's house?

2   Why does she have to leave the house so hurriedly?

3   What do you think will become of her, after the close of the story?

More than just the Disease

07 *the scholarship examination*   examination taken by some pupils who wish to enter fee-paying schools. A pass would mean entry and possibly financial assistance.

08 *psoriasis*   skin disease which shows itself in areas of reddish spots covered with silvery scales.

Guten Morgen, mein Papa   (German) good morning, dad.

09 *get heavy*   become unpleasant.

10 *secateurs*   shears used for pruning plants.

boule(s)   originally a French game, in which metal bowls are thrown as near as possible to a target bowl.

114 *a rum bird* peculiar woman.

115 *l.b.w.* leg before wicket.

---

1 How old do you think Neil is?

2 Why is he staying with Dr Middleton's family?

3 What, besides his psoriasis, makes him uncomfortable?

4 Why do you think he feels able to reveal his 'secret' to the Duchess, Mrs Wan?

End of Season

120 *gibbets* gallows, on which the bodies of hung criminals were left for all to see.

121 *sloth* laziness.

123 *Troubles* euphemism, or less emotional word, for the sectarian violence which has erupted in Northern Ireland.

125 *toupee* wig.

134 *chivvied* harassed or nagged.

ferrule metal point of the umbrella.

Muzak bland, mostly instrumental music found in some hotels and restaurants. Played largely to relax or entice customers.

---

1 Why has Mr Maguire returned to the Bradley sisters' home?

2 Why does Kathleen become increasingly bitter?

3 Do you think that Mary was right to refuse Mr Maguire's offer?

4 After she answers Maguire's letter, will that really be the finish of it — their relationship?

Words the Happy Say

8 *English Roundhand...Chancery* two styles adopted by calligraphers who specialise in the art of beautiful handwriting.

9 *tendrils of vermilion* thin red lines.

subscribers people who contributed money.

0 *paltry* poor or meagre.

1 *E Dickinson* (1830–1886) Emily Dickinson, an American poet. For further information, see the 'Study programme' (page 219).

3 *awl* specially pointed hand tool for making holes in wood or leather.

5 *artisan* skilled workman, a craftsman.

---

1   What has contributed to the loneliness felt by the man – the calligrapher?

2   What seems to have made his visitor similarly isolated?

3   Does this meeting serve to increase or decrease their sense of loneliness? Why?

Across the Street

60 *verve* liveliness, sparkle.

cry wolf from the old story, when a boy, to cause trouble, called danger from an imaginary wolf. When the real one appeared, no one turned out to rescue him.

61 *kaftan* long, loose dress with wide sleeves.

62 *cornet* the flute is a wind instrument, largely played in orchestras. The cornet is a brass instrument, like a trumpet, used both in orchestras and bands.

County Roscommon district in Ireland.

64 *hernia* medical condition caused by muscle strain where the intestine protrudes through the wall of the stomach.

doily mats little mats for laying under plates, made of lace or crochet.

165 *dandelion clock*   when the dandelion flower turns to seed, the seeds can b
blown off. The number of puffs taken, according to the old story, told th
time.

166 *the best of crack*   good times, good conversation.

paradiddles...flam-paradiddles   elaborate sequences played on the band'
instruments.

167 *Tyrone...Omagh*   Omagh is the chief town in Tyrone, a district in Norther
Ireland, Ulster.

172 *Dr Scholls*   sandal-like footwear.

173 *hawed*   breathed.

---

1   Why does Mr Keogh watch Una playing her flute?

2   Why do you think Una has attempted suicide?

3   Why does Mr Keogh begin to play his cornet at four o'clock in the
morning?

The Great Profundo

176 *Prows*   bows of a boat.

glissandi   series of notes played very quickly and clearly.

177 *balustrade*   ornamental rail on the riverside.

épees   thin swords with large hand-guards.

bedouin   arabian.

akimbo   downward, his hands on his hips, elbows outward.

cruciform   shaped like a cross.

178 *palaver*   showmanship.

Claymore   large, broad, two-edged sword.

179 *undergraduate*   student preparing for a university degree.

180 *coup*   brilliant success.

87 *asceticism* the practice of self-denial; someone who deliberately avoids comfort and pleasure.

animated lively.

88 *roustabout* an unskilled labourer or trainee.

hooring selling one's art for audience appeal.

89 *in the pawn* used to raise money.

Matisse famous French painter and sculptor (1869 –1954).

---

1   Why does the student narrator decide to invite the Great Profundo to the university?

2   Why does he wish to interview him for the student newspaper?

3   What brings about the end of Profundo's career?

4   Why has the interview transcript been included at the end of the story?

▨ Study programme

Detailed study of the stories

Father and Son

▣ This story contains two narrative voices, interspersed with dialogue. Trace the sections in which the father's narration, the son's narration and their dialogue actually occur. Do you find the narrative technique effective, and if so, why?

Would the story have been better if it had been told from the father's point of view, or the son's point of view, only?

▣ The impact of the story clearly depends on a sense of increasing tension, desperation and the sudden violence of its ending. It appears to show the horrifying effects of involvement in drugs, crime and/or terrorism in Northern Ireland.

However, the two characters are not named, the details of what has actually happened – and why – are few, and the title suggests that there may be wider issues to explore. Think about:

The relationship between father and son

The son says about his father:

You're a coward. (page 3)

He is an old woman. (page 4)

I would like to slap his face and make a man of him. (page 4)

- Do you agree with his view?

The father says:

I taught him how to tie a blood-knot, how to cast a fly, how to strike so the fish would not escape … (page 3)

I let you go once – and look what happened …The boy curls his lip as if snagged on a fish hook. (page 4)

- Think about the images in the lines above. Do these suggest that the father should have let go, untied the knot between him and his son a long time ago? Should he still feel responsible for his son?

- Why does the father's concern seem only to fuel his son's hatred?

Isolation

Him pestering me with questions. (page 3)

Talk to me, son. (page 3)

My son with friends. Talking. What he does not do with me. (page 6)

- What has led to the breakdown of communication between father and son? Which of the two is more isolated?

Compassion, love and forgiveness

- Quote evidence from the story to show that these continue, despite despair and horror.

- The last line in the story echoes a previous one. Try to find it. Why do you think this is effective?

3 Write an appreciation of **Father and Son**. Briefly summarise the events of the story, then explore the wider issues at some length. Finally consider the writer's narrative technique, the significance of the ending and your personal reaction to the story.

4 Write a story of your own which uses the technique of dual narration. You could perhaps feature a mother and daughter as key characters.

Then prepare **Father and Son** or your own stories as dramatised readings for radio in a series called: *Two Voices*.

5 *It is ten o'clock. The news begins.* (page 6)
The news has come to my door. (page 6)

Role-play or script the interview between the father and a reporter who appears later. Then prepare and read the script for a ten o'clock news feature.

6 **Some Surrender** (page 80), is similar to this story in a number of ways. Read the story carefully, then list the similarities and – just as important – the differences under these headings:

- Character relationships;
- Theme;
- Tone;
- Narrative technique.

Which of the two stories do you prefer, and why?

A Time to Dance

1 • This story contains both poignancy (sadness and distress) and humour. Try to find and list examples of both.

- Nelson is a drifter, he seems 'lost' in his world. How does the writer gain some sympathy for him?

- The story contains many references to Nelson's eyepatch and to blindness. Why do you think the writer has included these?

- Why might the passage from the Bible, read by Nelson's teacher, be significant?

2 Decide: does Nelson continue to drift through school, and perhaps life, or is he likely to turn over a new leaf?

Continue the story to include another incident, or incidents, in Nelson's life as he grows older.

3 There is a special meeting of the Childrens' Panel to decide what may be done about Nelson. Present are Ms Skelly, Nelson, a social worker, Mr MacDermot and the reporter (chairperson). Role-play or script the proceedings, ensuring that a decision is arrived at.

4️⃣ Script the story of **A Time to Dance**, in a number of scenes, as a theatre performance, a radio play, or a video production.

The Beginnings of a Sin

1️⃣ For most readers, the revelation of Father Lynch's secret, or sin, probably comes near the end of the story. It's only after a second reading that we realise how subtle the writer has been in introducing clues as to what it may be. The first paragraph contains two or three!

Re-read the story carefully, listing the clues which are given concerning Father Lynch's problem.

2️⃣ Colum is an innocent and sensitive boy.

- Find evidence from the story which shows this.

- But – do you think that he too may have in him, the beginnings of a sin?

3️⃣ How much sympathy do you have for Father Lynch? Consider the significance of:

With a Priest it is the opposite. He wears so much to hide himself … (page 25).

He wasn't dressed like a Priest but was wearing an ordinary man's collarless shirt, open at the neck … (page 30)

Father Lynch began to cry with his mouth half open. (page 31)

4️⃣ *What a mess for the boy.* (page 32)

Write the thoughts which would occupy Father Lynch's mind, after Colum has been shown out, and he gathers himself up from the floor.

OR

He ran all the way home. (page 32)

Write the thoughts in Colum's mind as he returns home.

5️⃣ Continue the story in the same style as Bernard Mac Laverty, but feature the 'wad of pound notes'. What will Colum do with these? Will the truth come out? What is his growing disbelief?

[6] Colum, now old, looks back on his youth. He describes the incident to a close friend: what he didn't know then, but knows now. Has he learned anything about life? What does he think of Father Lynch now?

Script their conversation.

[7] Write a short memoir of your own, based on personal experience, in which you recount a discovery made about a place or an adult. Be sensitive and discreet!

OR

Write a fictional story of your own featuring an incident when an innocent character makes a discovery about life in the real world.

Remote

[1] This is a very moving portrayal of loneliness; a widow's isolation. The writer, perhaps to highlight her state of mind, contrasts the brash, noisy village at Christmas with the silence which must fill her own home.

Find and note examples of these contrasts.

[2] A distinctive feature of Mr Mac Laverty's writing is his careful selection of precise details. These help to enhance authenticity, the realism of character or setting, to make us feel that we are actually there, watching, and to add significance to the story itself. The details often add information which stimulates our curiosity about and our understanding of the characters and themes in the story.

The extracts at the top of the next page contain such selected details. Say whether these help:

- authenticity;
- significance;
- both.

She walked round the front of the shuddering engine and climbed up to sit on the split seat. Mushroom coloured foam bulged from its crack. (page 38)

...the single track bulging at passing places – points which were marked by tall black and white posts to make them stand out against the landscape. (page 39)

...the top sweet was soiled, the relief letters almost black. She prised it out and gave it to him. The white one beneath she put in her mouth. (page 39)

'He's dead this long time'. She cracked the ring of the mint between her teeth. (page 40)

All that day the radio had been on to get rid of the dread. When 'Silent Night' came on the tape ...(page 41)

She looked down at the loch in the growing dark. The geese were returning for the night, filling the air with their squawking. They seemed like a dance-hall full of people laughing and enjoying themselves, heard from a distance on the night wind. (page 42)

3 Write the thoughts (interior monologue) which go through the old woman's mind as she waits in the growing dark for the lift home.

4 Write a short story which centres on a train, plane, bus or car journey. Include carefully selected descriptive details to highlight character, setting and, if possible, themes. Include dialogue too, of course, and try to show that what occurs at the end of your journey is different from what you expected! You could begin like this:

A green light suddenly snapped on and glowed brightly ...

5 Another portrait of a lonely woman can be found in the story Eels (page 96). Compare how Mr Mac Laverty reveals the circumstances of both women, the horror which lies beneath the surface of their lives, and how he evokes our compassion for both.

My Dear Palestrina

1 Timeline

This very long, highly accomplished story covers a period of precisely one year in Danny McErlane's life, in which his musical talent is discovered, matured, then prematurely brought to an end.

- Work out a timeline, charting the main events in the story. You can use the diagram below, and begin like this:

Page	Time	Events
	January - - - - Monday before Christmas	Danny is dragged, protesting, to Miss Schwartz.

- Consider when the relationship between Danny and his teacher is at its best, most productive, and when it is brought to an end. In each case, is the time of year significant?

- When do you think the story is set? Think of the international news at the time.

2 Creating character

- Working in a group, produce a series of character cards, like the one at the top of the next page, for Miss Schwartz, Danny, the blacksmith, Mr Wyroslasky, Mingo, Mrs McErlane, Mr McErlane. You will have to research the story very carefully.

Name:

Probable age:

Background:

Personality:

Two quotations which illustrate personality are:

- On which characters were you able to find most information?

- Choose one of your characters. Was personality mainly established by what the person said, did, or what was said about him or her?

3 Character contrast

Both the blacksmith and the music teacher try to influence Danny in very different ways. Outline what each would wish him to be. Which, if any, has the more powerful influence on Danny? Which other two characters are clearly contrasted in the story?

4 View point

Now note down how each character sees Miss Schwartz, like this:

Name:

View point on Miss Schwartz:

Two quotations to illustrate this are:

Who sees Miss Schwartz as she really is?

⑤ Suggestion

Some of the effects in Mr Mac Laverty's stories come not only from what he says, but also from what is suggested in our minds subliminally (unconsciously). Look at how Miss Schwartz and her music are often described as black. She is a 'dark figure' with 'jet black hair' who wears a 'black silk gown'. Indeed, the name Schwartz means black. There are black notes on the piano and on the sheet music, the composers are black silhouettes, the records are black.

* Suggest reasons as to why this is the case.
* Are there references to any other colours? If so, why?

⑥ Significance

* The following sections in the story seem to have little real relevance in the main narrative. Find and re-read these carefully. Suggest what the writer's purpose may have been in including each one:

  the description of Danny, ill, lying in bed (pages 50–51);

  the scene after Danny's sister's wedding, in the McErlanes' front room (pages 57– 61);

  the scene when the satellite is spotted (pages 69 –70).

* Find and read the following extracts and the contexts in which they occur. What is the significance of each of these? What is implied beyond the literal (actual) meaning?

  Miss Schwartz had pointed out to him when the flowers had fallen off the tree and each week they inspected the swelling fruit. (page 61)

  Lavish love and attention on growing things and they will not let you down. (page 63)

  The apples on the tree had become ripe and she had given Danny one. (page 67)

  'How utterly lonely,' she said, 'the immensity of it all frightens me.' (page 69)

'Caught between the heavens and the earth. How knowledgeable you are, Danny.' (page 70)

On the road Danny waited for the hammer blows so that he could walk in step but none came and he had to choose his own rhythm. (page 72)

Black loam spilled out and the dislodged plant fell from the pot, displaying its tangled skirt of white roots. (page 76)

'You are one of us, my love.' (page 76)

'Come into the heat, love …come in from the night. Join us.' (page 78)

- Why do you think the author may have chosen **My Dear Palestrina** as the title?

🎜 Issues

This story is especially rich in ideas. Decide which of the following statements, if any, most accurately describe what you think are the main issues in the story, then list your choices in order of importance. Feel free to add other statements of your own.

- Music can help to heal the divisions in the world.
- We can never quite overcome the barriers of social class or nationality.
- Having children outside marriage is wrong.
- We can never quite overcome the prejudice of others.
- The system can only be changed by force.
- Growing up involves more pain than pleasure.
- Isolation is the result of the prejudice of other people.

🎜 Appreciation

Use the information, insights and structure which you've obtained from the previous work in this section to write a detailed appreciation of **My Dear Palestrina**.

OR

Letter

Danny, unable to meet Miss Schwartz again, writes to her. Discuss first what you think he might say, then write his letter.

9 Alternative narrator

Write the events of the story as these may have been told by Miss Schwartz or Mrs McErlane.

10 Television production

You are an independent film producer. My Dear Palestrina is earmarked for filming. You have in front of you a file of items from your production team:

- a memo indicating, with reasons, that Bernard Mac Laverty's story could be filmed successfully;
- the start of the screenplay, covering the first four pages of the story;
- notes from Casting indicating what 'image' will be required of the actors and actresses in the main roles, and whose agents should be approached;
- notes and illustrations from Costumes and Set Design indicating what will be required.

Working as a team, neatly put together this file and decide whether filming should begin.

11 Read The Beginnings of a Sin (page 24). In this story, another innocent youth, Colum, learns about the realities of life. Write an essay which compares and contrasts the central characters in both stories.

12 Write personally about a time when someone older than yourself influenced the direction of your life.

Some Surrender

▣ This story reveals a troubled family background indirectly through memory and dialogue.

- Trace the relationships and religious background of the two generations by compiling a family tree.
- What has caused the breakdown of family relationships?

▣ Why may the setting, the Hill, be symbolic? Consider carefully the final paragraph of the story.

▣ The story is narrated in the present tense. Why do you think Mr Mac Laverty may have chosen to do this?

▣ The tone of the conversation is at times tense, yet also humorous and even optimistic. Find examples of each and say whether you find this confusing or appropriate in this situation.

▣ Why do you think Roy refuses to meet his mother again? Do you think he is justified in his decision?

▣ Compare and contrast the central relationship in this story with the one in **Father and Son** (page 2). Which story do you find more optimistic, and why?

▣ Discussion

> *What matters is our identity.* (page 87)

- Does national identity matter to you?

> *For evil to flourish all that need happen is that good men do nothing.* (page 88)

- What can good men – and women – do in the face of terrorism?
- Should decisions be left to politicians?

> *The principle of living stacked is a perfectly sound one.* (page 89)

- Is it? How would you design homes for the next generation?

🔟 Point of view

Re-tell the story from the point of view of Roy's father, mother or wife.

🔟 Hot seating

Place Roy in the hot seat. Which questions would his father, mother, wife and son really like to ask him, and what do you think his answers would be?

Eels

1️⃣ This story is a very moving portrait of an old woman, now close to death, whose life 'hadn't come out. Not the way she wanted' (page 104).

Incidents from her past life are narrated apparently at random, like the memories which filter through her mind as she secretly re-occupies 'her' house. The significance of these only become clear at the end of the story.

Read from 'And what makes you so different?' (page 104) to the final line, then consider carefully the function or effect in the story of the following:

- the moon, which is in 'its last phase';
- the eels: 'out of the depths, into the depths';
- the game of solitaire: 'it hadn't come out';
- the lough: 'she saw nothing but blackness';
- the meeting with the student: 'beneath her feet continents were moving';
- 'her coat unbuttoned'.

2️⃣ That night, Brian discusses his mother with Bernadette. He feels a little guilty. Think carefully about what you know of the personalities of both, then role play or script their conversation.

3️⃣ Read **Remote** (page 38) which is also a portrait of a lonely widow. Write an appreciation of both stories outlining similarities and differences and saying, giving reasons, which one you find more accomplished.

4 Write a story or a poem of your own in which someone visits a place which holds memories, only to realise that in the game of life – chance – things have not *come out*, or *perhaps later could come out*.

More than just the Disease

1 To help you think more clearly about the story, discuss the following fully.

- The first sentence tells us that Neil kept hearing his mother's voice. Indeed, her voice echoes through the story. Find what he hears: what can you deduce about his mother's personality and the influence she's had on Neil?

- Neil seems to be on the edge of life, but afraid to 'swim' in it. Find evidence of:

  what his problem is;

  his shyness;

  his excuses.

- Does the title help you to see the story, and Neil, in a new light?

- Re-read the last paragraph carefully. Do you think it provides a suitable ending, or do you find it puzzling? Will Neil in the future always be left in the warmer shallows, while others, like Michael, will be further out? Is this ending optimistic or pessimistic?

2 Next morning, Neil, still excited and relieved, writes a letter to his mother describing his holiday so far. Think what he might say about:

- Dr Middleton, Mrs Middleton, Anne and Michael;
- their house and their lifestyle;
- Mrs Wan and how she has helped him;
- how he feels about his holiday so far;
- what he thinks could happen during the next few days.

3 Next morning at breakfast when Neil is still asleep, Michael tells the others in his family what he saw at the caravan and where he and Neil had been the night before.

Script or role-play the conversation, ensuring that each person shows how he or she feels about Neil and the events of the previous days.

4 Neil, now twenty-nine and married with children of his own, looks back on this holiday as a turning point in his life. One evening he tells his wife all about it – the Middletons, his problem, Mrs Wan, and how each made him see life differently.

Script their conversation.

5 Read the story called **A Time to Dance** (page 10). Then try to record any similarities and differences you can find between the two boys, Neil and Nelson. Use the following headings: *Background*, *Personality*, and *Outlook on life*.

Now think about the stories, especially the ending of each, and write an evaluation of both as follows:

• Briefly summarise **A Time to Dance**.

• Briefly summarise **More than just the Disease**.

• Compare and contrast the two central characters, Nelson and Neil. Both are lonely figures. Why?

• Compare and contrast the endings, the mood and tone evoked by the writer.

• Say which of the two stories you prefer and why.

OR

Danny, in **My Dear Palestrina**, is also given help and encouragement by an adult, Miss Schwartz. But the outcome is very different! Write an evaluation of this story and **More than just the Disease** using the outline given above.

6 You are a feature writer for a glossy weekly magazine. Do some research and conduct interviews. Then write a humorous, tongue-in-cheek article about holiday embarrassments and what your readers should do when faced with these. Think of a snappy headline, consider your layout carefully and include, if you dare, a photograph or illustration which will 'hook' your readers.

7 Write a story or poem which, like the one you've read, centres on someone who stands on the edge of adulthood, a little afraid to 'swim' out into life. You could use the title *On the edge*. Try to create a clear picture of your key character. If you select to write a narrative you could structure it like this:

- a meeting or encounter;
- the problem;
- the conflict or tension;
- the solution.

8 • Publishers have produced a series of books for very young children called *Worries*. The idea is to help them cope with having to go to hospital, visiting the dentist, the death of a grandparent/loved one, Mum or Dad leaving. Write a short article for young children on one of these 'worries'.

- In a group, discuss what worries your age group most. Make a list of top five worries. Discuss what you and others can do to help and contribute an article to a teen magazine on *Stress*.

OR

Prepare a radio script, including interviews, on *Students' Stress*.

End of Season

1 The romance genre

This seems a fairly typical romance story which borrows from the conventions of Hollywood films. The plot seems to move forward in three stages: Normality – Disruption – Normality. The Bradley sisters' everyday life is disrupted by the arrival of a gentleman, Mr Maquire, who proposes marriage. This unleashes varying emotions and in the end normality is restored.

But it's not as simple as that. We would expect the happy ending; romance should blossom, but it doesn't. Or at least it doesn't seem to. Or could it, later? Do you think it will?

② The question

Mr Maquire has proposed marriage. Mary seems to have refused, for a number of reasons. Which of the following reasons do you think were most important in her mind?

- She is too snobbish, she finds Mr Maquire's attitudes rather 'common'.
- She is too comfortable in her own life to change now.
- She wishes to keep control of her own life.
- She prefers the security of everyday life, with her sister and her job.
- She can't desert her sister, or her responsibilities.
- She is probably near the age of fifty and so may be afraid of a new relationship.
- Mr Maquire doesn't fulfil her more romantic notion of what love is.
- She was really in love with Herr Hauptmann.

③ The outcome

Read the second to last paragraph carefully, then write Mr Maquire's letter to Mary, and her reply.

OR

If you find the ending of this story too inconclusive, continue it in your own way, adding your conclusion.

④ Write your own romance story in which someone from the past reappears. This person creates doubt, or even disruption, in a perfectly ordered life. Consider your ending carefully.

⑤ Write a personal essay, after thinking clearly about one of these titles:

- What makes my life really worthwhile.
- The most embarrassing silence I have ever known.
- Books should not be a means of escape.
- Don't do something you'll regret for the rest of your life.

Words the Happy Say

☐ This narrative seems to encircle the poem which provides the opportunity for a meeting between two very lonely people. It's worth reading the poem again and thinking about what it means.

It was written by Emily Dickinson, who lived in Amherst, Massachusetts, from 1830 –1886. She lived quietly, and for the last twenty-five years of her life actually lived in seclusion, seeing only the closest of friends. She never married and only created lovers in her imagination. Emily Dickinson wrote more than a thousand poems; most of them written in an intensely creative period between 1858 and 1865. She sought advice and criticism by sending them to Thomas Higginson, an essayist and critic who wrote for the *Atlantic Monthly*. He discouraged her from publishing any of her poems. It was only after her death that she and her work became widely known and praised.

Does any of this information help you to understand the poem, and perhaps the story, better?

☐ *Would you do a poem?* (page 149)

Why do you think the woman has chosen this particular poem?

☐ How does the poem seem to comment on the man's situation? Think about:

He further surprised himself by using his precious gold leaf. (page 151)

Instead of working in the morning he was tidying the flat. (page 151)

and when the story ends he:

punched the table hard with the knuckles of his fist ... turned up the volume and filled the flat with the noise of voices he could not put a face to. (page 157)

☐ Write a story of your own which is based on a poem which you particularly like.

OR

Write a story which focuses on a meeting which has promise, but ends with none.

⑤ Explore possible connections between this story and **End of Season** (page 120) and **Remote** (page 38). Report your findings to your group.

OR

Try to find out more about the life and work of Emily Dickinson. Report on your research to your group and read two of her poems which you particularly like.

Across the Street

① In this story the lives of two contrasting characters, who are unlikely ever to have met, briefly intermingle: Una, the nineteen year old ex-student, and Mr Keogh the old ex-policeman. The link between the two – or part of it – is their music.

Re-read the beginning and the end of the story, noting similarities and contrasts.

② The personalities of the three main people in the story are carefully established as information is gradually revealed to the reader.

- Which of the following words describe which character? You may wish to include other words of your own, but find the evidence in the story which backs up your choice.

  nervous, short-tempered, compassionate, unstable, endearing, fussy, a voyeur, a perfectionist, polite, insecure, timid, practical, caring, a coward, domineering, vain, guilty.

- *Mr Keogh ...wondered why that memory, more than all the others, frightened him so much.* (page 169)

  This is a memory of how he had saved someone from injury. Why should it frighten him?

  - *He wondered why it had so affected him – he had seen much worse things, a mush of head after a shotgun suicide ...*(page 172)

  Why has this incident, involving Una, so affected him?

③ Imagine that Una kept a diary. Using evidence from the story, and the same time-span, write some of the entries she may have made.

220

④ Mrs O'Hagan speaks to Mrs Payne – Una's landlady. They try to make sense of what has happened, of Una herself and of Mr Keogh's strange behaviour. Role-play or script their conversation.

⑤ Write an appreciation of **Across the Street**, examining how the writer has portrayed characters clearly and say what you may have learned about them – or people in general – as a result. Remember to include quotations from the story to illustrate points you wish to make, but set out these quotations accurately within your text.

⑥ Write a story in which the lives of two strongly contrasting characters touch briefly, but the meeting is not likely to be forgotten by one, or both.

The Great Profundo

① Irony

This is a term used to describe when someone uses words to imply the opposite of what he or she really means; or when we, the readers, grasp the significance of what is said or done, but the person saying or doing this doesn't.

- In what way is the title ironic? To help you, read the second paragraph (page 176).

- In what way could the last two words of the story, 'thank you', be said to be ironic?

② Theme

So absorbed was I in this illusion. (page 176)

- How many illusions can you find in the story? How many illusions, or expectations, are shattered?

- The theme of a story is a unifying idea which the writer has developed throughout it; there may be more than one. Is it *illusion and reality*, or is it *exploitation*? Which of these people are simply preying on the Great Profundo:

audiences, for cheap excitement?

the narrator, for his own ends?

Jimmy, for money? (Note that he is ransacking the dying man's home.)

- Work out what you see as the main theme, or themes, and show how the writer has developed it.

3 The narrator

The story-teller is actually a young student, who is also a character in the story. He influences events and comments on these in a very detached, almost clinical *tone*.

- Do you find this method of narration satisfactory?

- Would the story have been more effective if it had been narrated by:

  Jimmy – the saw player?

  The Great Profundo himself?

4 Narrative structure

Why do you think the interview appears at the end of the story, as an appendix? Why wasn't it placed on page 182 when it actually took place?

5 Tone and character

- Do you find this story to be a black comedy, or moving and compassionate, or simply sick and tasteless?

- Is the story essentially a joke in poor taste or a portrait – like the one done by Matisse – of someone who is also an artist, who despite faults has some integrity, a personal honesty?

- Read the interview again. Find examples of what there is to admire in the Great Profundo. Find also examples of his failings. Which outweigh the other?

- In New York the Great Profundo, immortalised by Matisse, is playing to another audience. Will the reception be different? If so, why?

6 Discussion

- Are circuses harmless entertainment or grotesque shows, or pure theatre?

- Is Art exhibitionism, or illusion, or entertainment, or exploitation of wealthy audiences?

Looking at the entire collection

1 Conflict

Compare and contrast two stories which focus on a conflict which is within one character, or is outside that one character, showing how the writer has revealed its source and, perhaps, its resolution.

2 Character

Discuss in an essay how the writer has created, for you, credible characters in any one of the stories you've read in this collection.

3 Themes

Explore in an essay how Bernard Mac Laverty has presented one of these themes in one, or two, stories:

- growing up;
- prejudice;
- isolation;
- insecurity.

4 Consider carefully which *opening* and *ending* paragraphs are most important in any one of the stories in this collection. Then, explore at greater length why you think these are particularly effective.

5 Style

Bernard Mac Laverty often develops his stories as a series of 'shots' or pictures. His writing if highly 'visual'. He narrates, as many story tellers do, through a selection of precise visual details and realistic dialogue.

Explore how, in your opinion, this technique is especially useful in one story of your choice.

6 Publishing

Two of the stories in this collection may be published in a new book under the title *Twentieth Century Short Stories*. You are members of the Editorial Board. Discuss which ones you would recommend, giving persuasive reasons why these stories should be included.

7 Interview

The Great Profundo contains an interview between the narrator and a single character. Script an interview between yourself and a key character in one of the other stories. Decide beforehand which questions will elicit the information you want and think carefully about what the responses might be.

8 Meeting the author

If you were given the opportunity to interview Bernard Mac Laverty, which questions would you most like to ask him on one story, on this collection, or on his work in general? Make a list. Role-play his responses, or better still, why not invite him to make his own replies?

9 Illustration

Apart from the cover design, there are no illustrations in this collection. Which story would you have chosen to illustrate? Design an illustration to highlight a key aspect of one story for future printing;

OR

A bookshop poster and blurb which would help to advertise this collection.

10 A writer once said:

A novel is like a jumbo jet; it may contain hundreds of characters and travel to

> *the end of the earth. A short story is like a hot-air balloon, containing few passengers, but it can ascend to undreamed-of heights.*

Write an appreciation of one or two stories which seem to ascend to such heights.

Suggestions for further reading

Other works by Bernard Mac Laverty

Lamb His first novel. The story of an escape to freedom by Michael Lamb, a Brother in a Catholic Reformatory, and twelve year old Owen Kane. The novel is also available in the Longman Literature series. Recently filmed for Channel Four.

Cal A powerful novel, also recently filmed, set against the background of the Ulster troubles. Cal's relationship with Marcella is born out of innocence but is doomed by his guilt.

Short story collections by other authors

William Trevor has published many highly acclaimed collections of short stories, some of which poignantly evoke rural Ireland, and some deal with the effects of terrorism in Ulster:
The ballroom of romance
Angels at the ritz
The day we got drunk on cake
Beyond the pale

James Joyce's *Dubliners* which is now a literary 'classic'. Stories of paralysed life in Dublin under British rule. Read especially **Eveline** and **The Dead**, recently filmed.

Flannery O'Connor was an American novelist and short story writer whose work has been admired by Bernard Mac Laverty. Try to find out why by reading her stories in these collections:
A good man is hard to find
Everything that rises must converge

Dip into any collection of short stories by Frank O'Connor, Sean O'Faolain, or Liam O'Flaherty.

Related reading

These novels are very readable and explore the human dimension of the Irish troubles:

Shadows on our skin, How many miles to Babylon, and *Fools Sanctuary* by Jennifer Johnston

Fools of Fortune by William Trevor

Under Goliath by Peter Carter

Wider reading assignments

▨ Select one of Bernard Mac Laverty's novels which seems to link in character or theme with any of the short stories which you've read. In an essay, explore the similarities which you've identified.

▨ Read a number of William Trevor's short stories. Select one which deals with the effects of prejudice or terrorism and compare this with **Father and Son** or **Some Surrender** in this collection.

▨ Write an essay which explores how Joyce has portrayed life in early twentieth-century Dublin in *Dubliners*.

▨ The short story has often appeared as a poor relation to the novel. Write in defence of the short story, saying what it can achieve and show, by taking two stories as examples, how this can be done in the hands of a good writer.